HIGHGATE

My life is like a broken stair
Winding round a ruined tower
And leading nowhere...
(Anon)

ALSO BY SHANI STRUTHERS

EVE: A CHRISTMAS GHOST STORY
(PSYCHIC SURVEYS PREQUEL)

PSYCHIC SURVEYS BOOK ONE:
THE HAUNTING OF HIGHDOWN HALL

PSYCHIC SURVEYS BOOK TWO:
RISE TO ME

PSYCHIC SURVEYS BOOK THREE:
44 GILMORE STREET

PSYCHIC SURVEYS BOOK FOUR:
OLD CROSS COTTAGE

PSYCHIC SURVEYS BOOK FIVE:
DESCENSION

PSYCHIC SURVEYS BOOK SIX:
LEGION

BLAKEMORT
(A PSYCHIC SURVEYS COMPANION NOVEL
BOOK ONE)

THIRTEEN
(A PSYCHIC SURVEYS COMPANION NOVEL
BOOK TWO)

ROSAMUND
(A PSYCHIC SURVEYS COMPANION NOVEL
BOOK THREE)

THIS HAUNTED WORLD BOOK ONE:
THE VENETIAN

THIS HAUNTED WORLD BOOK TWO:
THE ELEVENTH FLOOR

THE JESSAMINE SERIES
BOOK ONE
JESSA*MINE*

THE JESSAMINE SERIES BOOK TWO
COMRAICH

This Haunted World: Book Three

HIGHGATE

SHANI STRUTHERS

This Haunted World Book Three: Highgate
Copyright © Shani Struthers 2019

Authors Reach
www.authorsreach.co.uk

ISBN: 978-1-9160626-4-1

Dedication

This book is dedicated to those who lie one beneath the
other in the unmarked grave at Highgate Cemetery:
Emma Jones, Anna Williams, Caroline Harriet Rhodes,
Emily Potter, Harriet Smith, Frances Lliffe, Maude
Clabby, Rosetta Edwards, Ada Rebecca Ingram and
Agnes Ellis.
Also for Christina Rossetti.
Remember.

Acknowledgements

Thank you, first and foremost, to Highgate Cemetery itself, for providing such inspiration. If you haven't visited it yet, make sure you do, as it is a place of peace and every bit as magical as you think it may be. Next up, a huge thank you to my beta readers: Rob Struthers, Kate Jane Jones, Sarah Savery, Lesley Hughes, Louisa Taylor and Amanda Nash – Amanda, your comments were amazing and inspired a whole new thread. Also thanks to Rumer Haven, not just an editor but a novelist too. If you want to read more about the Magnificent Seven, her book What the Clocks Know set at Brompton Cemetery, is a must. Gina Dickerson, thank you so much for helping with the cover, for formatting, and for always being there to help with so many things, you are such a good friend. And last but not least, thank you to my brother, the artist David Henty, for painting the weeping statue that graces the front cover – check out his website: www.davidhentyart.co.uk for more of his world-famous outstanding pieces.

Prologue

There it is again, a rustling amongst the leaves, so faint that if you breathed you would have to forego such an act in order to hear it. Silence, and then she comes a little closer.

I wait as I have waited for so long, but the footsteps – such as they are – retreat.

Why is that? I wonder. What, in the end, deters her?

Is she afraid? If so, she has every right to be, for there exists amongst us dark things, impure things that we run from. We hide whenever they break away from the shadows to stalk these grounds, which were once so grand. Does she hide too? What if she doesn't?

I want to shout at her, to scream: *The darkness waits; it pounces. Once it has you in its grasp it is so hard to break free. Run! Now! Be on your guard! Never let that guard down.*

I have no voice, however. And I never have had. The words I utter are for my ears only. There has been no one to smile or nod their head in kind understanding of my wretchedness.

No…wait… There was someone, long ago. But it was all so brief, and she is but a shadow too.

Would this woman who ventures near bend her head to listen? Is that her purpose? Not just to me but to others as desperate?

Don't turn away! Don't go! You're one of us!

Too late. It is only her sorrow that remains, settling like dust motes in the air.

I sit and weep. Amidst such crumbling grandeur, so many have faded from memory. In this land of granite and stone, of towering monuments and deep sarcophagi, of weeping angels and broken columns, there are some that have no marker at all. Instead we lie, one beneath the other, so deep.

We cannot rest. There is no peace. For *many* there is no peace, and no hope either.

This is now home. This is our domain. The lost, the bewildered, the arrogant and the insane, the guilty and the innocent. And aside from the darkness I have talked of, there is the living too.

Of the living, where is the other one? For I can sense her as well.

I halt these tears to go in search of her. What else am I to do with this endless ribbon of time? I know where to find her. My tread is also light as I follow more hidden paths – their many twists and turns, the knotted trees that cloak them, the ivy, the weeds, and the bracken no hindrance at all. To tread the main path is to be too exposed. I pause when I hear screeching.

"Where are you, you little swines? Come here! You deserve what you got and what I'm going to do to you still."

It's the old woman, in the open for all to see, her body plump and hair unkempt. She wears a long dress with a tattered hem that reveals tight black boots. Around her midriff is an apron, white in colour but with splashes of red upon it – the blood of the children she searches for.

"Is that one of you? Is it? Hiding. You're always hiding. Come 'ere, you little rat. Vermin, that's what you are. You need to be culled before you overrun us."

There is laughter – an echo that drifts. Childish laughter that infuriates the old woman further.

From the pocket of her apron, she retrieves a butcher knife, the blade also smudged with red. "I'm coming to get you! There's no escape, not now, not ever."

I watch as she rushes past me, oblivious to all but those she seeks – once a murderer, always a murderer. Is she buried here, this slayer of children? What about those whose lives she ended? If they are or if they are not, this is where they play their endless game of hide-and-seek, the young ones continually outwitting her. In death, they have grown so much cannier.

But it is not the old woman or her wily victims that concern me. And so I carry on, watching both my left and my right, noting the stony gazes of so many winged creatures that will never take flight.

The sun is fading, and what scant warmth it yields will soon give way to night's chill. I have felt both on my skin in the past, and remembering them is a torment and a pleasure.

At last I have reached the steps. Below me is the curved colonnade that overlooks the grounds where horses, black of course, their headdresses weighted with feather after feather, would turn the carriages of those that society deemed worthy of a burial service, affording them the utmost pomp and ceremony. How I loved to see those horses! How magnificent they were! How solemn too, such intuitive creatures. I would stand, just as I am standing now, and gaze at them. They would stare back at me. They would notice me when so many didn't.

And she's staring too – the other woman – from a building across the courtyard, the glow of light from within so different to the glow that is cast by candles. It is harsher, more brittle.

I can sense the weight of her scrutiny and how puzzled she is. Also, how intrigued.

I feel the same.

Both women mystify me; both capture my attention wholly.

Who are they? Who am I?

Why do we converge here when the world and what lies beyond is so vast?

I know it's you out there...

Is that what she's saying even though her lips don't move? So often I say the same thing.

I know it's you out there in the low light.

Chapter One

Lucy – current day

"Another gin and tonic?"

Lucy Klein checked her watch. It was past 10.30p.m. already. She had work in the morning, full tours booked. But this man, Zak, who was offering to buy her another drink, was nice, and it wasn't often she went on dates, not anymore.

In her early forties, she perhaps wasn't striking enough to be highly visible – something that, if she were honest, didn't perturb her. She'd never been an attention-seeker. Getting ready tonight, taming her dark curly hair and applying a touch of lipstick, she'd thought she looked okay. She'd *hoped* so. Zak, at forty-three, was a year older than her. He'd been married, apparently, and was now divorced, the father of a teenage girl and boy. He came with baggage, whereas she came with nothing. Sometimes she thought the former was better. Baggage fleshed out a person, it gave them depth, whilst all she ever seemed to have was the moment. But if that were true, why should she care about an early start in the morning? Why not simply make the most of now?

Yes, she decided, she would have another gin, inwardly marvelling at the enthusiastic response her acceptance elicited.

"Brilliant! Thank you, I'm so glad. Wait there, okay? Don't move! I won't be a minute."

The Queens in Crouch End, with its art nouveau décor, was busy for a midweek night in November. Only a ten-minute walk from her ground-floor flat in a Victorian terraced house, it was both a pleasant and convenient place to meet. Zak Harborne was a friend of a friend, someone she'd met on the aforementioned friend's birthday night out a fortnight ago. Cornily, just like they portrayed in the movies, their eyes had met across a crowded bar. They'd exchanged tentative smiles, and then, to her delight and surprise, he had made his way over. They'd got chatting, although the noise levels surrounding them made conversation difficult. Eventually, he'd taken her mobile number. She never thought he'd actually phone her, was stunned when he did.

"Here you go, budge up a bit."

Zak squeezed into the seat beside her. Previously, he'd been sitting opposite. She straightened her back, steeled herself. God, she was terrible at this, so out of practice! It'd been years since her last date, two, or was it three? More likely the latter. And that had fizzled out pretty quickly, just like so many others.

Surreptitiously she studied him; he looked like the cat that had got the cream. Could it be true? Was she reading him correctly? He thought that much of her? That she was a prize of sorts?

"This is nice," he said, having taken a swig of his beer.

"Uh huh."

"Good boozer. Your local, is it?"

"That's right, it's just down the road from me."

"Do you come here often?"

The trite comment caused her to laugh and him to do a facepalm.

"Sorry. Did I really just say that?"

"I'm afraid you did. But in answer to your question, no, I don't come here often, although I walk past it every day on my way to and from work."

And during the evening walk she would glance inside, at people who were sitting together – couples, friends, on occasion a solitary man or woman staring intently at their mobile or a laptop – the lively atmosphere such a contrast to her life and how she'd spent her day. But did she envy them? The sociable, the revellers, those who visited establishments such as these on a regular basis, whilst she more often than not returned home alone to cook a dinner for one and watch a bit of TV, or read a book, before heading to bed? Perhaps. On occasion. Not tonight, though. Tonight, she was one of them.

"So this job of yours, over at Highgate Cemetery, tell me more."

"Well…" She shrugged. "Apart from all the usual boring admin that I suppose comes with any job, I organise tours there. The West Cemetery, I mean."

Zak's reaction surprised her. Had he just snorted? "Who the heck would want a tour of a cemetery?"

"It's an historic place," Lucy countered, working hard to suppress a bloom of indignation, "home to some of the world's finest Victorian funerary architecture. Not only that, several notable people are buried in the West Cemetery: Michael Faraday, Radclyffe Hall, Christina

Rossetti…" Rossetti, sister to the Pre-Raphaelite artist Dante Gabriel Rossetti, was one of the reasons for her interest in Highgate in the first place, given Rossetti's connection with it and the surrounding area… How Lucy loved the woman's poetry, in particular 'Remember', for the beauty of it, its sheer haunting quality.

Remember me when I am gone away,
Gone far away into the silent land…

Is that what she had sought, a silent land? One in which she lived, both night and day.

"You're doing it again."

Perplexed, Lucy glanced at him. "What?"

"It's as if…as if you keep drifting."

"Do I? Oh, I'm sorry."

Zak reached out a hand to tuck some hair behind her ear, hair that she was sure hadn't come adrift. "It's no problem. As long as you're not getting bored of my company?"

"Oh God, no! I'm…enjoying myself. Tell me more about *your* job."

He had already mentioned he was in construction, but now Zak went on to explain that he was part of a large firm that worked mainly in central London, detailing several current projects and becoming quite enthusiastic about them. All the while, Lucy nodded encouragingly, only occasionally sipping at her drink, not drifting at all but noting the hand gestures he was given to when describing certain things, the way that his mouth moved, the stubble on his chin, and how piercing his blue eyes were, almost cerulean in colour. He was a handsome man, cultured and clever, a man who was interesting and in turn showed so much interest in her.

"So there you have it. That's me in a nutshell: work, eat, sleep, repeat. It's pretty run of the mill. Pretty mundane, really. Well…it is in comparison to what you do. I've never met anyone who worked at a cemetery before. Do you find it a bit…? I don't know how to put this… Depressing?"

She shook her head; it was anything but.

"Describe a typical day for you, then."

As he'd gone into detail, so did she. This was her chance. She told him about the tours she organised for visitors who turned up every day, come rain or shine; that the West Cemetery, unlike the East Cemetery, could only be visited by arrangement; and that some – the obsessive, as she used to be, perhaps – visited more regularly, not to listen to the tour guide, as they knew the history well enough, but to immerse themselves in the atmosphere that only Highgate could offer, to admire the wealth of Gothic imagery, to sit awhile and do what? Feel closer to death and the mystery of it?

Is that what I did? What I still do? Why?

Maybe it was because they, like her, found it more comfortable amongst the dead. The deceased didn't ask questions, for a start, or demand anything from you; they simply let you be, unlike this man sitting close to her, who was edging closer still. His arm had also moved and now rested lightly across her shoulders. Had he noticed how flustered she'd become by this close encounter or that her breathing had grown slightly irregular? If so, he made no comment, which she was grateful for.

"And that's it." Her laugh was nervous, at least to her ears. "That's me in a nutshell too."

"It's a step up from being a mortician, I suppose. I've never gone out with one of those either."

Lucy tried to make light of it. "We're not a breed apart, you know."

Thankfully, Zak's reply was lighthearted too. "I know that, and it's great, you know, to be…different. Perhaps you could give me my own private tour one day?"

"A private tour? I…"

"Relax. I was joking. But I would like to learn more about this famous cemetery." As he frowned, several creases appeared in the folds around his eyes. "Odd, isn't it? In this part of London, we live side by side with history and yet, for most of us, it's…invisible. Yet, if you look for it, if you meet the right person who's interested in it, they can open up a whole new world for you."

Never mind about laboured; her breath lodged in her throat.

"Yes, I suppose," she eventually managed to say. Did he mean that *she* could open up a whole new world for him? He was a clever man, she'd already decided that, but regarding history she was perhaps more insightful. She could teach him, if he was genuinely interested, and he could teach her, about a life such as this – one where she belonged rather than feeling like an outcast, only truly comfortable when wandering the lone, ivy-stricken paths of a cemetery in North London, as if continually searching for something that eluded her. Could it be that she'd been looking in the wrong place all along? What she needed was a future, which was to be found right here, in a pub, next to this man, Zak Harborne, his gaze intent, his lips parting slightly, as if…as if…

That heady feeling after he'd kissed her – his lips so soft against hers, his tongue toying ever so slightly with her tongue – lasted the entire journey home. Time had been called, forcing them apart, and they'd left the pub, Zak insisting on seeing her to her door.

There wasn't any physical contact between them en route, however, and she felt disappointed by that, keeping her hand by her side in case he should reach out and clasp it. In fact, he was quiet on the short walk, contemplative. Immediately, she started to worry. Was he regretting his actions and how intimate they'd been? Strangely, from being nervous in the pub, all unease had vanished, the kiss awakening something in her, a longing that she knew was there but had never realised was quite so alert. She *wanted* to belong, to be a part of something, a couple. And he was nice; he had *smelt* nice when he'd leaned closer, a clean smell, soap and water.

"This is it!" she said, stopping outside her flat, chasing confusion from her voice and forcing brightness into it.

"Yours is the ground-floor flat?"

"Yes." She'd already told him that, in the pub.

"You own it?"

"Yeah."

"Who lives upstairs?"

She frowned. What a strange question to ask! "A young guy. He works in the City." She glanced upwards at the closed curtains. "Looks like he's gone to bed already. Either that or he could be out. I think he goes out a lot, actually. I hardly ever hear him move about up there."

"I see," he said, that look of contemplation returning.

Lucy shuffled from foot to foot. "Thank you for a lovely

evening."

Zak smiled at her, but there was something odd about it. "I've really enjoyed myself."

"Good. Perhaps…we could do it again sometime."

"Definitely."

The silence between them was heavier than any she'd encountered at the cemetery.

Eager to break it, she said, "Goodnight, then."

"Goodnight."

Would he? Wouldn't he? The anticipation of even a peck on the cheek was causing knots in her stomach.

Zak took a step back and then another. There was no one else on the street, the other occupants of Crouch End tucked neatly inside their respective houses – their 'boxes', as she tended to think of them – either asleep, watching TV, or sipping at a final cup of tea before lights-out. It was just her and Zak, caught in the glare of a streetlamp, the light brighter than she remembered.

You don't have to go…

But he was already walking away, leaving her feeling quite bereft.

A gentleman, that's what he is. She kept telling herself this as she made her way to her front door, fished out her key from her shoulder bag, and inserted it into the lock. He had bought her drinks all night, ensured her safe arrival home, and kissed her just the once. *Leaving you eager for more.* Of course, that was it! It was all part of a game she was unused to playing. And he wanted to meet again; when she'd suggested it, he'd said *definitely.* She just had to be patient and wait for his call – or take the bull by the horns and call him, not be a martyr to her natural shyness.

As she entered her flat, walked straight down the hallway to her bedroom and kicked off her shoes, relishing being free of them, she once more noted the silence. *As quiet as the grave.* It always was, despite people living upstairs and on either side of her, despite being in the centre of London, come to that, with *millions* of people around her. It was so, so quiet.

She shook her head. She'd best get some sleep, ready for that early start. But sleep that night refused to come easily. She lay for hours, turning one way and then the other, the silence getting louder as not even a car passed along her road or a fox squealed in the darkness. All she could think of was Zak.

That kiss… It was such a tender kiss, leaving its mark.

That smile… His last smile, not all those he'd bestowed on her in the pub. What had been so different about it?

The answer reached her as, finally, she drifted towards oblivion.

The smile, it had failed to reach his eyes. That's what had been different.

Chapter Two

Emma – 1972

Did they think she couldn't hear them or what they were saying? They were wrong. She could.

"Don't worry about it…you know…what she's like."

"…so intense."

"Some people are."

"…a drag, man."

"Yeah, yeah…said…don't worry about it."

"It's her eyes…

"…about…eyes?"

"Hollow."

"Yeah…you mention it…they are."

In the hallway of the digs she shared with her fellow university mates, Emma took a step backwards. She'd been about to enter the living room, to encounter not just them but that huge haze of dope-tinged smoke that seemed forever suspended above her so-called friends' heads. She thought perhaps she'd sit with them awhile and have a smoke too – force herself to inhale that noxious substance that so often just irritated her throat. Make conversation, laugh a little, blend in.

But how could she do that now? Although no names had been mentioned, it was her they were talking about. She could sense well enough how odd they found her. Not just because of her accent, which was perhaps a little more refined compared to theirs – although she tried hard to modify it – and it wasn't the way she carried herself either, tall and straight, the set of her shoulders perhaps too rigid on occasion. It wasn't the way she dressed, in bell-bottomed jeans and cheesecloth tops, just like the rest of the girls. And she wore her fair hair long and free-flowing. On the surface she *did* blend in, perfectly, but her eyes – the windows to the soul – gave her away.

What soul?

It was this question that burned in her mind as she entered the bathroom, locking the door before turning to stare into a slightly mottled mirror that hung over the sink.

What was on the outside was presentable enough, but whenever she imagined what lay beneath, all she saw was stark-white emptiness. How long had it been like this? She closed her eyes for a few seconds and tried to think. Soon the force of drums interrupted her, the beat trudging like something from ancient times, something ominous, before she realised exactly what it was – Led Zeppelin: 'When the Levee Breaks'. They played it all the time, her flatmates, anything by Led Zeppelin, really. Collectively they worshipped the band. She liked them well enough too, but this song, right now, she hated it. The lyrics and what they implied, it was too close to the mark: *Cryin' won't help you; prayin' won't do you no good...*

Briefly she closed her eyes. *Take a deep breath, Emma. Just join in.*

How many times had she said those words to herself? Convinced herself that *this* time it'd be different, it'd be better; not only would she act the part, she'd feel it too. Leaving home and going to university to read History – the only subject she was really any good at – was supposed to herald the good times, a fresh start, a brand-new Emma. Amongst strangers she'd be able to be whoever she wanted to be, with no expectations attached. She could be free, finally, from the restraints of her childhood and parents that so obviously hated each other but stifled her, always competing for her attention, using their only child as a means to score points off one another.

Even her dog, Daisy, hadn't been immune to the often alcohol-fuelled games they played. *It's me she favours,* her father would roar, pointing at the poor dog. Her mother would laugh, a horribly brittle sound. *No, it isn't. That dog's like the rest of us – it can't stand you.*

Poor Daisy. The front door had been left open one day, whoever had left it that way probably meaning to return to shut it, but too late. Daisy had run straight out into the road to be hit by an oncoming car that never bothered to stop to see the damage it had inflicted. Emma, aged twelve, had been the one to hear the brief squeal of brakes and had gone to investigate. Oh, how she had wailed at what she'd discovered!

Despite what her parents used to say, Daisy was *her* dog, the only living thing that had loved her with no conditions attached. Even her parents had had the good grace to look ashen-faced about her untimely demise, although neither owned up to who'd left the door gaping. Instead, the whole thing descended into farce as each so readily blamed the other, the accusations becoming more heated until it wasn't about Daisy at all, but them. As it always was. And all the while Emma hugged Daisy's cold body to her, praying that they'd stop, just stop, so that they could get on with the sorry task of burying the dog, consigning her to the earth, a spot in their garden, where at least Emma could visit, she could sit awhile, remembering not just what she'd lost but also what she'd never had from anyone else.

It was whilst her parents continued to argue, her mother reaching for a glass of wine and guzzling it, that a terrible thought had occupied Emma's mind and refused to abate: Daisy had run into the car deliberately, because she *wanted* to die, to escape a sorry home life. A ridiculous thought, really; a dog tended to accept its lot, not rail against it. Nonetheless, the thought persisted. Not only that, Emma found she *envied* Daisy.

"Em! Em! Is it you in there? Come on, open up, I gotta take a leak."

No longer in the living room, Kev was banging on the bathroom door.

"Em! Come on! I'm being serious."

Taking one more look at herself and the emptiness that wasn't just confined to her eyes but actually seemed to mark her entire being, Emma turned towards the door and opened it. Kev pushed past her and raced to the toilet bowl, where he unzipped his trousers, took his penis out, and proceeded to pee right in front of her, as if she weren't there at all, as if she were invisible.

"Oh Christ," he said to himself, not her. "I was that desperate."

The sound – like someone emptying a bucket into a bath – caused her to grimace as she finally made her way to her bedroom, a room only big enough for a single bed and a chest of drawers, with hardly any floor space in between. A bleak room, that's what it was, with its scuffed white paint, thin curtains, and bare light bulb, but a room in which she spent the majority of her time, reading, sleeping, and thinking...

The more communal areas of the house, which comprised the living room and the kitchen, were dominated by the others: Kev, Danny, Angela, and Louise. They hardly ever spent time in their bedrooms, not as far as she could tell. They slept in them, that was all, and had sex in them too, of course. Not with each other; none of her flatmates were couples. But on occasion someone would bring a 'friend' home and disappear for a while, the banging of the bed frame against the wall or moans and cries drawing sniggers from the others but leaving her red-faced and agitated.

God, she wished she could chill out about it all! What was wrong with what they were doing? Nothing. They were young, *she* was young, nineteen years of age as they all were, or thereabouts; Kev was slightly older, nearly twenty-two. This was a time in their lives to have as much fun as possible, with no strings attached. But the banging, the moans, it reminded her too much of them, her parents...and how noisily they would make up after an argument, not caring if their child was in the next room, again as if she were invisible, a ghost rather than flesh and blood.

More Led Zeppelin occupied the air – 'What is and What Should Never Be' this time. Robert Plant's voice sounded like he was being tortured, as far as Emma was concerned. She'd gone to close the bedroom door when an arm shot out to grasp the door edge, preventing her. Startled, she saw it was Kev, his grin revealing the gap between his two front teeth.

"What you doing?" she asked.

"Wondering what you're up to, that's all. Not hiding again, are you?"

Was that a slight sneer in his voice, or was she imagining it? Was this just simply his way of being friendly? After five months of living with him, she still couldn't tell.

"I've got some reading to do."

"Little Miss Swot," he commented.

She shook her head. "Not really. I'm behind, actually, if you must know."

Realising he wasn't going to budge, she stood aside, a silent invite that he could come in if he wanted to, even though there was barely enough room for two – unless you were horizontal, that is. His eyebrows rising a little, perhaps in surprise, he took her up on the offer, making his way to her bed and settling himself down upon it.

That grin of his did nothing to banish her unease, which grew more potent when he gave the space beside him a short, sharp pat. "It's okay," he told her. "I don't bite." When she did as he asked, almost teetering on the bed's edge, he added, "Much."

She laughed when all she wanted was to tell him to leave, to get out of her private space, the only sanctuary she had.

Kev's gaze moved from her to a stack of books piled neatly on the floor against the opposite wall. "What you reading? Is it really something to do with your course or some steamy novel?"

"Steamy novel?" Leaning over, she picked up one of

several textbooks and handed it to him. "This is what I'm studying: the Victorian period. I've got an essay to write by the end of the week."

He took the book from her. "*The Victorians and the Cult of Death,*" he read. "Cheerful."

"Interesting," she corrected. "It's...fascinating, in fact."

"Sounds like a horror film, if you ask me, one of those cheap ones. What does it mean anyway, the Cult of Death?"

"You really want to know?"

"Yeah. Why not?"

To her surprise, when she studied his face to see if he was being genuine or mocking her – after all, it had been his voice that mentioned the hollow eyes – it seemed it was the former. Maybe she shouldn't have been so shocked. He adored Led Zeppelin, after all, and there was no one more into the Victorian Cult of Death than its guitarist, Jimmy Page. She'd read about that in a magazine.

She swallowed. Perhaps she'd been paranoid earlier; perhaps they hadn't been referring to her at all. It could be that Kev really was making an effort to get to know her properly, even if he hadn't done so up until now. Either that or he was as big a faker as her.

Slowly she began. "You're probably well aware of this, but in Victorian times, life expectancy was low. If you came from a fairly well-off background, the middle classes, I mean—"

"Like you do?"

"Me?"

"Yeah, the way you speak, the way you act, your parents must be pretty well off."

"I..." She had no idea what to say, or whether to deny it.

They *were* well off, financially at least.

"You close to your parents?"

She shrugged. "Not particularly. They're okay…"

"Got any brothers or sisters?"

"No."

"Thought so."

"Sorry? What do you mean—"

"Nothing. Go on, you were saying."

"It was just…if you came from the middle classes, you could expect to live 'til around forty-five, but with the working classes it was half that age, and as for children, many were lucky to survive their fifth birthday."

"Grim," was all the comment Kev gave.

"So…inevitably, death was a big part of their lives. You could even say they were obsessed with it. Queen Victoria herself was *totally* obsessed with it. She mourned the death of her husband, Prince Albert, for forty years, dressing in black every day and keeping their home exactly as it was the day he died, like…a shrine, and…if it was good enough for the Queen—"

"It was good enough for everyone else."

She sat up. "Exactly."

Whilst Kev contemplated this, she studied him, albeit furtively. She supposed that many girls might consider him good-looking. He had a mop of unruly hair, but there were curls in it, she noticed, which rested lightly against his shoulders. His tight blue tee shirt emphasised how toned his arms were, and his jeans, flared only at the ends and tight elsewhere, emphasised something quite different. Embarrassed where her thoughts were leading her, she quickly continued.

"The Victorians created a variety of different rituals to help them cope with the loss of their loved ones. These included everything from being photographed with the recently deceased so that they could keep their last picture together as a memento, to having death masks made or items of jewellery like…lockets or rings, where they would put strands of the dead person's hair. When it came to the day of burial, they'd sometimes hire professional mourners to follow the cortège, who'd do all the weeping and wailing. It was important to them that the final send-off was an impressive one, a bit like keeping up with the Joneses. A lot of money was spent on burial sites."

She inwardly winced when Kev's grin faded. Damn it! Had she gone too far?

"And this is what you're interested in?" he said. "Death?"

"Not so much death as how people dealt with it back then. It's what my essay's about."

"It's incredibly morbid."

"It's history! It's what I study, remember?"

"Yeah, yeah." Kev was an engineering student. His focus was on creating projects for the future, so little wonder he didn't get it. She was busy thinking that when he inched his entire body forward, effectively closing what little gap there was between them.

"What you doing?"

He looked slightly indignant she'd asked. "Nothing."

"Oh, right."

He pulled out a crumpled roll-up from his jeans pocket and offered it to her. "Fancy a smoke?"

"No. No, thanks."

"It'll relax you."

"I'm fine."

Lighting the cigarette for himself rather than her, he took a long, deep drag. "Ever been to Highgate?"

"The cemetery?"

"That's right."

She knew about it, of course. It was a short Tube ride away. But no, she'd never been there. Why would she? Once the jewel in the crown of London's Magnificent Seven cemeteries, built by the Victorians in the early to mid-1800s, it had long since been abandoned, nature claiming not just the bodies buried there but the glorious tombstones that accompanied them. As soon as she admitted she hadn't been there, Kev's greeny-grey eyes lit up.

"We should go!"

"What? We can't. It's not open to the public."

"So?"

Emma frowned. "So that means we'd be trespassing if we did. No one's allowed in there!"

How amused he was by her. "You're such a good girl, aren't you?"

"What do you mean?"

"Don't smoke, don't drink, study all the time, abide by any rule going."

"I do smoke—"

"You said no just a minute ago."

"Because sometimes it…"

"Burns your throat?"

"Well, yeah, actually. It makes me cough."

"Lager doesn't do that, though."

"I don't like lager, okay? Just because I don't doesn't

make me a good girl."

"But you are. A *really* good girl. A posh girl."

She'd had enough. "Look, if you're going to get funny with me, Kev, you can leave—"

That grin of his was wider than ever. "Hey! Come on! I'm messing with you."

"I really do have work to do."

"All work and no play…"

"Yeah, yeah, I know what the saying is."

"Then let's go to Highgate and play awhile."

"I've told you, we can't—"

"Not today, I don't mean that. Man." He paused a minute to look at his cigarette. It was clearly not the first one he'd smoked today. "I'm too wasted anyway. Soon, though. And we'll go at night; we won't be discovered then. No one in their right mind goes near a graveyard at night."

She started to shake her head, but Kev was having none of it.

"We'll invite the others, Danny, Ange, and Loo. It'll be fun. You're studying the Cult of Death. Where else is that more evident than in an old Victorian cemetery? You know what, if we do get caught, if they've got some barmy old night guard patrolling the grounds, we can plead the student card, say we're there because of research. That'll get us off the hook."

"I'm not sure…"

Her voice faded as Kev blew a smoke ring straight in her face. She held her breath and waited for it to disperse, kept her eyes open instead of closed, a gesture of rebellion no matter how small. With all her heart, she willed him to move away, to put some space between them.

When finally, *finally*, he leant back against the wall and closed his eyes, his shoulders slumping slightly, relief washed over her. Relief mixed with dismay. He looked as if he was settling himself in for the duration despite the fact she'd told him repeatedly she had to study. There was nothing more she could do. She'd just have to be patient and wait it out. Perhaps one of the others would call him soon or he'd grow tired and bored and wander off.

There was no use protesting further about going to Highgate either. In many ways Kev was at the helm of this little band that lived in this little flat, and she was right at the other end of the spectrum. A boy from the South Coast, a town called Brighton – whereas she was from the far reaches of Kent, a more rural location – he was cheeky as well as street-wise, boasting a confidence that even she'd admired on occasions. He was charismatic, she supposed. People took notice of him. Her flatmates certainly did, so if he wanted them all to go to Highgate at night on a jolly, to Highgate they would most likely go, a place that was indeed the epitome of the Victorians' obsession with death. As she watched a lazy grin appear on his face, his eyes still closed, his words resonated.

It was research going to Highgate, *valid* research. And another chance to get more involved.

Chapter Three

Grace – 1850s

"Get out of it, you little runt! Go on, I said, bugger off. And don't steal nuffin' either, else know what I'll do? I'll chop your bleedin' hands off."

Grace backed away from the ruddy-cheeked man who stood there in clothes almost as tattered as hers, clutching a tray of baked loaves that he was selling on the streets of St Giles, the area of London she called her home. Here, every squalid inch was packed with hawkers, gin shops, drunks, and prostitutes, all of which she'd run the gauntlet of, day in, day out.

It was hunger that prised her from the tiny room she shared with her mother and two younger brothers, in one of the tenement buildings a mile or so distant. Not her own hunger. That she could bear. Grace Derby was eleven years old, nearly twelve, and, although slight of build, was robust in nature. As long as she could find some clean water or some leftover ale that someone had left in a tavern somewhere, she could go two or three days without eating. But Michael and Patrick were just eight and three respectively, and Patrick in particular would howl when the hunger got too much – his cries joining so many in the rookery, their mother's milk long since dried up.

She needed some bread for him, at least. Mam had given her what she could from the wages she earned as a seamstress, but it was never enough, not even for bread as stale as that which the ruddy-cheeked man sold, something only barely edible that tasted like sawdust. But never mind; it would fill their stomachs, it would stop Patrick from howling, if only for a short while.

And yet it had been denied her, despite her pleading, despite that it was bread from yesterday that had hardened overnight. Once he'd started shouting at her, she had no choice but to turn and run; his cries would alert the peelers otherwise. They'd assume she was stealing the way he was carrying on and chuck her in the clink, where she'd remain, branded guilty, because no one listened to you, not when you were penniless. If that should happen, if she should be locked away, what would happen to her mam and brothers then?

As she ran, she ignored the pain of the stones that littered the ground, that bit at the bare soles of her feet. His cries and her subsequent fleeing had captured the attention of some but not the peelers, although that was only a small mercy, considering. As she veered down a side alley – one of those her mam had told her to keep away from, fearing what manner of person lurked in the shadows there – she was grabbed by the shoulders. Without thinking, without even looking, Grace started to fight, kicking her legs and punching out.

Her attempts at release were met with laughter, a chorus of cackles that made her skin crawl.

"Ooh, she's a lively one."

"Got some fire in 'er."

"That's what they like, don't they, the gentlemen. A bit of fire."

"Let go of me! Let go!" They were holding her, pawing at her, grabbing at her thick hair, examining her. "I said let go!"

Three women, their faces chalky white, a red gash where their lips should be, and eyes that looked like they'd been blackened with coal – either that or it was a man's fist responsible. Not just women; these were the ghouls her mam would also warn her about as they'd sit hunkered close to the fire, trying to eke what warmth they could from flames that would only grow weaker.

"There are bad things out there," she'd say, "on the streets of London. Be careful, Grace, so careful."

Her two brothers would be asleep in their cot in the corner, Patrick coughing intermittently, drawing worried glances from both his mother and sister.

"What kind of things?" Grace would ask.

"Evil things. Things that have no heart, no soul, that are godforsaken."

Grace remembered looking into her mam's fearful eyes, sure that hers were just as wide. "Ghouls?" she questioned further.

"That's it, Grace, that's right! The streets are packed with 'em."

And she was right, they were. So, why, oh why, had Grace veered off the main artery to come down here? The inner alleys were like warrens, drawing you ever inwards to a hell within a hell, one worse than even she could imagine. These creatures that still had hold of her were laughing in her face. They had about them such a strange smell, at once sweet but sickly too. Would they ever do as she bid and let her go? Or would they be the ones to drag her towards that hell, their fingers like talons, scratching at her skin, not only grabbing her hair but yanking at it, pulling it from the roots, trying to force her to be like them – wretched women of the night, those who sold their flesh, their bones, to the 'gentlemen' they'd mentioned. She wouldn't. She'd rather die. She was a good girl. Her mam was always telling her that: "Don't let anything change that, Grace."

"LET GO!"

As small as she was, Grace still managed to summon up the strength from somewhere to kick and punch with renewed vigour. One of the women fell against the wall, a look of pure shock on her face that this scrap, this urchin had been able to do such a thing. The two other women appeared surprised too, their attention captured by their felled colleague – perhaps only briefly, but it gave Grace time enough to bolt forwards and down the length of the alleyway, which she had indeed been dragged further into, her feet yet again crunching against sharp stones, making her wince but not slowing her at all. The end was in sight, although the three women continued to scream like harridans behind her. "Get back 'ere! Just wait 'til we get hold of you! There's no escape! Who'd ya think you are anyway? There's no escape from any of this!"

For a moment she closed her eyes. *There is. There has to be. I can't bear it if not.*

Finally, she emerged into a day that was just a few shades lighter than the gloom of the alleyway: the main thoroughfare, a hustling, bustling place, full of sellers shouting out their wares, and raucous laughter and chatter.

Except it was none of those things. A hush had descended, a silence. Even the screaming of the women behind her had faded to nothing.

Noting that people had stopped, that men had removed their hats to hold them respectfully in front of them instead, she turned to the left, the direction in which everyone was looking. Black horses were coming towards her, though not galloping as the carriages ferrying people from one destination to another tended to gallop, making it treacherous to cross their path. She'd seen many like her trampled, their bodies mangled by hooves and wheels. No, these horses were travelling at a much slower pace; they were so graceful, so…mournful. On their heads, plumes of huge black feathers swayed in the breeze, bigger than any feather of any bird she had ever seen. They drew behind them a black carriage, and behind that, on foot, she could see the semblance of an entourage, people clad in black and beating at their chests.

A funeral procession, and such a grand affair. Someone important must have died. A lord or a lady, perhaps, from the upper echelons of society, for it was only their deaths that were mourned in this manner, the wails of the entourage breaking the silence at last, and containing such bitterness, such angst.

Grace had known a great many people die in her short lifetime, including her father and two more siblings: another brother, who'd died just before his first birthday; and a sister, Althea, who'd died not even two years before. There'd been no performance such as this; rather, their bodies had been taken in the early, freezing hours of the morning or under cover of the night to lie she knew not where. No pomp, no circumstance, no ceremony. There would be no names to mark their graves either, perhaps just a *P* on a wooden stake. *P for pauper.* What had been similar, though, were the tears. Not just her own; her mam had cried enough to fill the Thames. She had wept and wept, and with each tear she had grown smaller, as though life were being sucked out of her, or at least the will to live it.

Staring at the procession as it came closer, moving further into the crowd that were also held rapt, Grace couldn't help but wonder: were the poor nothing but a scourge, their deaths welcomed if anything? Certainly, London was stuffed to the gills with them. In the rookery, whole families were crammed into rooms above, below, and beside her. In one room alone there were ten people – a mam and dad and all their children. She knew this as, one day, she had stood and counted as they'd emerged from within on their way to church on a Sunday morning. In the dwelling the Derbys occupied, there were four – or, rather, four remaining – and even that was a squeeze.

"'Ere, move out the way so I can see better."

A stout woman next to her had begun jabbing her elbow in Grace's face. Quickly she ducked, not wanting to remonstrate with anyone further this day, and moved forwards. The carriage was in front of her now, and she could see into it – faces as white as the women in the alleyway. Five of them sat in there, a woman and a man and three younger people – their children, perhaps? Behind them were the mourners and then more horses and another carriage. This one, glass-sided, would hold the deceased, and it was this that people were straining their necks to see. Were they looking at the size of the coffin, trying to determine if it belonged to an adult or a child? She found herself doing the same thing, edging further and further to the front.

What an elaborate carriage it was! There was gold upon the roof and so many flowers inside, all of them white in colour – the colour of innocence. A child, then, it had to be. Her age or younger? She marvelled that it should be so. So many died in the rookery, but even if you had money, it was no barrier against fate. If death wanted you, it claimed you, regardless of your status in society. The words of one of the women who'd molested her took on new meaning: *There's no escape from any of this.*

And of the deceased, some were mourned publicly whereas others were thrown silently into the ground, earth heaped upon them, one less mouth to feed and one less burden. Grace felt not sadness within her but indignation at that – every life meant something! Every death should be treated with the same respect!

The crowds dispersed as the cortège continued, on its way to Highgate, perhaps? A cemetery that lay on the outskirts of the city, that was guarded both day and night against the Resurrection Men, those that stole fresh cadavers to give to hospitals so that doctors could experiment on them. It was a dire fate that everyone feared, from the wealthiest to the poor – not being laid to rest at all but dissected like an animal. Highgate was therefore likened to a fortress; she'd heard tell that iron bars and high walls surrounded it.

The spectacle over, the street gradually filled with noise again, with shouts to buy bread and pies and milk. Horse dung joined the other more dubious fragrances. There was also laughter, cruel laughter, and every bone in her body froze to hear it. Was it the women from the alley, come to find her, relentless in their pursuit? She shouldn't have lingered, she should have continued running, back to the rookery and her mam, although to bear witness to the disappointment on their faces as she returned empty-handed would be hard. She had to get food from somewhere, some gruel, perhaps, that Mam could warm over the fire.

"Mind where you are going."

Grace blinked. Because she'd been so preoccupied, she hadn't realised she'd stepped into the road and straight into the path of a…a…

She looked the man up and down. Entirely in black, his attire consisted of a tall hat and an overcoat with a cape; even his cane was black, as was the jewel in the ring on his middle finger. Was he one of the mourners of the cortège that had just passed? Had he also lingered?

Immediately she apologised. "Sorry, Mister. So sorry."

As she hurried to get out of his way, his hand shot out and grabbed her by the arm. She flinched, the touch reminding her too much of what had happened so recently. But then – curiously – she found herself relaxing. No, his touch was nothing like that of the women; it was far gentler. More curious still, she dared to look into his face. She supposed he was a handsome man, his skin remarkably smooth and his eyes a soft shade of blue. Miracle of miracles, instead of scowling at her, he was smiling, something that had never happened before. Gentlemen didn't smile at street urchins, not in all the years she'd lived.

Grace tried to say something, perhaps to apologise again,

but words failed her, especially when his smile only grew in width, when a slight, almost delighted laugh escaped between moistened lips that gradually opened to speak.

She braced herself. Did his smile belie some deep anger, perhaps? Would he scold her for the collision? Worse, summon a peeler after all and declare her a nuisance? *Please, God, help me.*

What he did say almost caused her to faint.

"Are you hungry, child?"

Chapter Four

Lucy – current day

"Hi, Bert, how are you today?"

"Hello, sweetheart. I'm well, thank you. How about you?"

Lucy smiled, not just at Bert as he approached but also his dog, Firecracker, a medium-sized black, scruffy mixed breed, so named because he was born on 5th November. Bert had just finished the last tour of the day and was busy shaking the rain off his shoulders as he came in. Lucy's office was a small room adjoining one of two chapels, the one originally intended for the Dissenters as opposed to the Anglicans, whose chapel was on the opposite side.

"All good here, I'm glad to report."

"Good, good. Tour took a bit longer than usual this afternoon," he remarked, "despite the weather. Had some right inquisitive ones in this batch. Asked all sorts, they did."

In the corner of the office, a small desk housed a kettle and various tins containing tea, coffee, sugar, and biscuits, made use of by the volunteers as well as the various groundsmen and gardeners that Highgate employed. Bert walked over to the desk, flipped the switch on the kettle, and then delved into the biscuit tin to feed not himself but the eager dog.

"Just the one, boy, no more," he muttered. "And a quick cuppa for me before we head off."

Bert was in his early seventies but looked older; countless lines marked his face, and his eyes, perhaps once blue in colour, resembled faded denim. As his hand reached out to pour hot water from the kettle into a mug, he winced. He tended to do that a lot, Lucy noticed, whenever he moved, causing him to shuffle rather than walk. And yet, he still insisted on conducting tours of Highgate several times a week, the threat of loneliness more painful, perhaps?

He didn't offer Lucy a cup. There was no need; he knew she rarely drank tea or coffee but preferred water instead, which she sipped at now from a sports bottle as Bert and Firecracker settled themselves briefly by the radiator, the dog ever hopeful of more treats.

It was just after three o'clock, but already the day was fading. It was low light. That's how Lucy thought of it – an in between time, not quite one thing or the other. In many ways, this was her favourite time of day. And this light, this *special* light, could linger for so long at Highgate, much longer than in the world around her, where night tended to fall so quickly.

Listening to Bert's appreciative sighs as he drank his tea, and Firecracker's continual low whining, she headed over to the window to gaze outwards across the courtyard. Her eyes travelled up steps leading to what was once described as a 'Garden of Eden', a paradise, to stare into the distance there, at what lay beyond – or what she *imagined* lay beyond, noting the trees swaying in the driving wet mist of the afternoon and the birds that swooped from tree to tree.

As they flew, they would be calling to each other, whilst below, in the thicket, there'd be rustling as more and more creatures woke from their daytime slumber: squirrels, mice, and rats, even, with moths and butterflies gliding gracefully by. She echoed Bert's sigh. In the low light, Highgate was just so *alive!*

"One lass wanted to know if she could be buried here when it's her time to shuffle off," Bert continued. "Only a young lass too, couldn't be more than twenty. A student, perhaps."

"Perhaps," agreed Lucy. They got a fair few students on the tours. "What did you tell her?"

"I said not unless you're famous, not on the west side anyway. The east side is different."

Bert was right. Although the west side was officially a working cemetery, plots were nonetheless limited; to request one, you had to be eighty-plus or have a terminal illness.

"I gather she was, to all appearances, fit and well?" Lucy enquired, still gazing ahead.

"Robust, I'd say," Bert answered. "It amazes me, you know?"

"What does?"

"How preoccupied the young can be with death."

"Young people die too, Bert."

"You're right there. Life is fragile."

"It is," murmured Lucy. So fragile, in fact, that it was extraordinary how so many survived into old age. There was so much that could go wrong at any given time, things you'd never expect.

Trying not to be too morbid herself, she focused instead on the faded majesty of all that lay before her, the Gothic corrosion that the Friends of Highgate Cemetery Trust, a charity she'd belonged to for so many years, had worked hard to reverse. They'd done a great job; between them they'd managed to save this spectacular piece of history from complete ruin, including, of course, all who lay within its confines: the famous, pillars of society, and those considered the dregs…

I know it's you out there…

"That's it then, love. I'm off. See you for tomorrow's tour."

"Yeah, okay, Bert. See you tomorrow."

Still her eyes remained on the horizon, a 'Victorian Valhalla' as the poet Sir John Betjeman had famously described it. The beauty of it, the feel of it, cast a spell on her as much as it ever did on him. Several moments passed before she heard a shuffling again.

"What is it, Bert?" she said, turning fully at last. "Have you forgotten something? Oh!"

It wasn't Bert but Zak Harborne – tall, as handsome as she'd thought him last night, and casually dressed in blue jeans and a jacket, his damp blond hair falling in an almost foppish style.

"Sorry," he said before she could utter another word. "The old man said to go right ahead, that you were in here. I just…I wanted to see you again. I did try ringing earlier."

Had he? She'd had her phone on her all this time, in her back pocket, and although she kept it on silent, she would have felt it vibrate. She could hardly check now, however, not in front of him.

"Hi there! I…erm…I don't know what happened about that call, sorry." Glancing at the clock on the wall, she continued, "I've still got a while to go before I finish, although…" There was no one in the office, all volunteers had gone home, and there were no groundsmen either, not today. She could close this side up early if she wanted to, come in a little earlier in the morning to complete any outstanding admin. Across Swain's Lane in the East Cemetery, Margaret would be on duty, nestled in the entrance booth, taking admissions until four but ensuring all visitors had left by five. She had her own keys, however, and could lock up. "Did you want to go for a drink?"

"A drink?"

"Or something to eat? If you're hungry…"

"I was wondering… I mean, would it be okay…" He gestured vaguely around him. "As you know, I've never been here before. Is it too late to take a look around?"

"A look around?"

"That private tour we talked about?"

Of course, yes, she remembered now, although he had also said he hadn't meant it when he'd asked, that he was joking. "It's just the time…"

"Never been out there in the dark?"

"Not full dark, no," she said, smiling. "I shouldn't think you'd be able to see much."

"Good job it's not full dark yet, then. And the rain has stopped. Reckon we've got about an hour or so until then, so whaddya say?"

"Erm…well…yes, yes of course, why not? Let's do it. It's… Wow! It's lovely to see you. I really wasn't expecting…" All the worries she'd had that he'd lost interest in her vanished into thin air. "We should take a torch, though, just in case. It's easy to lose track of time out there."

"Whatever you say. You're the boss."

Opening a drawer in one of the chest cabinets to retrieve the torch, she felt bad about lying. She *had* been out there at night before, but only briefly. It was a good few months ago now, during an evening in February, and she'd heard a cry, a tortured sound like an animal in pain. She'd been leaving for the evening, and half of her had been tempted to carry on, to walk down Swain's Lane to Archway Tube station and go home. Highgate during the daytime was one thing – even during the low light, when it became something akin to magical – but in the darkness, it wasn't a place she particularly wanted to linger. If she was honest, as much as she loved it here, when the light had faded completely, she was sometimes uneasy, as if…as if someone was watching her.

But you felt that just now, as if someone was watching you, someone just beyond sight.

That was true, she had. Quite often she'd get such a sensation, but it never unnerved her, it intrigued her, during daylight hours, at least. The night when she had gone to investigate, unable to ignore the pitifulness of such a cry, she'd grabbed a torch as she was doing now, went into the courtyard and climbed the steps to Highgate proper. The torch had been bright enough below, but having stepped over the threshold – as she thought of it – the light had dimmed somewhat, unable to cut through the swathes of darkness that hung like a heavy cloak over such hallowed ground.

"Hey there!" she'd called, not wanting to venture any further into the cemetery, instead tucking the torch underneath her arm and clapping her hands. "Hey there, shoo! Come on now!"

If the cries were from two animals fighting, she hoped her actions were enough to scare them apart. Listening, silence reigned. Total silence. The kind that could trick the imagination…

Whatever it was had gone. But then another sound struck up, echoing all around her, like people calling to each other but in hushed, whispery tones. Was it truly imagination, or were the voices real? Yes, she loved this place, but this place was a cemetery filled with those who had passed, their remains. *Just* their remains. Still, she couldn't help but wonder; it was human nature to wonder…to be afraid of the unknown as well as fascinated by it. And so much had taken place here in the years it had lain neglected, when it had fallen out of favour during the fifties, sixties, and seventies. There were rumours of rituals carried out and spectres raised, sightings, *documented* sightings…

She had turned and hurried back down the steps, her breath coming in short sharp gasps as she re-entered the office in order to make her way out of the front door and into Swain's Lane. She'd continued to hurry all the way to Archway, where amongst the hustle and bustle of ordinary life, she felt she could breathe normally again. Once she'd reached home, she was cross with herself for becoming so badly spooked, feeding off the stories that abounded about Highgate, tales of horror. Even so, she'd never ventured back into it at night, but night might yet fall again if they weren't careful.

She hadn't realised she was stalling until Zak held his

hands up in a gesture of surrender. "I've been really forward, haven't I? Turning up out of the blue like this, with no notice at all, asking you to show me round. Strange thing to do for a second date, I suppose."

A second date? "You said you'd called."

It was Zak who hesitated now. "Ah yeah, do you know what, I'm thinking now I might have accidentally dialled the wrong number. It just went straight to voicemail. Can you check?"

Lucy took the phone from her pocket. "No missed call," she confirmed.

"It was on the way over here – I drove, by the way; I've got the car outside – but now I've realised my mistake. I'm sorry. I'll go."

"No!" The word was out of her mouth before she could stop it, but once uttered, Lucy was glad it had burst from her in such a manner.

Zak Harborne seemed a nice man, a friend of a friend, that particular friend thrilled when she'd heard they were going on a date. "He's gorgeous," she'd said. She was right, he was, and he'd also made an effort to see Lucy twice in twenty-four hours. Last night, when he'd said goodnight, when he'd backed away and hadn't kissed her again, maybe he'd just been tired. She certainly had been. She still was, not having slept well, but there was something else stirring in her stomach too – excitement?

"I don't want you to go," she said. "I want you to…stay. I'm honestly very happy to show you around."

From the way his shoulders relaxed and his smile became brief laughter, she could tell how relieved he was to hear her say that. "It's just, when you talked about your job last night, you were so passionate about it. It was clear you love what you do. My job? I enjoy it, I do, but it's nothing out of the ordinary, is it." Clearly not requiring an answer, he continued. "I wanted to know what it was about this place that lights you up."

That was a curious way of putting it, slightly ironic too, that the dead could do that.

Gesturing for him to follow her, she led him out of the office and into a hallway, acutely aware of – and embarrassed by – the musty smell that always occupied it. She stopped at another tall cabinet. "Got to change my footwear," she explained. "It's muddy out there."

Whilst she hurriedly exchanged shoes for ankle boots, he nodded at his own feet. "Timberlands okay, I presume?"

"They're perfect," she said, her smile shy again, she knew it. This simple act of dressing and undressing, even if it was only footwear and her rainproof jacket, felt intimate somehow.

Once attired correctly, she straightened up, intending to unlock the door, but his hand on her arm caused her to pause. She turned to face him, their eyes locking, another act that felt intimate.

"Zak…?"

"Thank you," he said, and his earnest expression made her catch her breath.

"For what? Giving you a private tour?"

"No," he replied, still so sincere. "For trusting me."

Chapter Five

Lucy – current day

As she climbed the stone steps to what she considered the threshold, Zak behind her, Lucy shivered. Although it hadn't been visible from below, she could now see well enough that there remained a layer of mist covering the ground – *shrouding* it, the imaginative might say. Inwardly, she smiled. That wouldn't be her, not today; she'd keep such fanciful thoughts in check.

Reaching the top, she stopped. She knew the spiel by heart, what to say; she could tell him all about the history of this place, the many people of note who were buried here, the first grave, the most recent, and those that had come in between. She shivered again. It really was quite cold, a sting in the air that hadn't been noticeable earlier. All around her, lining the main path – the one that would eventually lead to the entrance of the Egyptian Avenue – were columns, crosses, and angels, as well as stone slabs that rose out of the mist, and mausoleums too, some choked with ivy or green with moss, others sheltering beneath the branches of a mighty oak tree or a hornbeam. Looking around at the sheer vastness of this otherworldly location, she found herself slipping almost effortlessly into the role of tour guide.

"When Highgate was first opened in 1839, this would have all looked so different. The lawns would have been manicured, and the view towards London breathtaking, as this was open countryside. People would come, and they would see what was tantamount to the ideal resting place. They'd want their loved ones to be buried here and, when the time came, themselves."

"At a price, though." Zak gazed around him. "Plots like these wouldn't have come cheap."

"At a price," Lucy agreed, beginning to walk. "Of course, it was people belonging to the middle classes and above who could afford to buy a plot here, mostly. There are other graves here, not quite so salubrious, those belonging to paupers and marked with a *P*. Some aren't marked at all…"

If she thought he'd ask for more information on that, she was wrong. Instead, he veered off to the side to one of the more decorative graves and hunkered down beside it.

"James William Selby," he said, reading the inscription that lay beneath a large cross. "What's this? There's an engraving, a whip of some sort."

"It's a coachman's horn and whip." She knelt also, the mist covering her knees. "You'll notice too on the surrounding posts that there are inverted horseshoes. James Selby was a famous stagecoach driver, who ran the route from Piccadilly to Virginia Water. He drove his stagecoach to a relentless schedule, through all kinds of weather; whether it was torrential rain or freezing cold, nothing could stop him. In the year 1888, he wagered that he could drive his coach from London to Brighton and back again in record time. With eight teams of horses and fourteen changes en route, he won the wager, completing one hundred and eight miles in less than eight hours. The strain was perhaps too much, though. A few months later, the flu hit him hard and fast, and he died. Highgate is full of symbolism, and those inverted horseshoes represent the fact his luck ran out."

Zak pulled a face. "It does for everyone, I guess."

"Sooner or later," Lucy said, rising.

Leading him back to the path, they continued onwards, Lucy pointing out the gravestone of Elizabeth Jackson, the first person to be buried at Highgate. Not a rich man's wife, not by any stretch, but her husband had already lost his baby daughter and then suffered the indignity of her grave being robbed in Soho. He was determined his wife wouldn't suffer that same terrible fate, and so somehow he'd raised the money to have her buried here, where it was more secure.

There were so many stories to tell, stories that would make you smile or cry, but Lucy could only cover so much in the time they had. The light might be taking its time to fade, but already she had switched her torch on, not because they couldn't see the path in front of them, but, rather, as a source of comfort, the memory of those whispers she'd heard still at the forefront of her mind.

"Whilst we've still got some light, I want to show you two things. The first is the Egyptian Avenue." Rounding the path, she came to a stop before a huge stone arch flanked by lotus columns and tall obelisks. She expected him to take a deep breath inwards – when she led the tours, everyone did just that, almost without exception, and this despite how faded it had become. The stonework was now cracked and crumbling, grey rather than colourful, but its grandeur was intact. Certainly, he was staring at it, but if there was wonder on his face, she couldn't detect it. Quickly she stifled her disappointment – was he enjoying this tour that he had come here asking for? Was she being perhaps a bit too formal in her delivery of its history?

"Do you… Are you sure you want to carry on? It's cold. We could go back."

"What? Oh no, not at all. Sorry, I was just thinking how flashy this is, you know, and about all the things that money can buy. I mean, what's with the Egyptian connection?"

It was a fair question, and he had a point – even in death all things weren't equal. "Because of very high mortality rates, it's generally held that the Victorians were obsessed with death. Historians tend to call this obsession the 'Cult of Death'." As she said it, she noticed his expression change again, from distaste back to intrigue. "Because death was such a normal part of life, they developed ways of honouring it, and, yes, one of those ways was to ensure a good send-off, the more ostentatious the better. During this era there was a strong interest in all things Egyptian, particularly how they honoured death, and, well…that's the inspiration behind this."

"It signalled how much the deceased was loved?"

"Yes. It was meant to. There was a lot of ritual involved. Everything had to be just so."

"But if you had no money, if you were poor, what then? You mentioned something earlier about pauper's graves."

She nodded; so he *had* been listening. "Poorer families often saved what they could in order to ensure a proper burial for one of their own, even if it meant that they by and large starved. If you had no money, however, nothing at all, then the Poor Union would step in and you'd be buried in a communal plot, without ceremony or a headstone, just a marker with *P*. No name, no date, and often no record kept that you'd ever been here, that you'd existed. A pauper's grave was feared, though, because who cared about them? It seemed no one but the grave robbers who got paid well for digging them up and delivering them to medical schools for dissection. It was the ultimate fear, that there was no rest in death, no peace and no dignity, just as there'd probably been very little peace or dignity in life. Times are hard enough now, we face so many uncertainties, but back then, if you were no one, you were doomed right from the beginning."

Having come to a finish, Lucy noticed Zak was smiling.

"There it is," he said. "There's that passion I was talking about."

She winced. "Sorry, did I...erm...go off on one?"

"Not at all," he assured her. "Believe me, it's quite incredible to have found someone like you."

"Like me?" Lucy queried.

There was a brief pause before Zak answered, as if he was taking time to cultivate his answer. "Someone so...fascinating."

Unable to hold his gaze, she lowered her eyes. Had anyone ever said that to her before, that she was fascinating? No boyfriend had, that was for sure. Even her parents, whom she had loved and who were now both deceased, hadn't. And yet here she was, aged forty-two, in a cemetery, in the low light, being told she was just that: fascinating, by a man who'd not long been in her life and whom in this moment she very much hoped would stay there.

Clearly aware of her embarrassment, he pointed to the archway. "So come on, enlighten me further. Who's buried here and why?"

Grateful to seize upon something more familiar, Lucy led him onwards through the archway, explaining that the passage ahead used to be covered by a roof that had long since crumbled, leaving it open to the sky. On either side of the passage were brick vaults designed to take multiple lead-lined coffins so that family members could be reunited in death. She further explained what some of the imagery on the doors to the vaults meant: the lotus flower, both open and closed, representing life and death; and the inverted torch, a symbol of an extinguished life. She also told him about what else inhabited the vaults: the bat colony, one of the biggest in London; and the Orb Spider, Britain's biggest spider, a creature that required absolute darkness in order to thrive.

Her torch was having to work in earnest now as they left the Egyptian Avenue behind them and encountered the Circle of Lebanon, which comprised more vaults, sunken this time and arranged in both an inner and an outer circle, each linked by a continuous cornice. What was truly awe-inspiring was the massive tree that towered over the circle, providing a daunting silhouette.

"That's the Cedar of Lebanon tree," Lucy explained, shining her torch at it. "It was here before they built Highgate, more than one hundred years before, apparently, and it's why this is called the Circle of Lebanon. The tree is very much a focal point, the cemetery spreading out all around it."

Now Zak did inhale, his eyes wide as he took it all in.

"See these walls?" she continued, going over to pat them. "In the nineteenth century these would have been milky white in colour, not grey."

"Incredible," Zak breathed.

"It certainly is," she replied, thrilled that he thought so. "Zak, it's…well, it's getting late."

"There's still so much to see, though."

"Like I said, you won't see much in the dark."

Reluctantly he conceded. "Yeah, I suppose not."

"I could always show you around properly another time?"

"A third date?"

She laughed, sincerely hoping this wouldn't be the end of the second one. Happily, it wasn't, as in the next breath he suggested drinks followed by dinner.

"That'd be lovely," she answered. "There's an Italian restaurant in the village, if you like Italian, that is?"

"I adore it."

"Me too."

As they retraced their footsteps back along the path, Lucy could feel the first drops of rain on her face and hair. She gazed up to witness a sky that had darkened even more dramatically, heavily swollen clouds suddenly conspiring with the night and a low rumble of thunder that she felt through her boots more than heard.

"Christ," she exclaimed. "I think it's going to pour down."

Zak looked nothing if not amused. "Better make a run for it, then!"

Without another word, he took off, Lucy hesitating for only a second. As she also broke into a run, she was laughing again, really laughing – shrieking, even, when it did indeed start to pour heavily, quickly plastering her hair to her face and her clothes to her skin. When a streak of lightning lit the cemetery around her, if only for a moment or two, followed swiftly by a proper clap of thunder, she shrieked a second time, not frightened, as she had been before in these grounds at night, but exhilarated. In this moment, still hurtling along the path, barely able to see, all around her just shadows cast by so many stone monuments and dense trees, she felt nothing but happiness – maybe even bliss. She might hardly know Zak, but somehow he had managed to bring this place even more alive for her. She could hear his laughter from up ahead, great gusts of it punctuating the loud hiss of rain in the trees and the crunch of wet gravel beneath her feet, his calls now urging her to keep up and enquiring whether she was all right.

"I'm fine!" she yelled back, but if he heard her or not she had no idea as yet more lightning struck and more thunder crashed. There weren't just shadows within the grounds; they seemed to be so much more substantial than that, turning towards her and staring. They were tall things, blacker than either shadows or the night could ever be. *Get a grip,* she told herself, but in a lighthearted manner because in that instant, even being scared felt delicious. It felt *right,* adding to the thrill of the situation.

When, finally, they reached the door to her office, she leant against it, trying to catch her breath. A small porch roof sheltered them both from the worst of the deluge.

"Bloody hell!" Zak said when he was able to. "The

thunder's loud enough to wake the dead!"

"I hope not," replied Lucy, still panting heavily. "We'd be severely outnumbered if it did!"

"Yeah, right, of course. This wouldn't be the best place for that to happen."

Any further reply died on her lips as Zak pulled her towards his chest and held her tight, his mouth covering her mouth, his tongue seeking hers. Again, she was surprised, not anticipating this happening – not yet, at least. Initially she was rigid, perhaps due to the surprise, but quickly she relaxed and began to respond. There was something about him…not just exciting but familiar too somehow. Was he the one she'd waited all her life for, even though she hadn't realised she *had* been waiting?

As his grip became tighter, his tongue probed deeper still. In response, her rain-soaked body melted into his until it was impossible to tell where she ended and he began. Only briefly did he pull away to stare into her eyes. Did he see the consent there, the longing? He must have, as he pushed her back against the door, lifted her skirt, and freed her before freeing himself. Next he was holding her, supporting her as he thrust into her, stealing her breath clean away.

Never had she done anything like this before, something so raw, so intoxicating. It took her time to form a relationship with someone, a bond, and even then it could be tenuous. This man, however, who'd turned up so unexpectedly, who'd wanted to witness her passion, was unleashing a new passion within her, one perhaps greater? Did he feel the same? Was it possible? *He sought you out, remember? Not just last night, but today as well.* As he continued thrusting, the guttural cries he emitted a match for her own, she opened her eyes as another bolt of lightning hit the higher ground in front of her.

It wasn't multiple shadows that she could see this time, not like those she thought she'd seen before, but *a* shadow, singular. It was small and quite alone, standing there for a moment, only a moment, and therefore easy to doubt. But what she couldn't doubt was what the shadow inspired in her, the very last emotion she should feel as her body reached its climax – sheer horror.

Chapter Six

Emma – 1972

"Shut up, Loo, stop making such a racket. We're not supposed to be here, remember?"

Despite Kev's warning, a snort escaped Louise, Angela and Danny laughing too. As for Emma, she didn't know whether to plaster a smile on her face or not. If she did, it would give the appearance she was joining in the fun, at least, whereas all she felt inside was trepidation. The five of them had arrived in Highgate, had walked up Swain's Lane, itself a drab and depressing place with no houses, no real sign of life. All it led to was a ruined place, one that housed the dead.

Kev took the lead again. "Danny, over here, I'll give you a leg up."

The wall they intended to climb was a high one, slightly taller than they were. Not a particularly solid wall, it looked in definite need of repair in places, but still, Emma couldn't fathom out how they were going to scale it and so stepped back so that she could watch Danny. With no hesitation at all, he hopped onto Kev's cupped hands and pulled himself upwards. From there he straddled the wall, pulling his second leg over and jumping down the other side.

"Whoa!" he shouted, his voice truly full of awe. "It's a

jungle in here!"

"Loo, you next."

Still with a big grin on her face, Louise was up and over the wall too, with all the ease of an athlete. Angela struggled slightly, making a fuss whilst in the straddle position and screaming that she was stuck. Danny told her not to be so stupid and helped her down the other side.

Kev then turned to Emma. "Your turn."

Emma could feel whatever colour she had drain from her. When they had left their flat earlier, it had been cool but not cold, a pleasant spring evening, but standing in this lane with nothing but darkness all around them, she'd begun to shiver. It was just so bleak, the air of decay so tangible that you could almost reach out and grab it, an abandonment that made her heart ache terribly.

"Emma?"

"I'm sorry, Kev, I don't think I can."

"Can't what?"

"Go in there, it's..." She struggled to explain. "Not right."

"You have to."

"Have to?"

"Yeah. It's 'cause of you we're here. What you going to do otherwise, stay this side by yourself?"

Emma bit her lip, her shivering increasing. It wasn't because of her they'd come; that was a lie. It was because of him, Kev. This was his idea. And no – once more she glanced around her, at the lane they stood in, the emptiness that seemed so vast – she didn't want to stay this side of the wall on her own. All she wanted was to be back at the flat, in her room, safe in bed.

"Oi, Kev, Em, what you doing? Come on, get over here."

It was Danny calling out again, such words not meriting the inane giggling they caused from Angela and Louise. They'd been smoking before they left the house but not much. Emma herself had had a few drags but hadn't inhaled; she'd discreetly blown the smoke out of the side of her mouth when the others weren't looking. The way they were acting, though – not Kev so much, but the other three – had they also taken something else, either in the house or en route?

"Emma!" Kev's voice held more of a command this time, one difficult to ignore.

"If I go, though, who'll help you over?" Kev just laughed.

"Okay, okay," she relented, lifting her foot into his clasped hands and emulating the actions of the others, screaming just as much as Angela when she practically fell down the other side. Danny heroically cushioned the fall, brushing off her apologies with more laughter.

Kev was next, clearly needing no assistance as he landed in front of them with a thud, a look of grim determination on his face. It seemed darker still this side of the wall, and the ground beneath them was spongy, covered as it was in so much bracken. A screech pierced the air, just an owl probably, but it nonetheless caused Angela to grab onto Louise, the pair of them screeching too.

"For fuck's sake," Kev barked, "this place might be patrolled. Keep it down!"

Danny wasn't so sure. "Come on, Kev, look around you. At the state of it, no one comes here, except lunatics like us."

"I s'pose," Kev replied, beginning to relax. "Blimey, you're right, it *is* a jungle!"

Emma took it all in too, not just the silhouettes of countless trees, their branches spreading far and wide, but the many tall stone crosses dotted in amongst them. *No—* the retort lay silent on her lips—*this is no jungle; it's a place of rest.* And here they were, disturbing the peace.

"Switch your torches on," Kev instructed. "And follow me."

Not everyone had brought torches, only Emma, Kev, and Danny. Angela and Louise hung onto each other instead but kept close to Danny. Because of so much undergrowth, it was slow going in the cemetery; they would need scythes to negotiate it more efficiently. Kev, though, wasn't letting anything put him off. He was here, at Highgate, and he was going to explore, the light from his torch bouncing in front of him like a yellow ball on elastic, haphazardly revealing a landscape awash with carved stone despite nature having done its utmost to rectify that.

"This place…it gives me the creeps." It was Louise's voice, a slight tremble in it that hadn't been there before. There was also something else in her tone. Wonder? Was that it?

Angela was clearly in agreement. "Yeah, but on the other hand, wow! Just wow!"

"Fuck!" Danny had come to a standstill and was pointing to the left of him. "What's that?"

They all turned to look, Emma's breath hitching in her throat as the outline of some sort of gateway loomed in front of them, yet more branches hanging over it and swaying slightly from side to side, as if beckoning them onwards, trying to entice them.

Kev swore too. "It's like the fucking gateway to hell or something."

Emma shined her torch at the building to get a better look. A gateway; it was indeed that, ornate with fat columns on either side of it. Within it, however, in the tunnel that lay beyond, the darkness had a thickness to it, one that inspired further dread.

"I don't think we should be here," she said, but her protest went unheard. Kev and Danny were already wading forward through the undergrowth, Angela and Louise too.

"Has anyone brought a camera?" Kev called. Emma had, and it seemed she was the only one. "Well?"

"Me," Emma said, joining them. Again, she couldn't bear the thought of being left behind.

"Get it out, then. Start taking pictures."

"Where are we going?"

"Where does it look like?" he responded, deliberately being dramatic. "Into the bowels of hell!"

With all four of them not just laughing but whooping and hollering, Emma still saw no choice but to follow. *Do as he says and take pictures. It's research.* Retrieving her Kodak Instamatic, she shoved in a flashcube and, rather than peer through the viewfinder, she held it almost at arm's length and fired, wondering what, if anything, she'd be able to capture in such gloom, the flash like a huge burst of blue lightning. Further ahead, Kev was kicking at something.

Shoving the Instamatic back in her pocket, Emma went to investigate. "What's up?"

"This vault door's not quite closed. I reckon we can get in here, see what's going down."

"What? No! You can't!" Trespassing was bad enough, but to vandalise as well? "Kev, stop!"

Ignoring her, he continued to kick at the door, which thankfully was holding fast…for now.

"Kev!" she pleaded, but it was no use. Kev seemed to be in a world of his own, as did the other three, who, no longer forming a huddled mass, had begun to drift away, heading further up the passage, their hands in front of them and one of them exclaiming yet again, "Wow!"

Distraught at what Kev was doing – the disrespect he was showing – Emma forced herself to reach out, placing her hand on his shoulder to pull him away. "You can't do this! It's wrong!"

Immediately she regretted the action. He swung round and grabbed her instead, fingers digging into what scant flesh there was at the top of her arms.

"Kev!" Any further protest died in her throat; she was simply too stricken to utter another word.

"What the fuck's the matter with you?" His teeth bared, he looked feral. "Why don't you loosen up? Have a bit of fun for once."

"You… You can't go around damaging property."

"It's property that no one cares about!"

"There are bodies in there!"

"Exactly. So they're gonna care least of all."

"But this wasn't part of the deal!"

"What deal?" This close up and despite the lack of light – both their torches had fallen to the floor in the struggle – she could see genuine confusion in his eyes, also that they were flickering slightly from left to right as if he was having trouble focusing.

"Kev, are you all right? What have you taken?"

"What do you mean, what have I taken?"

"What drugs?"

His arms dropped to his side, something she was thankful for, although she could still feel well enough their throbbing imprint. "Don't judge me."

"I'm not!"

"Look at you. You think you're so much better than us, don't you?"

She shook her head. "Kev, that's not true." Turning her head slightly, she scanned the horizon for Danny, Angela, and Louise. They'd disappeared completely, been swallowed up, it seemed. It was just her and Kev – in hell, as he'd described it. Where had the others gone? Why had they left them like that? Surely they should stick together? There was safety in numbers.

Like a dog with a bone, Kev had got the bit between his teeth and wouldn't let go. "Why are you so high and mighty? Did your parents spoil you, their *only child?*"

God, the sarcasm in his voice! "I've told you, I'm not close to my parents."

"So what are you, then, estranged?"

"Look, just forget it. I'm an ordinary girl from an ordinary background, that's all."

"Bullshit! There's nothing ordinary about you. You look down on us, on me in particular."

"I honestly don't know where you're getting all this from."

"You never join in."

"I do! Before I came out, I had a smoke with you all."

"You didn't inhale. Not once."

She was amazed. How could he have noticed? She'd been discreet; she knew she had. And if he had noticed that, then what else? How she had flinched when he drew closer to her whilst sitting on her bed? The terror he'd instilled when he'd just grabbed her? Terror even she didn't understand, and why it should be so.

"Come on, Kev, let's go join the others."

Her attempts at moving him on fell short. "I'm not going anywhere," he growled.

She swallowed, praying his temper wouldn't get out of hand again. "Kev, I think…I think you don't feel too good, and, to be honest, nor do I. It could be this place…it's having a bad effect."

"Oh, really? You think so? But you love this sort of thing, don't you?" He started to swing his head from side to side, glancing wildly around him. "This place suits an *extra*ordinary girl."

She frowned, not just scared, not just bewildered, but baffled too.

"That's why you're so obsessed," he continued, gesturing round him, that too a frantic action. "Because here's where you feel at home. You're one of them. You belong here."

"It wasn't me who wanted to come."

His eyes were on her again. "I see you, Emma. Really see you. And do you know what—"

"Kev, we need to find the others."

"You're dead inside."

There was silence, as heavy as a cloud full of rain. What could she say, how could she respond to that? Could she deny it, when she had thought it too, time after time? The silence continued, his gaze not unfocused anymore; instead, his eyes bored into her, seeing everything and missing nothing. Never had she felt so vulnerable, so naked. "Kev..."

More cries, more whoops pierced the air, preventing her from continuing the vain task of placating him. Grateful for the distraction they provided, she pushed Kev away from her, quickly bent to retrieve her torch, and ran to catch up with the others. Kev could follow her or he could remain where he was, take his anger back out on the door rather than her. She no longer cared.

The path led to a circle, one set just below ground level, and within it there were yet more vaults, all of which looked thankfully intact. Above the circle, on a flat of land, there was a tree, quite different from other trees she'd seen in this cemetery. It was so much taller, much wider. Regal, almost, a sentinel that presided over its many sleeping charges.

"What's happening?" she asked, aware that Kev had indeed decided to follow her, that he'd reached her side. "What are they doing?"

Danny was running round and round the circle, almost as if he was trying to outrun himself. Louise could be heard declaring that what was before her was "amazing, just amazing," but she could not be seen. Angela was closer, standing in front of Emma and Kev, her hand outstretched and tracing the patterns on two columns that stood on either side of a chamber door.

"Angela?" Emma said, stepping closer, if only to put more distance between herself and Kev.

"Look," Angela replied. "See how the stone sparkles,

how it shimmers."

Emma shined her torch directly at the columns and stared at them too, just as Danny completed another circuit, beating at his chest like he was champion of the world. The stones were far from shimmering; they were blackened with dirt and grime accumulated over years of neglect. They had symbols on them too, strange symbols – graffiti, she assumed – deeply etched.

"It's beautiful," breathed Angela, running her hand over one of the symbols, a star of some sort, "all so beautiful." Suddenly she whirled round and held her hands out in front of her instead. "It's like paradise here, everything is so…abundant."

Emma turned to Kev. She should never have agreed to come here and especially not with them, her flatmates, in the state they were in. They'd taken more than dope; now she was certain of it, leaving her to deal with them stone-cold sober.

"We have to leave."

Kev's gap-toothed grin normally lent him an air of cheekiness. Right now, however, he looked stupid, plain stupid, a goon. "Em," he answered, "we're only just beginning."

Without another word, he took off and joined Danny in his manic race, the pair of them no longer worried about security but making such a racket. *Stop,* she wanted to scream, *all of you!* But she knew how futile her words would be; there was no stopping them, not yet, not until they began to come down from whatever they had taken. Right now, they were in the grip of it.

To avoid being knocked over by Danny and Kev, Emma

took a step back into the doorway of one of the chambers to shelter there in the recess, the smell of lichen, of damp – despite it being a dry night – redolent. And something else too…a more perfumed smell, at first not unpleasant, but then it became so; the more you breathed it in, it became nauseating.

Louise had rounded the corner, coming back into view. Petite in stature, she appeared almost ethereal. "It's magnificent!" she insisted. "Everyone is so friendly. Look! Look at him, Emma, he's just a child! His hair, oh, it's beautiful. He's got blond curls, just like a cherub, and there are others that surround him, more cherubs. They're all so beautiful. I love it here! I love it!"

The space she pointed at was empty. Whatever she could see, Emma couldn't. There was just darkness, so much of it, pooling in corners and, with hers the only torch still beaming – Kev clearly hadn't picked his up, and Danny too had discarded his – it seemed only to be creeping closer, ready to engulf them. Briefly she closed her eyes, Kev's words appearing in her mind again: *You're one of them. You belong here.* She didn't. She hated it. Unlike the others, who were all caught up in their own versions of reality. Even so, she had to get them out, get them home. This wasn't research; this was madness, or at least it could turn to madness soon.

Danny had stopped. He was also pointing at the walls and the chamber doors. "The walls are rippling," he muttered, practically breathless. "There…there are hands in the walls. Oh wow, hands and…and…they're coming out of the walls. So many of them!"

Kev stopped beside him and was looking too. "They're

dead people."

"No, mate," Danny vehemently denied. "They're alive!"

Emma was about to beg them all to come with her, to trace their path back out of Highgate, when screams filled the air. "Get off me! I said get off!"

It was Louise, bolting forward and grabbing Danny and Kev. "Someone's here," she declared. "We've got to go!"

"Yeah, Loo, whatever," Danny started to say, but she tightened her grip on him and started to drag him forwards.

"I'm not joking, Danny. Someone else is here! A tall man. He's got a cape on, and a hat, and...I don't know...he's just weird. Christ, Danny, it's the smell of him. He stinks. Come on!"

She started to run, and Danny, who had no choice in the matter, started running too, grabbing at Kev and forcing him onwards as well. Emma looked for Angela. Where was she? They couldn't just leave her, high on drugs and at the mercy of some stranger.

Although the last thing she wanted to do was lose the others, Emma darted back into the circle, all the while calling out Angela's name. "Angela! Angela!" Reaching some steps, she took them two at a time, only briefly registering how jagged they were, how chipped and broken. There she was, thank goodness, not far; she was at the top of the steps, standing still and simply gazing into the distance, towards yet more buildings, yet more graves. As she drew closer, Emma could make out the expression on her face, one of delight, so pure that it stopped her in her tracks and, for a moment, she stood as still as Angela, wondering what it was that her flatmate could see now...a new feeling rising up within her, obliterating all else, that of envy. The girl was serene, perfectly at peace. Something she herself had never been.

"Angela, it's me," she told her, her voice a whisper this time. "It's Emma."

When there was no reply, she reached out to touch Angela's arm, a part of her hoping that in doing so, in making contact, something of what she was experiencing might rub off on her. *I want to see what you see; I want to feel it...something good, something...worthwhile.*

"Angela," she implored again, "what can you see?"

Although there was no answer forthcoming, contact with Angela, as Emma had hoped, had a positive effect. With no laughing, screeching, or shouting to disturb or distract her, this was the calmest she'd been since she'd scaled the wall – both of them in harmony amidst the decay.

"Angela." There was nothing beseeching in her voice now, just acceptance. They would have lost the others, but that was okay; she was happy here, she belonged, as Kev said.

As Angela started to sway, Emma could feel herself swaying too, caught in the throes of some silent rhythm, the beating heart of Highgate, perhaps? She closed her eyes briefly, wished she could keep them closed, the darkness a welcome oblivion; it held such promise. Of course she could keep them closed, why not? Wasn't that in line with so many others here?

Peace – what a strange feeling, what an incredible feeling it was in this silent land.

Still swaying, lulling herself deeper and deeper into plush, velvety folds, the shock of being forced back to reality was harsh. "What the...?" she managed, her eyes snapping open.

Angela looked far from sublime; her eyes were as wide as could be, her mouth open in panic. "There's a man here! A tall man!"

Before Emma could respond or look to see if Angela was indeed right, she was suddenly running, being forcibly dragged out of Highgate too.

Chapter Seven

Grace – 1850s

It was a wonderful sight to see! Her brothers' eyes were nearly popping out of their sockets, Michael's especially, whose stomach also rumbled in anticipation. As for her mam, it was the first time Grace could remember seeing her smile in such a way; it brightened her whole countenance, dispelled some of the years, the grief, that had ravaged her. Just for tonight, they wouldn't have to worry or endure a hunger that tore at your insides.

The second encounter she'd had earlier that day had been so different to the first, terrible one – those women that had dragged her further into the alleyway, who'd talked about her as if she were nothing but a hunk of meat, who'd prodded her and laughed at how she'd struggled, their cackling so hideous to hear. She was so grateful to have escaped them. No, the second time, it was as if a miracle had occurred.

The tall man, wearing a tall hat and a cape, was a true gentleman. At first, she had thought him forbidding, someone to be even more afraid of, but how wrong she'd been! He had saved her. It *was* a miracle! No doubt about it. He had marched up to the baker who had refused her, almost as if he'd known, as if he'd seen how that other man had treated her earlier, and he had bought the rest of his loaves for her. The baker, his cheeks even redder than before, anger clearly suffusing him, nonetheless hadn't said a word. He just took the gentleman's money and handed over the loaves, although he'd glowered at the child by his side – briefly, mind, so that the gentleman wouldn't catch him. Grace had torn into one of the loaves there and then, had stared right back at the baker, willing him to say something.

Her bold actions seemed to please the gentleman, as he began laughing, his blue eyes filled with mirth. As if it were infectious somehow, she began to laugh too, couldn't help herself.

The man hadn't stopped there either; he had then taken her to another costermonger, had bought her some apples, big red rosy ones. He'd asked her how many she wanted, and she'd replied four; that would be one for each of them: herself, Michael, Patrick, and Mam. She couldn't believe it when he handed the package over to her, her hands hugging it to her chest in case he should change his mind. She didn't like to tell him that she'd never tasted an apple before, not one such as this, fresh and juicy, only a rotten piece that someone from one of the inns had thrown at her once when she'd been in there scavenging.

"Do you eat meat?" the man had gone on to ask.

"Sometimes." The truth was – and she suspected he was perfectly aware of this – it was rare that she ate meat, and that tended to be on the rotten side too.

"Let's get you some."

As he'd continued to walk, she had stopped. "No," she said, hardly believing her own ears.

He'd turned on his heel, inclined his head, and looked at her.

"I...I can't go home with all this and meat too. My mam, she'd wonder."

"Wonder what?"

"What I'd been doing to get it." She was being bold again, but this man had been so kind to her, and in return she wanted to speak nothing but the truth.

Instead of berating her, the man – she wished she knew his name, but it was a step too far to ask him – smiled. "Where do you live?"

"St Giles, the Riley tenement."

"With your mam?"

"And my two brothers, Michael and Patrick."

"No father?"

"He's dead, along with another brother and my sister."

"Does your mother work?"

"Sometimes, when she can."

"Why is it that she cannot work?"

"She gets ill easily. She has this cough..."

"I see," the man responded, and Grace nodded. He *did* see; he understood. But then hers was a common enough tale.

"Well...you had best get home, had you not?"

"Yes, sir."

Once more, he laughed, as if how she'd just addressed him was another source of amusement.

"We'll eat well tonight," she continued, "thanks to you." Again, she added, "Sir," wanting to please him further.

"It is the food of the gods," he replied, "bread and apples."

Grace avidly agreed. About to turn, to run off, he stopped her with yet more words.

"There is more if you want it."

"More, sir?" she queried, unease returning.

"You do want more, do you not?"

Yes, of course she did.

"Your family would want more…"

They would.

"Then meet me here tomorrow."

"But—"

"*If* you want more."

He had been the one to turn away on that occasion, his smile still in place. A kind smile. That's what she'd told herself then and she reminded herself of now as she handed over the packages to her family. Unwrapping the apples, Michael immediately bit into one, a look of sheer bliss as well as surprise on his face as flavours hitherto unknown exploded in his mouth. Patrick was more tentative, staring at the apple that their mam had handed over to him, full of suspicion.

"Go on," their mother gently encouraged. "Just try a bit. You'll like it, I promise. Everyone likes apples fresh from the orchard."

Patrick did as he was told, but his teeth weren't sharp enough to pierce the skin.

"Here," said Grace, reaching up to one of the shelves to find a knife there, one with a carved wooden handle that had belonged to her father. Wiping its blade against her clothes, she took the apple from Patrick in order to cut slices from it, the first of which she held out to him, suppressing an almost overwhelming desire to snatch it back and fill her own mouth with it instead. How trusting the child was! He took this piece of fruit he'd never seen before and finally bit into it. At first his expression was somewhat horrified, but then it dissolved into pleasure, into amazement that something had taste to it when all they were used to was the blandness of bread.

Grace's mother took the third apple. "I haven't had one of these since I was a girl," she said, but more to herself than her children. "Where'd you get them, Grace?"

The lie came easily. "There was a woman, a costermonger. She said they were on the turn. Took what money I had in exchange."

"On the turn? They look fresh enough to me."

Feigning nonchalance, Grace shrugged. "I wouldn't know."

"And the bread?"

"Cheap too, on account of it being stale." She almost thanked God that it *was* stale; her mam might believe that lie more readily.

"I see." She took another bite of the apple. "You're a good girl, aren't you, Grace?"

"Yes, Mam! I am!"

Her mother smiled. She'd caused affront and she knew it, but she also believed her daughter. "Sit down, take your apple, and eat it."

"But the fire needs stoking."

"It does. But eat first."

Oh, the taste of it! It was at once tart yet sweet; no wonder it had made Patrick grimace initially. It felt full of goodness, as if…as if…it could cure all the ills that might afflict a person's body. Maybe it could. If her mam got to eat more food like this, her cough might go away, might disappear altogether. It would be another miracle. Today seemed full of them.

Michael devoured his apple, Patrick ate two pieces of his, and then Grace carefully stowed the rest of it away. She and her mother left not even the core of their own apples before all of them ate the bread, sitting in front of the fire that Grace had at last teased into life. Replete, the evening passed peacefully, none of them speaking much, just content to be in each other's company. Around them, in the other dwellings, various cries and screams drifted towards them, a fair few of them caused by hunger. What else caused them she wouldn't think about, didn't want to; in the confines of their room, at least, all was well. Thanks to him – the man with the bright blue eyes.

Her mother was sleeping now, sitting upright in her chair, her head having fallen forwards. Her brothers were dozing too, Patrick occasionally coughing and Michael's legs jerking as if he was chasing something in his dreams...or running away. As the last of the flames flickered, Grace drew her shawl around her – a tattered thing, but nonetheless it offered a semblance of warmth. She closed her eyes too, keen to gain some respite from the cries that still drifted on the air, as well as a stray dog barking and feral cats hissing.

Her mind was churning, however. Would she do it, go and meet him tomorrow? Was he really a kind man? There had to be some kindness in the world, although she knew so little of it. But even if he was, why would he bestow such kindness on her, someone from the gutter, whose life didn't mean a thing to the upper echelons of society and whose death didn't either? Vermin. That's what she was, what all her kind were. And what did you do with vermin? You destroyed them. Everyone knew that. You didn't feed them or encourage them. Not unless...unless...

No!

He'd given her food, for her and her family, and hadn't asked for anything in return. You couldn't disguise benevolence, not when it shone in your eyes like that.

What he'd done for her, the joy she was able to give her family because of it...

She replaced her doubts with memories of her brothers' faces as they'd eaten, her mam's too, even now as they slept, their contentment, the kind that only a full belly could bring about. And her mam wasn't coughing now, but it would start up soon enough. It would get worse as the night wore on; it would wrack her body. She needed food, good food, the sort that could save her. *She* could save her – Grace could.

All she had to do was meet the tall man tomorrow.

Chapter Eight

Lucy – current day

Not just the cemetery at Highgate was fascinating; Highgate Village was equally so.

"Swain's Lane itself is one of London's oldest trade routes," Lucy told Zak as they lay in her bed together, their roles as lovers firmly cemented over the past fortnight. "It was once a drovers' road leading to Spitalfields Market. There've been scores of murders, suicides, and other tragic deaths associated with it over the years. There've also been numerous sightings of a spectre."

"A spectre?" Zak laughed as he traced a finger down her torso, running straight through her breasts and causing her insides to quiver. "What kind of spectre?"

"A man. He's tall and dressed peculiarly, in Victorian clothes, I think, a cape and a tall hat. He comes out of nowhere and rushes at you before disappearing. Hey, why are you laughing?"

"Me? Laughing? I'm not."

"Yes, you are! It's true! Honestly. As I said, there've been numerous sightings, all through the years. Even today people swear they've seen him. Some think he's a vampire."

Quick as a flash, Zak had her on her back, his teeth gnawing at her neck.

"Stop it!" she yelled in between bursts of laughter. "What are you doing?"

"Showing you who the true bloodsucker is!"

As his teeth grazed her neck just that little bit harder, Lucy's laughter turned to squeals. She couldn't believe it, that she was falling in love. Because that's what was happening here, in between the lovemaking and the bouts of playfulness and all the talking they would do, sometimes into the early hours of the morning, forming a bond that had become so intense so quickly, nothing tenuous about it at all.

As his lips moved away from her throat, following the same path his fingers had earlier, delight enfolded her. Is this what it felt like to be a part of something? No longer on the outside looking in, curious and lonely, because that's what she'd been: lonely, despite a busy life and her job – a job which still seemed to fascinate him, the uniqueness of it. But, in truth, over the past two weeks, she was becoming more enamoured with the business of living.

Her breath beginning to come in short, sharp pants, she closed her eyes and relaxed into him. His mobile, when it rang, was a rude awakening.

"Damn!" he muttered, breaking away from her and turning his head to the right.

"Can't you ignore it?"

He pulled a face. "It might be one of the kids."

She hadn't met his kids yet – Joe and Maia, who were seventeen and thirteen, respectively. He'd told her a bit about them, and they sounded fairly typical for their ages: one minute charming, the next surly. She'd seen a picture of them too. Maia had blond hair, just like his, whereas, in a separate picture, Joe was darker, clearly unimpressed with being photographed as he scowled at the camera. Zak was a good dad, one who saw his kids a lot and who still provided for them. When the phone rang, he was always prepared to answer it, just in case it was one of them and they needed something. A good dad and a good man; she was lucky to have found him.

She watched as he leant over and grabbed his jeans off the floor, quickly retrieving his phone from one of the pockets. Glancing at it, he then turned to her to indicate it was indeed one of his children before rising to leave the room, stark naked, and take the call elsewhere in the flat.

The reason she hadn't met his kids was because they didn't know about her, not yet; he wanted to break the news to them gently and in time. Although they hadn't discussed his ex-wife much, she had the impression that the breakup had been somewhat traumatic. Who'd decided to leave whom, she still had no idea about and nor had she probed. It seemed...inappropriate to do that. She was just thrilled he intended to introduce her to Joe and Maia 'someday', that he was taking their relationship that seriously. The *L* word hadn't been discussed, not openly, not yet, but she prayed he felt the same. That he wanted to see her and so often was an indicator that perhaps he did. In fact, this past fortnight, they'd hardly been apart, and it was he that had instigated every single meeting, her flat becoming something of an after-work refuge as his flat was out of bounds – again because of the children, should they turn up unexpectedly.

Alone in bed now, she glanced at the clock. It was after 7.00 a.m., time to get up soon and get ready for work. For now, though, she simply listened to his voice and the tone of it. It was quiet. Was he whispering? Why would he do that if it was one of his children? Curious, she sat up, swung her legs over the side of her bed and reached for her dressing gown. Wrapping it around her, she padded across the carpet to her chest of drawers, strewn with makeup and a mirror, which also happened to be closer to the door. There she stood, wincing slightly as she caught sight of her face, which was still puffy from sleep. Her hair was mussed too, and she reached up to calm it with her hands before dragging a brush through it. Yes, he was definitely whispering, standing in the kitchen, probably, with not a stitch on, engaged in something clandestine. Holding her breath so there'd be no other sound to distract her, she couldn't help but try to listen further.

"…no…not now…I can't…listen to me…soon."

What was it that was being demanded of him?

"…have to go…yes, call…later. No…won't forget. Look! Told you…won't forget."

There'd been anger in those last words, she was certain of it. She didn't have kids, but she had friends who did, and on the occasions she managed to see those friends, they looked and sounded harried too. She was an aunt, at least – she had a niece and a nephew, but she never got to see them as her younger brother, her only sibling, lived in Hong Kong with his native wife.

As Zak re-entered the room, not even glancing at her as he went to fetch his clothes, she pulled what she hoped was a suitably sympathetic face. "Problems?"

"What? Yeah, yeah, you know how it is."

Having kids? No, but she was willing to imagine.

Walking over to him, she placed her hand on his back, immediately wishing she hadn't. Had he just flinched at her touch? She withdrew her hand and hugged it to her chest instead. "Look, I'm sorry. If something's wrong, I'd like to help."

Dressed in his jeans now but only halfway into his shirt, he stopped for a moment, became quite still.

"Zak?" she said, another apology in her voice. Family matters could be sensitive; whatever had happened between him and one of his children had clearly upset him, as had her prying.

She took a step backwards, completely unsure of what to do, tears pricking at her eyes. She *had* been nosy, deliberately moving closer to the door so she could eavesdrop on him, and now she felt bad about it, as if he'd guessed what she'd done. Was he suddenly cross she wanted to be a part of his life so soon, even though, she reminded herself, he'd done all the running so far?

He swung round, shrugging his shirt on properly now so that it covered his shoulders. There was indeed anguish on his face, and he was clearly struggling to conceal it. Lucy waited, wanting him to be the first to break the awkward silence that had settled between them.

"Joe," he said at last. "He's having...a few problems."

"What kind of problems?"

"It's just..."

"Look, you don't have to tell me, not if you don't want to. I'm sorry he's having problems, and I'm...well, I'm concerned for you too. It can't be easy."

"Easy is one thing it isn't! Teens...they can be a liability. And his mother, well, let's just say she allows certain things that I wouldn't, you know, if he lived with me. But he doesn't live with me, he's with her, and... God!" He clenched his fists as, briefly, he screwed his eyes shut. "Why does the law, why does *society*, always favour the mother? If he lived with me, if they both did, those kids would be on the straight and narrow, I'm telling you."

"The straight and narrow?" Lucy was shocked. "Is Joe in trouble with the police?"

"Not yet. But he will be if he carries on the way he's going."

"I'm so sorry." It was the third time she'd apologised.

The laughter he emitted was bleak. "None of this is your fault, Lucy!"

"I know, I know." She couldn't help it; she stepped forward and put her arms around him. He had a child, but in this moment he was like a child himself. She wanted only to comfort him, to protect him somehow, to try to make what pain he was suffering disappear. "If there's anything I can do to help..." she whispered, relief filling her that he was at least letting her hold him.

"It's fine," his voice was muffled too. "It'll be okay."

She realised that he was shaking. "Zak?" she said, pulling away slightly. Oh God, he was crying! Silent tears pouring down his face. "What is it?"

Pulling him to the edge of the bed, she sat him down before kneeling in front of him and taking his hands in hers. "Please tell me what's wrong."

Unable to look at her now, he shook his head.

"Why won't you?"

"I...I don't want you to think I'm bringing problems into your life, that's why."

"Problems? No, no, I wouldn't think that. If you're suffering in some way or suffering because of someone, I'd want to know, of course I would."

"You know how complicated it can be with families."

She didn't know that either. She was a single woman, after all, living on her own…up until two weeks ago, anyway. Zak knew that her parents were dead; she'd told him that, also that she rarely saw her brother nowadays – she hadn't for three years, in fact. Her life was simple, whereas his life… She could see the toll it took. From being happy earlier, playful, he was now wretched.

"Zak, tell me." Her voice was gentle but firm. "Sometimes you just need someone to listen."

When he lifted his head to finally hold her gaze, she was relieved to see something akin to trust in his eyes. More than that, they seemed to have a light behind them.

"You're amazing. You know that, don't you?" were the words that left his mouth.

"Me? I—"

"No, don't do that, don't shake your head. You are, you really are. I *will* tell you what's wrong, I promise. Not now, though, this isn't the time, we've both got work to get to. But…soon."

"Promise?"

"I promise."

"Tonight, maybe… I'll cook, get us a nice bottle of wine."

"That sounds lovely."

She smiled and he smiled too; whatever despair he'd been feeling, he was clearly doing his utmost to push it to one side. More silence reigned, but this time it was expectant somehow, although she couldn't quite determine in what way.

"Lucy." Again, his voice was a whisper.

"Yes," she could barely reply, her voice was so choked.

"These last two weeks—"

"They've been wonderful. The best two weeks I've ever had."

"Me too. Every minute of it's been brilliant. You're so…perfect."

This time words failed her entirely.

"And so there *is* something I want to tell you," he continued. "Right now, before I have to go."

She nodded, biting so hard on her lip she feared she might draw blood.

"I love you."

Chapter Nine

Emma – 1972

"Here you go, love. Hope you've taken a few good 'uns. Must have done, a pretty girl like you."

Emma gave a reluctant smile as the chemist assistant handed her a paper wallet of photographs, noting the way his eyes lingered on a certain part of her anatomy. With her head low, she scurried out of the shop and headed over to a bench in the distance, sitting down as people rushed past her, all of them seeming very determined, as if wherever their destination, they'd be shot at dawn if they didn't reach it soon. That was London for you, she supposed, full of people having to be somewhere, not even glancing up from the pavement half the time or noticing others caught on the same treadmill.

At Highgate, it had been so different; it was a place of peace. Eventually she'd realised that, and this despite the lunatic antics of her flatmates, the sudden fright that had caused them to run, to scale that wall again and hurtle along Swain's Lane, the length of which seemed endless. As they'd reached the Tube, fright had forcibly turned to laughter, the boys pushing at one another as they'd tried to convince themselves they were only having fun.

"You pansy!" Kev had said to Danny.

"Hey, man, it wasn't my fault. Loo grabbed me, said she'd seen someone in there, some tall geezer."

"Yeah, yeah, I did," insisted Louise, although she was giggling about it now, the black of her pupils practically obliterating the green of her eyes. "He *was* tall, really tall... God, he reeked... I remember that...like...ugh! It made me feel sick."

"Some old tramp, then," Danny concluded. "You must get a few of 'em in there."

It was only Angela who wasn't laughing quite so much; she appeared to be in a daze still, unsteady, kept shaking her head and muttering to herself.

Emma had reached out to her. "Ange, you okay?"

"Yeah, yeah, I'm fine. Just leave it," had been her terse reply.

Surprised by her aggression, Emma had tried to find a reason. Maybe whatever high she'd been on was over, and the come down seemed too high a price to pay, especially as all of them had lectures the next day with no opportunity to snuggle beneath the sheets and ride such a tedious wave in relative comfort. That feeling of peace, though... Just like Angela, she'd felt it too, no drugs required, drugs that hadn't even been offered to her in the first place. Even though she would have refused anything harder than pot, it hurt to be left out again. Had Kev been speaking on behalf of the others when he'd said what he had? Did they all think the girl with the hollow eyes was dead inside?

Not wanting to think about that particular part of the evening anymore, she broke the seal on the packet of photographs. It had been four days since Highgate, and she hadn't seen much of Kev, as if he was lying low. If that was the case, she was glad of it. The less she saw of him, the better, as far as she was concerned. She'd seen the others, but again only briefly, and she'd noticed there'd been no nighttime congregation in the living room to smoke pot and listen to Led Zeppelin since. Whatever had happened that night, the drugs they'd taken, it had made an impact.

She hadn't used the camera in a long time, so the first photographs she looked at were ones from about a year or so ago, when she'd been living at home. There were pictures of her alone, in her bedroom, silly pictures, like her posing against a poster of David Bowie as the 'Man Who Sold the World', pretending to give him a kiss on the cheek. Normal pictures. Teenage pictures. Perhaps her trying *too hard* to be a teenager, turning the camera on herself as there was no one else to take it.

Another picture showed her with her mother. She was surprised by this, had to try hard to remember the occasion. They were in the garden at home, sitting in deckchairs on the patio, neither of them looking particularly happy at being caught on camera, her mother especially. Her father must have taken it, grabbed the camera that had evidently been within arm's reach and just snapped it. There was another of the same composition, her mother's face not changed but her own having developed a smile, clearly forced. They had drinks in front of them – she a glass of orange squash, it looked like; her mother wine, of course.

Here were the photographs she was looking for. Those she'd taken at Highgate, outside that huge archway. Seven in total, more than she'd realised. She'd used the flashcube, but still, what was depicted was grainy. The darkness had been far more intense than shown, especially in the passageway that led beyond the arch. She'd thought of it as impenetrable. Crazy, really, as Kev and the others had penetrated it well enough, Kev stopping to mess about with one of the chambers. Thank goodness he'd finally stopped.

The archway, although obscured by the branches of trees and ivy as well as the night, was magnificent. *It's Egyptian, that's it!* Yes, it was, with fancy columns on either side. How exotic it must have been once upon a time, the finest of resting places. It made sense that the Victorians would have utilised Egyptian splendour, that a society obsessed with mourning would, in turn, be obsessed with another society that had equally embraced mourning and its rituals. Their example was one to follow. Certainly, she knew scarabs were utilised in women's mourning jewellery, with obelisks on tombs, mausoleums, and cemetery gates.

Research. Yes, she could use this, write pages on it. The photographs, although not great, inspired her nonetheless. Emma was disappointed she hadn't taken some of elsewhere in the cemetery; it might've been a veritable treasure trove. The circle of sunken chambers that the passageway had led to and the tree that had overshadowed it, the sheer size of it – that had been magnificent too. And then just beyond the circle, the patch of ground she'd stood on with Angela, it had felt as if she'd taken root, as much as any woody vine.

She hugged the photos to her. Oh, to see it in daylight! She wanted to. She had to. And to go alone, without the distraction of others. Leaning into the bench, she raised her head again. All these people – so many of them – but one day they and their concerns would be no more. *She* would be no more. Whereas the Victorians realised that, embraced it, even, death being such a big part of life, in today's society, it had become a subject to be wary of, a taboo. You had to live, be *seen* to be living, to be laughing, partying; you had to belong. If you didn't, if you were remotely different, if you shied away from all that, then you were considered dead already.

Vehemently, she shook her head. It was nonsense what the others thought of her! She couldn't wait to get out of the flat she shared with them, get her degree, a job that she enjoyed, and grow up finally, be independent, of her parents, of her flatmates, of everything and everyone. To achieve that, she would work hard, study hard, go the extra mile. The Victorian Cult of Death – yes, she'd need more pictures, more inspiration. She'd excel in that module if she could just get more, and do a better job this time.

She glanced at her watch. It was midday. Highgate wasn't so far; she could be there in under an hour, finding a wall that was easier to negotiate, perhaps, to take more photos with a fresh film cartridge. Research. That's exactly what it was; she wasn't being morbid. If there was a tramp lurking somewhere in the grounds, as Louise and Angela had said, she'd keep an eye out for him. It wouldn't be too difficult, not in daylight. There was no need to be scared.

In fact, she wasn't scared at all.

* * *

It was a bright, sunny day – or, rather, it had been. As soon as Emma began to ascend Swain's Lane, however, the sun disappeared behind a thick swathe of clouds, giving it the appearance and feel of a winter's day rather than spring.

Clothed only in jeans, a long-sleeved tee shirt and a crocheted waistcoat, Emma shivered, wishing she'd brought her jacket with her too. At least her footwear was sensible, as she was clad in a favourite pair of Green Flash tennis shoes instead of her open-toed Dr Scholl's.

She'd had the chance to read up a little about Highgate since her first nocturnal visit. She knew why it was derelict, at least – both the more ornate West Cemetery to the left of her as well as the East. By the turn of the century, demand for elaborate funerals was on the wane and, with the outbreak of the Great War, many of Highgate's workforce were called to serve, although those who remained behind did what they could to maintain the grounds. People continued to purchase plots into the 1930s, but most were opting for less expensive graves elsewhere. As families died out or left the area, the graves at Highgate became abandoned. In an attempt to raise necessary revenue, the cemetery sold off its superintendent's house and stonemason's yard. The two chapels were also closed. The London Cemetery Company ultimately declared bankruptcy in 1960, and although the United Cemetery Company acquired the land, funds eventually ran out for them too. Since then, nature had run rampant behind tall walls and iron gates – gates not yet in view as she continued walking.

Footsteps behind her prompted her to step to the side.

"Sorry," she said, expecting a reply of some sort or someone to appear. When neither happened, she turned around and looked back down the road, her eyes straining to see someone. She was alone, quite alone, the throng of people left far behind. *But…*

She shook her head. There was something about this lane that unsettled her. At last the gates came into sight. They'd bypassed these on that previous night and gone a little further up the lane, and she would do the same. Would there be an easier way in? She hoped so, or this would be a wasted journey. Apart from those strange footsteps she'd heard, it was deathly quiet, a figure of speech that caused a wry smile. She'd need to keep a lid on her imagination if she didn't want to experience any more strange encounters of the invisible kind.

Walking past the area of wall that Kev had hoisted her up onto, she rounded a corner, the lane becoming even steeper, even leafier, and thus even darker than before. Ironically, although it was early afternoon, it felt later than it did on that first evening. She only hoped the clouds might part once she was inside, so that any pictures she took would be clear and focused. Reluctant to go much further – it really could be described as quite murky now – she was relieved to find a section of wall that was as decrepit as all that lay inside. Bricks had either tumbled from this section of their own accord or been knocked down deliberately.

Drawing closer, it was definitely a way into the West Cemetery, the side that had stood there originally and best showcased Victorian melodrama. But tramps, vandals, and groups of kids messing around were very real problems. If she went in, she'd have to keep her wits about her, make a note of her route so that she could double back with no confusion or delay.

If you go in? There was no 'if' about it; she *was* going in again. She could hardly wait, in fact, climbing over the rubble and lifting herself upwards and over with relative ease.

When her feet thumped onto the ground, covered as it was in a plethora of greenery, a smell assailed her. Not that strange, sweet smell of before but something altogether more natural than that, a familiar scent: wild garlic, a plant that was abundant in the woods she used to walk in at home. She breathed in its heady aroma, spied the long, dark leaves that surrounded her and accounted for much of the foliage, along with acres of ivy.

As she stared, the sun did indeed reappear, the clouds above her obviously parting. What it revealed was breathtaking. Not just a cemetery – it was more akin to an enchanted forest! She couldn't recall hearing the sound of birds whilst in Swain's Lane, but on this side of the wall, it was practically deafening. She looked upwards – were they crows? Ravens? Whatever they were, they flew from branch to branch, very high up, seeking out the nests they had built, whilst at eye level a butterfly, its wings such an array of glorious colours, jittered past. Nature had also softened the harshness of the stones, had turned some of them pale green, the most delicate shade she'd ever seen.

After walking forwards a few steps, she bent down. An added bonus of daylight was that she could read the inscriptions, those that weren't covered entirely by bracken or worn by time. *Sarah Ashton, beloved wife, mother and daughter, born April 1862 – died March 1898.* She continued to read. *James Darling, a friend to all; Beatrice Allen, wife of George Allen, reunited at last; Isabella Dryden, delivered into the arms of the angels; James Arbutt, sleep softly.*

Swathes of headstones soon yielded to more elaborate monuments. There were columns, she noticed, left unfinished – deliberately so, she knew from research – which symbolised a life that had ended too soon. Box-like caskets known as sarcophagi would often detail several family members, all of them 'much missed' and 'beloved'. There was more symbology; it was everywhere to be found. Birds again, so graceful even though they were carved from granite, and doves too, a hopeful sign of peace. The crosses, she knew, were associated with resurrection – the body may have failed, but the spirit never would; it would rise and soar. Grapes – *What's the meaning behind them?* she wondered. An hourglass: that must represent the passing of time.

Her camera at the ready, she began to compose her first shots, getting as close as she could, careful of roots that broke above the surface of the ground and threatened to snag her ankles and topple her. *Imagine that,* she thought, *if I stumbled and fell. There'd be no one to rescue me.*

She'd meant it in a jovial sense, but actually nothing but sadness descended upon her at the truth of it – there would indeed be no one to hear, and there never had been.

Stop being so maudlin!

In here, where so many men, women, and children had been buried and then forgotten about, it was easy to let sadness dominate. One grave she'd stopped at was that of Joseph Yeats, who'd been six weeks old when he was taken; another, Janette Winters, had been three. Emma spun around on her feet and took in just how many tombstones there were – too many to count, of course. Where were their surviving families, their ancestors? Lack of funds may have forced closure, but did no one come to visit those they had once known and loved, and tend to their resting place?

Out of sight, out of mind. The old adage proved true.

There it was! In front of her, the archway, and now she could see just how splendid it was, in spite of the neglect it had suffered. Raising her camera, she clicked and took what she hoped were better shots. Should she venture through the passageway? It still looked so dark in there, daylight seeming to eschew it. Through there the circle, however, and that magnificent tree, as well as the steps leading up to the patch of higher ground where she'd stood and experienced such profound peace. *Be brave, Emma!* No matter how much she urged herself, trepidation still remained. *Nothing will happen during the daytime.* Not in the land of the dead.

She took one step forward and then another, forcing herself to first stand beneath the archway and then to walk through it. Once through, there was nothing but a complex network of branches above her, although she suspected there had been a roof once. There were eight burial vaults both sides of her, numbering sixteen in total, the door that Kev had kicked at still open just an inch or two. She stopped to inspect it. On its almost ruined door was more symbology, an inverted torch this time. If she shoved at it with her shoulder, would it budge? Would she be able to do as he had wanted and see inside? How many coffins did it contain? The name above the vault was Forsythe; would there be a mother, a father, and their children in there, sisters and brothers too? A fluttering from above made her cry out. She tilted her head. It was just a crow, come to rest on one of the branches and peering at her through a gap in them, its beady eyes fixated.

"I'm not going to do any more damage, I promise," she

said, and the crow cawed and tilted its head, as if it approved of the choice she'd just made.

Hurrying now, she entered the circle and could see the tree that towered over it, breathtaking in its majesty, a sentinel indeed, its ancient limbs enlivened by the breeze. Standing in such subterranean depths, being surrounded by many more vaults, she felt at peace – safe, even. This was the Cult of Death in action, the Victorians at their most beguiling.

Keep walking. Reaching the steps and beginning to ascend, she spied another strange building in the distance. This one also had an arched entrance but in the Gothic style rather than Egyptian. What was that building used for? To house more of the dead was the obvious answer.

It must have been here that she'd stood, on this patch of grass. On either side of her, as far as the eye could see, memorials trailed off, a haphazard collection leaning into each other, ivy-encumbered too. But this was it; this was where she'd closed her eyes, where she had swayed. And so she did the same now. If only she could find that peace again. And solace too, some sense of herself and her purpose for being. Would it happen? Would she be so lucky twice?

How long she was there for she had no idea, but when she opened her eyes, the clouds had covered the sun again, casting so many shadows upon the land in front of her.

She had to face it, even though she hated to. What was the use in pretending?

She felt nothing at all.

Chapter Ten

Grace – 1850s

There wasn't relief in her mam's eyes this time; there was
suspicion, thinly disguised. Grace did her utmost to ignore
it as she unwrapped yet more food packages, this one
containing meat, and not scraps either – those that would
normally be thrown to the dogs – but a decent slab of it.
They'd never had meat like this before. No wonder it had
provoked such a response.

"Where'd you get this?"

"From the butcher's, Mam."

Her mother, small as she was, frail as she was, shot to her
feet, the chair she'd been occupying scraping back against
bare floorboards. Michael was in the yard playing with the
other lads, and he'd taken Patrick with him. There was just
the two of them in this room they called home.

"What'd you get it with, girl? That's what I meant.
What *with*?"

Grace stood her ground, although she could feel well
enough the tremors coursing through her. "There was some
wood, down by the river. I collected it, sold it on. That's
what with."

Her mother reached out and grabbed her by the arm.
"You're lying to me…"

"I'm not."

How hard her mother's eyes were, like flint. "I won't have you bringing shame on this family."

"I was lucky. I fetched a decent price for the wood. Where's the shame in that? I thought you'd be proud of me, that you'd be pleased. We've got meat to eat, Mam! Decent meat. It'll do you so much good; it'll make you stronger so you can get rid of that cough."

No sooner had she mentioned it than her mam's body started to shake, wracked by the cough that plagued her. Grace was released as her mam grabbed a rag from her pocket and covered her mouth with it.

"Mam?" It was Grace who reached out now, guiding her mother back into her chair. If only she'd fetched some ale alongside the meat. Her mother needed something to drink, and there was nothing but rainwater captured in a cup she'd left out on the ledge. Better that, though, than water from the Thames, which could make you sick even to smell it. "I'll fetch the water."

At the ledge, Grace hauled the window open, so ill-fitted that it resisted her efforts. It was summer, and there'd not been much rain lately, but a drizzle last night had yielded two or three mouthfuls at least, and this she took to her mother, having to gently ease the rag from her lips before replacing it with the cup. As her mother sipped, she noticed specks of red on the cloth in her hand and peered closer. Was it blood?

"Oh, Mam," she whispered.

Her mother lifted a hand and waved it, her coughing easing at last. Even so, Grace's eyes became teary.

"You need good food. That's what'll help you. And

medicine. I'll sell matches, fetch bobbins under the looms, anything, Mam."

"Anything?"

Grace lowered her eyes.

"Are you intact?"

"What?"

From somewhere, her mother found the strength to raise her voice again. "Are you intact?"

Almost unconsciously, Grace pulled at the hem of her shift. "Yes, Mam, I am."

"Because I've told you what exists on the streets of London, haven't I?"

Grace nodded. "Yes."

Her mother's voice lowered to a whisper. As it did, it seemed the room darkened too, despite evening being a long way off. "Men and women that prey on others, that will burn in hell for the harm they cause. If you fall into their clutches, you're lost, forever. You'll burn in hell too—"

"Mam!"

"If you succumb, I will turn my face, do you hear? I have named you Grace, but if you choose a path that is grace*less*—" she coughed, but only slightly this time "—I will turn my face."

Unable to withstand her mother's glare any longer, the anger that set fire to otherwise dull eyes, Grace turned and fled from the room, leaving the slab of meat on the table, wondering if her mother would give in, if she would cook it or if it too would be thrown to the dogs.

Flying down the steps of the rookery, Grace let the tears roll freely down her cheeks. She heard screaming and crying from the alley in front of her, and she skidded to a halt, fearful that the cries were from Michael or Patrick. They weren't. Her brothers were nowhere to be seen. A scuffle had broken out; several lads were squaring up to each other, pushing each other and shouting insults. Around them other kids stood, enjoying the spectacle, cheering them on and shouting for the boys to not just hurt each other but go one step further.

"Kill 'im! The other one too. Tear their 'earts out!"

Their eyes held something similar to what she'd seen in her mother's. Her mam talked of evil, said it was out there, on the streets of London, but it was much closer – it was on her doorstep. No matter where Grace looked, she could see nothing to redeem this place, just further squalor.

Picking up pace again, she continued to run. She hoped Michael and Patrick hadn't wandered too far. If they'd gone to the river, then Michael had best keep hold of Patrick and keep him safe. If only she could afford to get them some schooling; they'd have prospects, then, a chance to escape the rookery and the chains of poverty that otherwise bound them so tightly. You were nothing in life without money, and they, just like so many others, had so little of it, her mam's failing health meaning she worked less and less as a seamstress.

And yet there were others who had so much. *He* had so much. The gentleman. Suited and booted with a voice as smooth as a pat of butter, he'd pull out a seemingly endless supply of coins from his pocket and give them to her, not asking for anything in return. All she had to do was meet him, down by Oldham's Market, usually, beneath the bridge there, in the shadows. It was always in the shadows, and yet, his eyes shone nonetheless.

Several times she'd met him now, and she'd been careful to conceal the money he had given her, bringing home only what her mother expected, apart from the apples. Today, though, she couldn't resist the meat in the butcher's window, couldn't believe she could afford it either, that he'd given her just that little bit more to spend, had encouraged what was already foremost in her mind: *your family need food, proper food, otherwise...* Cholera, consumption, and other diseases were rife both in the rookery and on the streets. A cough that persisted and blood on your kerchief were the signs of something terrible, perhaps the same kind of terrible that had killed other members of her family. Mam needed a doctor, but what would she say if a doctor did come visiting? What questions would she ask of her daughter then?

Are you intact?

Yes, she was. And she intended to remain that way. Not every soul that trod these streets wanted to take advantage of another. She refused to believe that. The gentleman didn't. She was sure of it.

In fact, she wanted to see him, despite another meeting not being planned for another day or so. She *had* to see him. And she knew where he lived. After their third meeting she had followed him, keeping at a discreet distance, careful to hide behind street vendors or other folk if he should happen to turn and look behind him. It was perhaps apt that he lived so close to Highgate, the cemetery she was sure the funeral procession had been heading to the day she'd first met him. He'd walked right past the entrance to it, picking up speed as though in a hurry, his stride so sure. On and on he went, past walls taller than him, his cape swishing about his shoulders.

He'd rounded a corner, and, fearful of losing him, she had hurried to keep up, tentatively rounding it also – another sudden fear descending on her: that he'd be standing there, waiting for her, demanding to know what she was about, following him in such a manner.

"Sir, I…"

Although words – an excuse – had started to form in anticipation, the road had been clear. Where had he gone? Was that a house further up, set back from the road, with wrought iron gates at the front of it? She hurried forwards. It was indeed a house, the strangest residence she had ever seen but undoubtedly that of a gentleman. It looked…almost churchlike with its arched entrance and arched windows fashioned from stone, and its roof so tall with a fancy chimneypiece attached to its side, stretching ever upwards. Had he gone in there? Had he walked up the stone steps – there appeared about a dozen – a servant greeting him?

She hadn't found the answer that day, but today she might. On that previous occasion, the gates had been left ajar…almost…almost as if issuing an invitation, and she had longed to go inside. The garden was an oasis, full of plants and flowers, more colourful than anything she had ever seen in her life, another high wall framing it that was impossible to see over.

But why do you want to know if he lives there? What business is it of yours?

That she couldn't answer either. All she knew was there was this burning desire within her to know more about the gentleman who had become her benefactor. Perhaps such curiosity would be the ruin of her...but perhaps it might be the making.

Without further questioning, Grace set off, taking the same route to Highgate that she had before, not needing to go as slowly or as cautiously. When, finally, she reached the house, she came to a halt. It was the only one hereabouts, and, as such, she'd encountered no other traffic on the stretch that led up to it, not this time – no coaches and no horses, no gentlemen or women entering or leaving the cemetery to pay their respects. Because it was so quiet en route, she had stopped to take a peek inside such hallowed ground, wanting to see for herself the place where those that were so deserving lay. It was only the courtyard she could see, and a building that looked to house a chapel. But in that courtyard she'd thought she'd spied a figure, rather a strange one, shadowy almost, dressed in clothes she'd never seen before – a woman, turning slowly, ever so slowly, towards her. Quickly she had scarpered, continuing up the lane. Behind those gates and walls, there clearly lay another world, one she'd probably never be able to understand.

Just like the first time she'd visited the house, the entrance gates were ajar. She knew it was fanciful to persist in thinking it was an invitation, but if not, it was at least an opportunity. All she wanted was to ascertain if this was where the gentleman lived, to find out at least something about him, to chip away at the mystery. She'd be a few minutes, no more.

Entering the gates, she crouched so that the shrubbery would hide her. There were thorns, and this despite the beauty of some of them. They tore at her flesh viciously, so she pressed her lips together to stifle any cries she'd otherwise emit. The smells that surrounded her were verdant, infinitely preferable than the smell that hung in the air of St Giles. There, it was ripe with the stench of multiple unwashed bodies and all that those bodies could produce: urine, excrement, and vomit. It was there from the minute you woke to the minute you fell asleep. The reek of poverty, she supposed. Unbearable. Little wonder, then, that they were despised so much.

She was at the window now, one of several with an arched stone surround. If she stood on tiptoe, she'd be able to glance in. She prayed to God no one would be peering out.

What she saw caused her eyes to widen. The room was huge, far bigger than she could have expected and filled with heavy furniture, several gilt-framed paintings on the wall, and case upon case of books. It was also unoccupied, which she was thankful for. It must be a sitting room, somewhere for the gentleman to retire to at the end of a busy day, a glass of port or sherry to hand.

Her curiosity mounting, Grace made her way to a second window. There was movement from within, and she ducked. It wasn't the gentleman, she'd been able to glean that much, but a woman in uniform, large and bustling – a cook, perhaps, and the room a dedicated kitchen?

Rounding the corner of the house, she was at the far side of it now, and there presented itself yet another window. Back to standing on the tips of her toes, she feasted her eyes. This room had a desk at the centre of it, upon which were laid sheets of paper and various writing materials as well as a bottle of something: medicine it looked like. As with the first room, more books lined every wall. If this was the gentleman's residence – and he was not just a visitor – he was a voracious reader. The room had about it a still quality, as if time were suspended within it. Solemn. That's what it was. The feeling it evoked giving rise to a sense of unease in the pit of her stomach. The sheets of paper that she had seen, cream against the green baize of the desktop, weren't bare; they had writing upon them. Not just writing, but drawings too. It was difficult to see from her position, but were those triangles etched upon them? Circles too, numbers and words placed within and beside the drawings – calculations, perhaps, for what she couldn't fathom.

As it was another unoccupied room, she drank it all in and then rested onto the flats of her feet. But no, unoccupied? It couldn't have been, not for long, as a fire was burning in the grate even though it was such a warm day. Surely it must be stifling in there!

A sound from behind startled her, and she swung round. There was nothing and – more importantly – no one there. It must have been an animal, a rabbit, perhaps, or a fox, nothing to worry about. Even so, she'd had enough for today. Guilt began to settle upon her. Although she meant no harm by her actions, what she was doing could be considered a crime. Who would believe it was just mere curiosity? They would call it trespassing instead.

Her breathing becoming heavier, she decided she'd best get home and face Mam. Michael and Patrick would be home by then, so perhaps she'd be lucky and Mam wouldn't say another word, at least not in front of them. Perhaps there'd be the smell of that meat, cooking in the pot…

Just one more look, that's all she'd take. Commit to memory those drawings she had seen, try to find out what they could possibly mean. She raised herself onto tiptoes again and looked through the window. When she saw the gentleman looking back at her, that bottle from his desk held up to his nose and a smile on his face, she screamed before swinging round and running full pelt out of there.

Chapter Eleven

Lucy – current day

In the courtyard at Highgate, Lucy turned right and walked on for several metres, deliberately averting her eyes from the steps directly ahead. The memory of what she'd seen that night a few weeks ago, at the very moment she'd cried out in ecstasy – a figure, that of a child, standing at the top of the steps – and how it had provoked feelings other than ecstatic in her, was still vivid in her mind.

She knew she'd find Bert a little further on, and Firecracker too, who'd be sitting obediently beside him. He had just finished the morning's tour, the guests all but gone now, having trailed out via the small gift shop, where some grabbed postcards or satisfied further curiosity by purchasing a book or two on the history of Highgate Cemetery and its surrounding village. There would be another tour after lunchtime, and Bert was leading that one too whilst Lucy got on with some paperwork. In between tours, he sometimes chose a bench under the colonnade to sit awhile and eat his lunch – either there or the place she was heading to now.

Sensing her approach, he looked up, the smile on his face tinged with sadness.

Coming to a halt by the Rossettis' family grave –

Christina Georgina Rossetti buried in the same plot as her mother and father – the stillness of the day again reminded her of the poem, 'Remember' and how Rossetti had begged to be remembered when she'd gone: *far away into the silent land*. In that silence, which felt exclusive to these surrounds, the world outside its walls having faded clean away, Lucy usually experienced such peace. Today, however…

"Lucy," Bert said, patting the empty space on the bench beside him, "come and sit."

She returned his smile, obeying his instruction.

"Crisp?" he said, holding up a bag of salt and vinegar, which caused Firecracker to wag his tail in excitement.

She shook her head. "No, thanks. I've just polished off a sandwich. I'm feeling a bit full."

He lowered the crisps, resting the packet in his lap. "Anything the matter?"

"No, I just…fancied a breath of fresh air, that's all." After a brief pause, she added, "And some company, of course. Good crowd?"

He nodded. "Yes, as always, fired off a lot of questions. Wanted to know where Faraday's grave was, whether Dickens himself was buried here, or just members of his family."

"If they could get a sneak peek at George Michael's grave?"

"That's it, that's the sort of thing. One was very excited about encountering Karl Marx's final resting place. I put him right and sent him over to the East Cemetery, said his marker gave a whole new meaning to the word 'headstone'. Still," he said, leaning back against the bench at the same time that Firecracker, realising he wasn't going to get a crisp, relaxed too and lay on the ground rather than sitting on it, "I kept them quite happy with tales of Selby, Wombwell, and Sayers."

Selby was the coach driver she'd told Zak about, George Wombwell a menagerist, and Thomas Sayers a bare-knuckle fighter who'd taken part in the first-ever transatlantic boxing match with an American boxer named Heenan – a fight so anticipated that even Queen Victoria had wanted to know the result despite it being an illegal match. In the end, there'd been no winner as it had descended into chaos. But, in true sporting form, both opponents had split the prize money and shared their title. His grave was much remarked on because it had a dog in front of it: a huge brown mastiff called Lion, carved in stone. The canine had been devoted to Sayers in life, and those who knew it sought to immortalise that devotion.

As Bert nodded to a patch of ground in front of him, only grass covering it, nothing more – no fancy headstone, and no marker of any sort – she knew what he was going to say next, what he *always* said. "Told them about those poor girls too. Some of them turned away, started checking their phones or their watches. Made 'em wait, though; made sure they heard all about it."

The patch of land Bert referred to wasn't barren, far from it. Beneath layers and layers of soil lay the bodies of children and women, one beneath the other, ten deep. Prostitutes, that's what they'd been, 'fallen women', and as such deemed unworthy of remembrance, their shame following them into death. Bert, Lucy tended to think, considered himself their champion. He and another Highgate volunteer had carried out some research regarding them – the youngest girl was thought to have been aged only twelve, whilst others were in their teens and twenties, their ages easier to find than their full names as so often this kind of woman was referred to as 'female' and nothing more.

He'd also found out that Highgate had only tolerated their burial on consecrated ground because the London Diocesan Penitentiary, also known as the Highgate Penitentiary or the House of Mercy, had bought the plot and insisted upon it. It was the same institution that Christina Rossetti had worked at for nearly twelve years, herself also a volunteer. Rather like Dickens, who'd been so concerned with the horrors heaped upon children during the nineteenth century that he'd unceasingly shed light on it in his literary works as well as his acts, Rossetti too had been something of a crusader. The home was devoted to rescuing prostitutes and unmarried mothers. The powers that be had tolerated the burials of these poor wretches, but one thing they wouldn't do – and still hadn't – was acknowledge them.

It was as if Bert had heard her thoughts. "No one cares, do they, not then and not now?"

"You do, Bert," Lucy pointed out.

He nodded. "And you do too. You always ensure this patch of ground is kept nice."

She did, having heard how overgrown it became when the cemetery had lain in ruins during earlier decades. Although the grave was unmarked, they knew the exact location of it due to census records kept by the penitentiary. That Christina Rossetti lay within such close proximity to them always amazed Lucy; was she still intent on looking over them, even in death? The idea made Lucy shiver. Could there be such things as lingering spirits? Was that what that figure had been on the night of the storm? Did it also account for her feeling of being watched sometimes? And if so, by whom? What was so interested in her?

No longer just shivering, iciness rushed through her veins.

Unable to bear it, to even understand it – after all, this was the happiest she'd ever been in her life: she loved a man and he loved her – she jumped up, went over to the barren patch of land and knelt before it, placing one hand on the grass.

"Lucy?" Bert questioned, grumbling slightly as he rose to join her. Firecracker too had a whine in his throat. "Love, are you crying?"

"It's like you say, these poor girls. I know Rossetti did so much for them, but, really, they must have felt so alone. And there were so many of them that suffered, that were forced into selling themselves to survive. It wasn't done willingly, oh God no! Far from that. Legions of them suffered, Bert, legions! Even nowadays, there are many that do, and in practically the same way." Another sob escaped her. "Nothing much changes, does it? The world pretends to get better, but it doesn't. Scratch below the surface and you'll find it's just as rotten."

There was silence. If her words, her tears, had shocked Bert, they'd shocked her as well. Yes, it was valid what she'd just said, but it was also bleak, without hope. Why was she feeling like this, when only this morning, on her way to work, she'd been so elated?

She forced herself to her feet, wiping almost savagely at

her face.

About to open her mouth, to apologise, perhaps, Bert beat her to it. "Let's go for a walk," he said, taking her arm.

It had begun to drizzle, but neither of them commented on it. He was right; she needed to walk, to find the peace this place normally inspired in her.

"I've met someone," she said as they proceeded up a gravel pathway, anticlockwise instead of the usual tourist route that followed the hands of the clock. 'Widdershins', their direction was called – unlucky in a graveyard according to superstition, as it could invoke if not the spirits, then the mystical fae, who might snatch you away and take you into their world, for you never to be seen again. Charming nonsense but nonsense nonetheless...hopefully. She carried on with what she was saying. "We've been together a few weeks now. His name is Zak."

"The man that came calling for you a while back?"

"That's the one."

"And?" There were no congratulations as she'd expected, just that one word. She took a deep breath. Should she tell him the problem that had recently arisen, even though Zak had begged her to tell no one? His shame when he'd admitted to it had been another terrible thing to witness. She struggled with her conscience. She had to tell someone, and, apart from their brief meeting the day that Zak had surprised her at work, it was unlikely the two men's paths would ever cross again. Where was the harm? It felt like something dirty otherwise, and it wasn't; it was just...sad.

"It's his children, his eldest in particular. A boy, Joe. He's taking drugs. A *lot* of drugs." She remembered the phone call she'd listened in on. "I think he's getting into trouble with dealers because of it. Zak is having to fend them off."

As they walked, taking the path past Faraday's grave, a structure of another kind loomed in front of them. Not a gravestone or a mausoleum, but a house, one that overlooked a leafy lane to the side of the West Cemetery. An architect's house – glass elevations in the main – built to replace another, much older house on land released in the sixties when the cemetery had tried to raise money. They hardly ever saw the owner, which was ironic as the house was akin to a goldfish bowl. He tended to keep to himself; certainly, there was no sign of him in the day.

The gasps this house elicited from those on a tour was always something to anticipate. It was the last thing you'd expect to see in a cemetery. "Who'd want to live there," was the general question asked, "with this as your back garden?" Sometimes Lucy would think it was *she* who'd want to live there; what lay around it was…enchanting. Often she'd think that. At other times, on grey, dreary days and cold days, she'd agree with them, her skin prickling as she wondered about the house that had stood there before, a neo-Gothic structure that had, even by the time it was razed to the ground, crumbled to ruins.

"Zak earns a fair amount," she continued, "but he's separated from his wife, who's taking him to the cleaners, apparently, over their divorce, wanting him to surrender all that they've built together over to her. What money he does have left, Joe's taking it, to feed his habit."

"So he's enabling it?" There was a slight note of derision in Bert's voice.

"He's tried to get Joe help, on many occasions," Lucy explained further, feeling immediately defensive of her newfound lover. "But he refuses it. The mother, Ellen, keeps chucking him out, and so he's spending more and more time on Zak's sofa, and...well...it must be so difficult, you know, dealing with something like this. If he doesn't comply, Joe is quite capable of getting violent. Zak's a strong man, but he doesn't want to engage in fights with his son. I just...I don't know what to do. I feel so sorry for him, for them both, really. Zak wants us to focus on enjoying our time together, but it encroaches, of course it does. Sometimes Zak is distraught by what's happening to his child."

Having walked past the house, they were now on what they called the Cuttings Road, home to some of the much larger tombs – Tom Sayers' included, with his dog, Lion, guarding his grave, ever mournful. Soon they would reach the path that led to the majesty of the Egyptian Avenue, passing through it, perhaps, to the Circle of Lebanon and then up towards the catacombs.

The drizzle was turning into light rain, but, as both of them had coats on, it disturbed neither of them. In many ways Highgate was suited to it; the heavens alongside them mourning the demise of so many. Bert was silent again, contemplative. Rather than disturb him, she allowed him that reverie, guessing what he'd say next and preparing her own answer.

"It's a sorry state," he began. "Round where I live, so many kids have gone the same route. Off their heads most of the time, they are, running riot and causing a lot of bother." He shrugged as they began their ascent – not through the archway after all but skirting around it, a path that led them to the farthest edge of the cemetery. "So many think there's no hope, no future. Trouble is, they don't *work* for it. They want everything handed to them on a plate."

Again, Lucy felt defensive of a child she hadn't even met yet. "Living in today's techno-world can't be easy. Everything's so readily available."

"But it's *never* been easy, that's the thing! You as good as said so back at the grave. There's a lot of ill in this world, a lot of people who are still taken advantage of. I agree with all of that, but there is also more choice, not for everyone but certainly for us here, in this country. And because of choices, there are consequences, dire consequences on occasion. And sometimes, just sometimes, the buck has to stop with the person who made those choices. They can't be nannied all the time. There comes a point when they have to take responsibility."

It seemed her earlier melodramatic mood had rubbed off on him. "Bert—"

"All I'm saying is, it's a lot for you to take on. It's a new romance, you say? Decide whether he's worth it, because it already seems to be all about the son and not very much about Zak."

It began to rain harder.

"The catacombs," Lucy said. "Come on. We can take shelter there."

Thankfully, they'd made enough progress round the cemetery that their flight there, with Bert only able to shuffle, took just a minute or two. Set aboveground rather than below, the Terrace Catacombs occupied the highest point of the cemetery. Bert and Lucy passed into its Gothic arched entrance – the door thankfully open – to rest awhile there. Firecracker had kept pace with them, and he also hovered at the arch rather than going deep within.

As Lucy blinked, she grimaced. The rain somehow intensified the smell that was unique to this structure, making her eyes water again. Not just damp; there was an undercurrent to it – decay, she supposed, and little wonder. There were over eight hundred recesses in the walls that lined the catacombs from floor to ceiling, and most of them contained remains, sealed with an inscribed slab or a small glass inspection window. It was the only place within the cemetery that could always make her skin prickle. Not one for horror films nowadays, she'd watched a fair few when younger, and some of them, particularly the Hammer Horror films, centred around a crypt of some sort, which the dead inhabited in more ways than one. It was in here that the 'Vampire of Highgate' had reputedly been seen; this was his bolthole too.

Also, though – and something she found far more chilling – a young man had been discovered dead here in the seventies, just at the entrance to the catacombs, by a group of kids. What he was doing there no one knew, but rumours abounded that his death had been down to drugs, as prevalent then as they ever were now, and that his body had been rigid, his hands held up like claws to protect his face, as though he'd died in a state of terror. Whether the latter was true or just dramatic fabrication, she didn't know; even so, she couldn't help but imagine him every time she came close to this building, her skin not just prickling but growing cold too, even on a hot summer's day.

As the downpour took hold, she shook her head, wanting to cast such a vision from her mind, and turned to Bert. "I've got savings," she blurted out. "I could help. I *want* to help."

"Feed his addiction more?"

"No, Bert!" This time she allowed her annoyance to show. "I just want to help. I'm no expert on such things, but maybe...I don't know...I could contribute towards rehab costs or something."

"Have you offered yet?"

"No."

"Does he know you've got money?"

"Zak? No. Why would he?"

"Because...because..." When Bert faltered, Lucy seized her chance.

"I love him. For the first time in a long while – oh God, I don't know how long; it seems like forever – I can see a future, a *good* future I mean, not one where I'm drifting along on my own. I've been happy enough, don't get me wrong, but it's nice to be with someone. It's...incredible, actually. And he loves me. He says so." A short but delighted laugh escaped her. "All the time, in fact. If we're going to make a go of it together, then doesn't it follow that his problems are mine too? Besides, what else is that money doing?" Money she and her brother had inherited from her parents. "It's just sitting in my account. How wonderful to use it for something...worthwhile."

From staring at the rain, at another mausoleum in front of them – one of the most beautiful in Highgate, built by a distraught father to commemorate the passing of his child, Ada Beer – Bert turned to look at Lucy, *really* look.

Scrutinising her, it seemed. "You love him?"

"Yes."

"And he loves you."

She nodded.

"But you've never met his son?"

"Not yet. I can't. It's difficult. You must realise that."

"Because of the ex-wife?"

"Yes."

"You said 'children'. He has others?"

"Just a daughter."

"And what about her?"

"Well, she's a handful too, apparently. Not as bad as Joe, nowhere near, but he's terrified she might go the same way." She reached out. "Oh, Bert, don't look so worried! I trust him. I really do."

"It's just when I met him, that time he came to surprise you—"

Without warning, the dog ran forwards, a howl in his throat.

"Firecracker?" Bert shouted, clearly surprised by the dog's actions. "Where you going? Come here, boy. Come on, come back here!"

This time Bert moved surprisingly fast, his concern for his dog overriding any aches and pains that he might feel. What had startled Firecracker? It wasn't the fact he'd bolted that gave cause for alarm – there was so much wildlife at Highgate that he may well have that spotted something, as he often did. It was more the cry he'd given and what it contained. *Horror?*

Before Lucy could follow, a scrape from behind caused her to turn her head. Along a passageway, one that veered off both to the left and the right, she thought she caught movement. She frowned. What was it, a punter from the next tour? Sometimes they did that; they nosed around because they wanted to explore on their own. Quickly she called out.

"Hello? Is anyone there?"

When there was no reply, she sighed heavily. It would take just a minute or two to make sure the place was empty. She'd better do it, if only to give herself peace of mind. This place attracted some strange people, both now and in the past. What she'd read about Highgate's murkier history surfaced again, this time evidence of black magic rituals and strange carvings found on tombstones... She rarely ventured in here alone, found any excuse not to, but now she had no choice.

"Hello?" she continued calling. "Hello?"

Having reached the intersection, she looked first one way, towards an arched window in need of repair, and then the other, where the bodies were kept. She could hear a scraping sound again, but there was no one to see and no real place for someone to hide either. Where was that sound coming from? Having to force herself through this sense of unease, she turned right, the smell of damp and decay becoming ever more pungent. There was nobody here, no living body, at least, but plenty of dead ones...

Lucy, stop frightening yourself!

Although it was daylight, there was so little light, and she had no torch with her. No mobile phone either; she could have used the light from that to penetrate the intense gloom. She would walk to the far wall, she decided, and then that was it. She'd turn and leave.

What a strange job this was at times – now more than ever she felt that – a peculiar one, *unique*, as Zak described it, making a living amongst the dead. That scraping sound, still she could hear it, but it had grown faint. What on earth was it? And the accompanying shadow – because her eyes hadn't deceived her, she'd seen movement of some sort, rounding the corner, fleeing from her – what accounted for that?

She reached the end, all too aware of what was piled on either side of her, name plaques in various states of deterioration, just as the bodies would be. Oh, the smell in here! It became an assault. And the walls seemed much nearer than before, as if they were closing in on her, suffocating her. It didn't feel like she was aboveground at all but entombed...yes, that was it...sealed in, her breath becoming increasingly laboured, her chest constricting.

This was ridiculous. She wanted out. Desperately. There was no one here. That scraping sound could be anything, probably a fox. All she wanted was to emerge into sweet daylight, into the rain. Let it pelt down, let it cleanse her, wash the stench of the catacombs and her fear away.

As she turned, what flew at her made her shriek even louder than Firecracker had.

Chapter Twelve

Emma – 1972

"What the hell?"

As Emma sat in the cramped confines of her bedroom, on the bed with her legs crossed, she reached for the lamp and switched it on. It was daytime, but the light was poor.

She was busy scrutinising the photos she'd taken at Highgate Cemetery – the root-strangled tombs, paths overrun with moss, and the route that led to the Egyptian Avenue. They weren't great photographs, admittedly. She'd taken the time to frame them properly, so at least she felt she'd captured the solemnity of the place, its sense of loss and abandonment. It seemed, however, she'd also captured something more: a shadow, a shape, and not just populating one photograph but a few.

How could that be?

Laying out these particular photographs in front of her, she peered closer. Was it a development fault? That would explain it, were it not for the fact that in some of the images, the shape was actually quite well defined. It was small, childlike in its proportions, and although more grainy than black, it was definitely there. In one instance, it was half hidden by a tombstone, so it was certainly something in shot. In another, it stood beneath the boughs of a yew tree. In yet another, the shape could be seen hovering above a patch of ground, a space between graves with a tangle of roots and weeds having run wild. This picture in particular made her shiver, although she didn't know why.

A knock at her bedroom door startled her.

"Emma, you in there?"

Damn it!

It was Kev, and, knowing him, he wouldn't wait for her to answer; he'd open the door, pop his head around it, and flash that grin at her before barging fully in.

"Hang on, Kev," she said. "Just wait a minute." Hurriedly, she gathered the photographs before twisting round and shoving them under her pillow.

As she'd predicted, by the time she turned back, he was halfway into the room. "All right?" he said. "Wondered what you were doing."

"Me? Nothing. Working."

"Another essay?"

"Uh huh."

"About this Victorian death thing."

"The Cult of Death, yeah."

"Mind if I sit down?" Why he bothered asking, she didn't know, as he'd already perched himself on the edge of her bed. "That was a blast, wasn't it, at the graveyard."

"Highgate? Yes, yes it was."

"Creepy bloody place. I don't know what it was that spooked the girls. Whaddya reckon?"

She shrugged her shoulders. "They were expecting to be scared; they set themselves up for it. It was a tramp, probably – just freaked them out."

"Yeah, the only place they can get some peace, I reckon."

He laughed as though he'd made a joke, settling himself in once again. Intrigued by the shadow, she'd wanted to carry on examining the photographs. "Kev, I've got a deadline…"

"Yeah, yeah. Me too. I hate essays, crap at them."

"You can't be that bad, not if you're at university."

"Used to bribe my sister to write them when we were at school," he said, laughing again. "And they say cheaters never prosper. That's a load of rubbish, that is."

"Do you have any help now?"

He nodded, his curls bouncing. "A bit. Loo helps me sometimes, and a few others too. What's the saying? I get by with a little help from my friends, that's it, and—" he reached into his pocket and pulled out a spliff, holding it aloft for her to see before lighting it "— a *lot* of help from this. At least after a few drags, I can relax about it all, not cave under the pressure."

As he pulled on the joint, she had to admit, she envied just how relaxed it did make him, what angst there'd been on his face disappearing entirely as he closed his eyes and smiled again, a languid smile this time, one of contentment. It reminded her of how the others had been in the cemetery – happy. *Amazed,* even. Not him, though, not that night. He'd been angry, downright rude – to her, at least. Something he still hadn't apologised for. He may have lain low since then, but so had she. Maybe he'd intended to apologise but hadn't been able to. And now, she supposed, the opportunity had passed. Even so, she was still curious.

"Kev, what were you all on when we went to Highgate? I know it wasn't just pot. Everyone seemed…really high, really happy. They kept saying how incredible the place was, you know, like, seeing things, *nice* things."

At first, anyway. After they'd all taken flight, Louise and Angela in particular had become agitated. "It wasn't a tramp," Angela had kept saying. "It was, like, spooky!"

"A ghost then?" Kev had teased, throwing his arms out and wriggling his fingertips. "Ooh, we've been to Highgate Cemetery and seen a ghost!"

Angela had shut up after that, and Louise had piped down too. As far as Emma knew, they hadn't said another word about it. Certainly, when they'd congregated in the kitchen afterwards, all they'd done was argue about who was using who's food in the fridge.

Kev now opened his eyes, his gaze intent. When he looked at Emma like that, her own agitation rose.

"Acid," he said. "That's what they were on."

"LSD?" A mind-altering drug, then, supposed to open doors and accentuate the world around you, let you see all the things you don't see ordinarily. "You hadn't taken any, though?"

"Doesn't tend to agree with me. I'd just had a few beers – and one of these, of course."

And yet his behaviour had been quite frenetic, aggressive even. If he was serious about the drug relaxing him, it hadn't done so that night.

"I wonder what it was that the others could see?" Normally she wouldn't continue to ponder out loud about such a topic, and especially not with someone like Kev, but she couldn't deny it: she was burning with curiosity. And whatever it was, something sublime, it had rubbed off on her, no matter how temporarily. What if... What if...

"Kev, did you get the acid?"

"Yeah, why?"

"Can you get some more?"

* * *

"Here you go. Put it on your tongue and then swallow it."

They were en route to Highgate Cemetery again, on the Tube, only her and Kev this time, his close proximity to her on the seat normally making her nervous, but she'd also had a smoke just before they'd left the flat, and her muscles and her senses had relaxed because of it.

From Archway they made their way to Swain's Lane. Although darkness had begun to fall, the night was mild enough, warranting just a light jacket. The drug that Kev had given her hadn't kicked in yet. It would soon, though; he'd guaranteed it.

When he came to a halt at the point in the wall where they'd gained entry as a group, she urged him on. "If we go further up, there's another bit of wall that's easier to get over."

"Really? How d'you know?"

"Oh." Quickly she had to think of an excuse. Kev didn't know she'd been here a second time. "When me and Ange were trying to find a way out, I noticed it then."

Although he nodded, his frown remained.

Once they were in the cemetery, she stood perfectly still, assessing how she felt. Still relatively straight. Kev brushed past her and started walking.

"Where'd you want to go?" he called over his shoulder.

"I don't know. We could just see where we end up.

We'd better be quiet, though, in case that tramp's still here."

"I never saw no tramp," he muttered.

He'd been 'friendly Kev' on the way over, but now she could detect a touch of surliness in his tone, and it worried her. He'd been awful to her the last time they were here and, although there'd been no repeat of that behaviour since, was coming here with him, and him only, a mistake? This place genuinely seemed to have a bad effect on him. What if he turned again? She'd be at his mercy if he did. But why would he act that way? She hadn't done anything to deserve it. Perhaps he'd simply been in a bad mood that night and seen fit to take it out on her.

As he strode on, she followed.

When she'd asked for the LSD, he'd seemed eager for her to try it. "Good on you, girl," he'd said, and inside she'd felt almost pleased, like a child who'd impressed her teacher. When she'd had second thoughts a few days later as he'd pulled her aside in the flat to tell her he'd got the 'gear', he'd also told her not to worry, that he'd remain straight when she dropped it – he wouldn't even have a smoke, not even a can of beer – that he'd look after her. He'd rolled a joint before they came here, however, and had a couple of tokes on it, but mainly he'd encouraged her to smoke it. There'd been more admiration in his eyes when she'd inhaled deeply. It was as if she had come in from the outside, was finally one of 'them'.

God, it was gloomy within the confines of Highgate Cemetery, their torches barely managing to make a dent in it. Whereas she was stumbling because of the foliage, his stride was confident.

"Wait up," she begged, now more scared of losing him than being with him. "Kev, wait."

He was leading her right into the thick of it – a jungle, as Danny had said, where stone and nature melded, so different to each other yet existing side by side and becoming one.

"Kev," she called again. He'd gained a fair bit of distance and was in danger of becoming nothing but a shadow. *A shadow?* He wasn't the only one, she realised, beginning to squint. There were several shadows, all hovering on the edge of vision. Graceful things, tantalising – things that swayed and rocked, that faded in and out of the gloom. "What the…" It must be the acid kicking in, with what she'd seen in the photographs as the prompt. Although fear would be her natural reaction, she still had the presence of mind to go with it. This was what she'd wanted.

"Kev," she repeated, but this time more half-heartedly. Instead, her attention was on all that lay around her. Shades of green were vivid when they shouldn't be, not when it was so close to darkness. There was so much depth to it, a richness to every single leaf, every blade of grass, and every bough that hung low. Enchanting, that's how she'd once thought of this place; certainly, it was enchanting her now, striking awe into the very heart of her and capturing her entirely. "Wow," she whispered, forgetting Kev, turning round and round on her toes, wanting to drink in every inch of the cemetery, to absorb it and become one with it as well.

The angels! She'd noticed them before, of course, the first time they had visited, and what forlorn figures they had cut, forever mourning their charges. What she hadn't seen then was how beautiful they were and how each one shimmered too. She ran up to the nearest one, an angel that wept, and reached up. "Don't cry," she whispered. "It's too beautiful here to cry."

Incredibly, the angel listened! Emma was able to take the angel's hands and pull them gently away from her face, silent tears dazzling like diamonds on the curve of her cheeks. She lifted her eyes, which had been cast downwards, to gaze into Emma's own. There was indeed sadness in them, but there was a light also, and wonder, and love, all emotions that wrapped themselves around Emma, just as tight as any vine might wrap itself around a stone. They understood each other, she and this glorious angel, one that Emma would fly away with if she could, all the way to heaven. As the angel straightened and let go of her, it occurred to Emma that perhaps she was in heaven already, an ethereal kingdom where so much love, so much life, existed.

She turned her head. What was that? Something had flitted past her, another angel, perhaps? Yes, yes, it was! Gliding through the grounds. Her elegance was impossible; she was a lavish thing, her gown made of gossamer, an abundance of golden curls tumbling past her shoulders as she threw her head back and laughed. All around Emma there was laughter, and there was music too: the blare of majestic trumpets, an announcement of something momentous. Her arrival, perhaps? She faltered. Was it conceited to think such a thing? She shook her head. There was no room for self-doubt or self-loathing, not tonight.

She gasped. There was a dog! Such a large dog! Where had he come from? Bounding up to her, it nuzzled the wet tip of its nose against her hand.

"I had a dog once," she told it, laughing as much as the angel had. "And you're just as beautiful."

Her hands sank deep into its fur, deeper and deeper, into its flesh as well. Not frightening, not really; again, it was as if she was connecting. Eventually the dog pulled away and ran off just as something swooped low, a bird of many colours, to hover briefly in front of her. Like the angel, its gaze was direct – it saw her, truly saw her, and nothing but love flowed from it, filling her veins, her limbs, and her senses. Never had she been anywhere as wondrous. That feeling she'd experienced before when standing with Angela? She was feeling it now, only far, far better.

With Kev forgotten about, she explored this way and that, following a haphazard path. Her torch had dropped to the ground further back, but no matter. There was light enough, real light. As far as she was concerned, Highgate *glowed*.

Before her was a place she'd been before, an archway, through which lay the darkest of passages, although now that wasn't so. There seemed to be a light through there too, one that called her onwards. No longer meandering, she headed towards it, focused and determined, passing straight beneath the arch, the doors to the vaults on either side of her bulging as if their occupants were straining to get out. She laughed further. "The door isn't a barrier," she shouted as she passed them, "just walk through it. It's possible. *Anything* is possible tonight."

She reached the circle, the one that Danny had run around and around. Her gaze not on the vaults but on the tree that sat above them, she could sense it breathing, in and out, in and out, and how powerful nature truly was. She could see all the years the tree had stood there before the cemetery was built, and she could see it would stand there when everything it overlooked finally tumbled to the ground. Its roots would drag those stones deeper into the ground, covering them entirely, reuniting them with each and every namesake. Oh, the energy it was imparting, that too filled her! She wanted to run, just like Danny, to whoop and to holler.

A whisper distracted her. Not just a whisper – there was also giggling, that of several children. She strained her eyes to see. Movement. Further round the circle. It was definitely children.

"Hello there, hi." As they moved out of sight, she moved towards them. "Don't go, please."

Their low, sweet voices led her up a flight of stone steps, out of the circle and onto the higher ground again. Ahead of her was another impressive structure, one with a pyramidal roof; it shone as though it were made of crystal or ice instead of stone. Another amazing house of the dead, and this time the grief that death had provoked was palpable. As she'd seen tears on the angel's face, the building was covered in them too – hence, why it shone, why it refracted what moonlight there was, because it was *drenched* in sorrow at the loss it commemorated.

She was about to start towards the tomb when the whispering, the giggling she'd heard before distracted her again, leading her away and into the thick of woodland to the left of her. As she followed them, their laughter increased. Such a delightful sound, so pure.

She started giggling too, just like a child. She hadn't

been this happy since… It was no use; she couldn't remember since when, suspecting she'd *never* been this happy.

The area into which she was going proved very dense; in order to pull her way forwards, she had to clutch at several slabs of stone projecting at awkward angles, each stone not cold but exuding warmth and leaning towards her as if eager to assist. Who did they belong to? If only she had the time to read each one, to get to know those that didn't wander but continued to lay in quiet repose. Perhaps they would tell her something about themselves, whether they had lived a happy life or a sad one, if they'd been mourned or forgotten about, their deaths nothing anymore, not even a memory. If they did rise, if they opened their mouths and held out their hands to her, she still wouldn't be afraid. She would listen, console them, and, finally, she would tell them that they were never alone, not in a place like this.

The giggling had ceased. All sound had. It was only the sound of her own breathing that punctuated the air, somewhat laboured from her recent exertions. She looked around, could hardly see for low branches that pointed like fingers and all in the same direction. Why had she been brought here? She took a few more steps, parted more of those strange, determined branches, and then she saw why: it was not an angel that stood before her but a saint.

The woman was kneeling above an inscribed stone plinth, her hands resting lightly in her lap, palms facing upwards. She looked to be wearing a dress of some sort, and her hair hung loose around her shoulders as her eyes gazed wistfully ahead. Emma drew closer. Of all the sights she'd seen this night, this woman was surely the finest.

She hadn't realised she was crying until tears started to drip from her cheeks. If only she hadn't dropped her torch, she could have shined it on the inscription. Instead, she drew closer still and knelt in front of the statue, holding her hand out to trace the raised letters in front of her: *A. M. E. L. I. A.* It was all the information she needed. This saintly woman, this paragon of virtue, her name had been Amelia.

Still kneeling, Emma laid her head upon the woman's lap, fitting into the mould of her hands perfectly, and sighed. This was comfort, the kind she had craved but never known. Tears fell again, practically choking her. She had never done such a thing with her own mother; she couldn't *imagine* doing it. But this was what every child wanted – what she had wanted – the simplicity of it.

She started. What was touching her hair? It was a gentle touch, the lightest of strokes.

Doing her utmost to halt her crying, she lifted her head. It was Amelia – as she knew it would be. It was her hands soothing her, now upon her shoulders, still holding her. If she'd thought she'd been awestruck before, it was nothing compared to how she felt now. The look in the woman's eyes and the gentle smile upon her face held a world of love, her breath lodging in her throat at the realisation that it was all for her. Amelia – now deceased but more real than any person she had ever met – loved her. And in turn, that calmed her aching heart; it *healed* it.

"Mother," Emma whispered, and Amelia smiled, for that's what she was, the mother of all things here at Highgate. And that was why the cherubs had led Emma here. "If only I could stay with you forever." Never had she wished so hard for something. Amelia's smile grew wider, but there was sadness in it too, something Emma couldn't bear to see: that her wish might prove futile.

She laid her head back down and closed her eyes, seeking only to revel in the solace that Amelia could offer. Bittersweet.

Far too soon, other hands were placed upon her shoulders, tearing her from Amelia, and the only paradise she had ever known.

Chapter Thirteen

Grace – 1850s

Whose hands were these upon her? Several pairs. They were ruffians, street urchins, just as she herself was an urchin, dressed in rags. Immediately Grace began to struggle.

"Get off me! Leave me alone!"

All that met her ears was laughter, loud and coarse.

The lane she was in, that steep, steep lane that in turn led to a house, *his* house, seemed a long way behind her. How fast she had run to escape the gentleman's gaze, how the sight of her should have disturbed him, and yet there'd been no surprise on his face, only that smile. Had he *expected* to find her there? How could that be? He couldn't know that she knew where he lived; she'd been so careful not to get caught when she had followed him before.

If only she'd been as careful on her flight *from* his house. These boys had seemingly stepped out of nowhere; then again, her eyes had been downcast, not fixed ahead.

"Oh, stop, please stop!"

She'd been scared when the three women in the alleyway had accosted her, but now she was terrified, her eyes frantically scanning their myriad vacuous faces but also her surrounds, to see if she could call to anyone for help. There was no one – no living soul, at least – only those that lay in their graves behind Highgate's tall brick walls, forever deaf to any pleas she might issue.

Having reached the bottom of the lane, she'd been dragged from the centre of the road into a leafy recess she hadn't known existed. The smell that rose up choked her almost as much as the smell of these boys: the smell of filth, of urine, a watering hole of the foulest kind. The boys had begun to tear at her clothing. She fought harder.

"Slippery fish, ain't she?" one of them said, causing more raucous laughter.

There were four of them, more than she could possibly tackle alone. Already she could feel what strength she possessed begin to wane. More hands were upon her, lifting the shift she wore, tearing and scratching at her. Her eyes watering, she closed them. The last thing she wanted these boys, these *brutes*, to see was her crying. She'd keep her eyes closed, try to detach herself. They might make use of her body, but her mind was her own; they could never touch that. Rapidly she built a wall around it, higher than those that enclosed Highgate Cemetery, knowing that like the occupants of that place, something not wholly alive would exist inside it forevermore.

One of the gang – a boy not much older than her, as none of them were – had his face close to hers now and was licking her cheek as one hand grabbed her breast, his other fumbling with his trousers, no doubt trying to release what lay coiled inside. The stench of his breath was as foul as the smell pervading this dark corner – she knew that she would never forget it, that it would taint all her memories, rising up to haunt her in the still, quiet hours of the night. *If* she lived, that is. She may not. She might die body *and* soul. In which case, was there more fitting a place than this, only feet away from one of London's newest cemeteries?

The boy stopped licking the side of her face and grabbed her cheeks instead, forcing her to look into eyes that held nothing but lust and stupidity. How she loathed him! Placing his mouth on hers, forcing her lips apart, his tongue was the first thing to penetrate her. As it did, she found herself wishing for death, the comfort of it. In it there'd be silence, surely? Not this terrible jeering that filled her ears.

A sharp, jabbing pain forced her eyes open at last. What was it? What was happening? Oh, how it burnt! *Dear God, what's happening?*

Blind panic pushed any further thoughts aside. She forced her head to the side again, away from his drooling mouth, and, finding the strength from somewhere, began to scream. The howls dredged up from her depths caused even the boy defiling her to falter and the jeers to quieten a little – before they renewed, trying to drown her out this time, to mask her cries, her yearning for help. If she made it home, what would her mother say to her? Because she'd know; the minute she looked at her, she'd know. How do you hide a thing like this?

Mam! Mam! She was all she could think of, her mother's face no longer ravaged but like a bright shining beacon in Grace's mind, that of an angel's, embodying the only home she knew. So many times she had told her daughter to be careful, to be wary, to keep an ever-watchful eye on those around her. *There's so much evil, do not fall foul of it.* But she'd done just that; she'd fallen so low.

Oh, Mam!

As the boy continued to heave, to grunt, the stones of

the flint wall he'd backed her up against jutting into her with every determined movement, she wished she'd never met the man in the tall hat, that she hadn't taken the food he'd bought for her, that she'd never followed him all the way to Highgate to find out where he lived. This was his fault, all of it. A feeling rose up in her, the blackest she had ever known. Hatred. Hatred for these boys, for the man who had fed her, and the women who'd grabbed her in that alleyway – vile women, fallen women, the worst.

It was also hatred aimed at herself.

The thwack of a whip as it sliced through the air, the subsequent scream that ensued – not from her but from the boy who was upon her – forced her back into a moment that she only sought to escape. There was another amidst them, dressed all in black, a tall hat upon his head and a cape around his shoulders. As he continued to use his whip, the boys did their utmost to scatter, but not the boy who'd licked her and then gone on to do so much worse. In an effort to pull up his trousers, he had fallen to the ground. He lay there, foetus-like, his trousers still around his ankles, revealing a flash of bare skin that she could hardly bear to look at.

The punishment this man inflicted upon the boy was yet another terrible thing to witness. Time and time again, the whip came down, drawing so much blood that soon the boy would resemble a hunk of meat on a butcher's slab, a red lump, raw and quivering. Hatred dissolved as fear took over. Was this man trying to execute him? Here in the street? No trial and no jury, although certainly the boy was guilty enough. He wouldn't go that far, surely? He mustn't! For then he would be the one to stand trial, for murder.

As his hand came up again, ready to bear down, Grace grabbed it.

"NO!"

She didn't expect him to listen; she expected to be cast aside. As he turned his head to look at her, she was sure she would see only madness in his eyes. Again, she could hardly bear to look. On the ground the red huddled mass was gibbering, begging for mercy, saying over and over that he was sorry, a lone felon now, abandoned by his cohorts.

Aware that she was shaking from head to foot, violent tremors coursing through her, she nonetheless pleaded, "Enough."

Her eyes closed but not before his image had imprinted itself on her brain. It was the gentleman, the one she'd followed, and who had clearly followed her too, all the way back down Swain's Lane, that steep, steep hill, to find... *this*. He was her saviour.

What she saw in her mind's eye, though, was it true? His face, kind and gentle, was ever so, his blue eyes with no murderous intent in them at all. But surely there couldn't have been amusement either?

* * *

She was in bed. This was a comfortable bed, not the crib she shared with her mother. That wasn't comfortable, and with two of them occupying it, it was also cramped, her mother often choosing to doze in the chair beside the fire, where it was warm. Her mother... How she wanted her by her side now, her cool hand on Grace's burning forehead, calming her, soothing her, telling her everything would be all right, that she forgave her. But it wasn't her mother's hand that touched her, it was another woman's, someone slight of figure and dressed in a uniform of some kind. A maid?

This fever! It caused such strange images to form in her mind. There were faces, those that must belong to ghouls, coming close and then receding, fading in and fading out. Some of them were screaming, their hands held on either side of their faces as if trying to suppress that scream. And their eyes glowed red – the devil's eyes. Then there would come another, far in the distance and dressed all in black, a tall man with a tall hat and a cape. Why was he smiling? Should the fact that he was unnerve her? He was always smiling, this man whose eyes were blue, not red.

She thrashed her head from side to side. How long had she lain like this? Mam would be so worried; she'd wonder where she was. And Michael and Patrick, who was looking after them when Mam dozed in her chair, her cough having exhausted her? There had been blood when she'd coughed; Grace remembered that now. A lot of blood. It seemed to her the entire world was drenched in it, in filth and in evil.

She tried to rise. It didn't matter how comfortable she was; she had to leave. She didn't belong here. She belonged in the rookery, the slums. That's where her family were and where she must be now that she was at its helm, if Mam was worsening. But what was wrong with her body? Why wouldn't it comply? It was like a lead weight. She had to try harder. Heaving and straining, she poured every ounce of effort that she could into the task, and still it got her nowhere. Frustrated, she cried out, the sound deafening to her own ears, but somewhere inside she realised what it really was: a mere whimper. "Help! Help!"

Someone stepped forward from the shadows that surrounded her bed. A woman. The maid again or…an angel; perhaps that's what she was.

"You're to stay there, you're not to move. Not yet. The master has said so."

Master? What master? Who was she talking about?

There was nothing she could do but obey, drifting back into sleep.

She opened her eyes, but now it was different. How many more hours had passed? How many days? There was strength in her bones, enough that she could move, at least – first one arm, lifting it a few inches off the bed, and then the other. The effort cost her, though, and she closed her eyes again and slept, those strange faces appearing, haunting her, the one in the distance especially, the man that kept to the shadows, the darkest part of them, the umbra.

What had become of the boy that had been beaten? Was he dead? Why should she care? Didn't he deserve to die for what he'd done? She screwed her eyes up at that, refused to think of the vile act he had perpetrated, and sank back into darkness.

No darkness now – there was daylight, a glow from the window in which so many dust motes danced. She opened her eyes more fully and scanned the room. It was small but pretty, the walls covered not in the grime she was used to but patterned wallpaper, roses upon them, perhaps? Pink against white. There was a dresser, a washstand, a chair upon which lay some clothing, heavy drapes at the windows rather than rags. Able to raise herself onto her elbows, the room should have caused nothing but delight. It was a young girl's room, or everything that a young girl could possibly dream of – how happy she would be in a room such as this! But happiness could not be summoned.

Sighing deeply, she pushed off the sheets that covered her to reveal the lower half of her body. She had a white shift on, a modest nightdress that fell well below her knees. Her legs were thin, her feet not the blackened things she was used to; they had, at some point, been scrubbed clean. She swung them over the side of the bed and sat awhile to catch her breath and let the room stop spinning, staring at her hands too as they supported her, noting how clean they were as well, the tips of her nails uniform rather than ragged. Who had been responsible for grooming her?

It required all her strength as she pushed herself to her feet and stumbled across the room towards the window, holding on to the bed for support and then what other furniture there was en route. It was just a few steps, but it felt like she'd sprinted the length and breadth of London. Struggling for breath, she leant her head against the windowpane, the touch of it as cool as the maid's hand. She savoured that coolness before drawing back to look outside.

The day wasn't a bright one, but it wasn't as gloomy as it usually was where she lived. There, the smog clung to the pavements and the river to sit as heavy as a blanket, so thick at times and brown like vinegar. Here, her vision wasn't obscured at all. A garden lay before her, and, yes, it was much like the one she had crept into however long ago, the one surrounded by walls. She hadn't been able to see over those walls at the time, but from her current vantage point, she could. It was Highgate Cemetery, in all its splendour, acres and acres of immaculate garden that stretched as far as the eye could see, a few trees dotted here and there, beneath the boughs of which the dead could rest in peace. There were slabs; there were columns and crosses, bright white most of them, marble, perhaps? And of course there were angels; numerous angels. Each and every one commemorating a life lived. But those lives were over now. And oh, she was envious.

Tears started to prick at her eyes as she realised for certain her whereabouts, although what those tears meant she couldn't fathom.

This *was* his house, then – the gentleman's.

Chapter Fourteen

Lucy – current day

His tears were proof that she'd done the right thing. Lucy had transferred an amount of money into Zak's account, not to enable his son to buy drugs, far from it, but to sort out rehabilitation – which, apparently, Joe was now willing to enter, having grown as desperate as his father.

At first Zak had refused the money. "No way, Luce. I'm not taking money from you. You work hard enough for it."

"But, Zak, these are my savings."

"Yeah, but you can't afford such a grand gesture. Bloody hell, who can nowadays?"

"Zak." She had taken his hands and forced him to look at her, hating the shame that was so prevalent in his eyes. "I *can* afford it. I… There's plenty, honestly, and I want to help." Shyly she'd added, "After all, that's what we're supposed to do, isn't it? Help each other?"

When she'd said that, that's when his emotions had got the better of him, when he'd wrapped his arms around her and sobbed into her shoulder. "You're amazing, you really are. I love you."

It was only money. She kept telling herself that as he held her. Money from the sale of her parents' house that had been divided straight down the middle between her and her brother and was now just sitting in an account, not doing anything except earning a bit of interest. She'd used some of it to pay off the mortgage on her current flat, which she could now upgrade if she wanted to, but why? This one suited her well enough. She also had enough clothes to wear, plenty of food to eat, and she could afford a night or two out when the invite came; her salary covered most of that. So it was empty money, really, dead money. That it could save a life was a good thing; that was what money *should* be used for.

Not only his actions had reaffirmed that conviction, but also the epitaph she'd read in the cemetery a few days back, one she'd never noticed before – peculiar, really, considering how long she'd worked at Highgate.

Firecracker had run off and Bert had darted after him. Lucy had intended to follow, but a noise had distracted her, coming from deep within the catacombs, where she, Bert, and the dog had sheltered from the rain. Worried it might have been one of the visitors having a nose around prior to the next tour, especially as she'd caught a glimpse of someone, or rather *thought* she had – a shadow, at the end of the passageway before it rounded the corner – she had gone to investigate. The accompanying sound caused her to shiver: a scratching, as if the remnants of those contained in the recesses, one of them, at least, was trying to claw its way out.

To be buried alive was a particular fear of hers, one she hadn't shared with anyone. After all, what a fear to have considering the job that she did! It was ridiculous. Well...perhaps not quite. People *did* get buried alive, once upon a time, when doctors couldn't quite determine if a person was truly dead or in a deep coma. Such was the regularity of it that a string was tied to the deceased's wrist and passed through the coffin lid, up through the ground, and attached to a bell. Someone would have to sit in the graveyard all night – the 'graveyard shift' it was called – and listen, in case a recent burial awoke. She shuddered again. To do that, to wake in such a confined space, the fear that must grip you, the sudden realisation of where you were and whether you would indeed be saved by the bell or if you were too late and there was no saviour after all…

Another noise had startled her, this one coming from directly behind her. She'd turned around, and out of nowhere something flew at her, something black and winged. How she screamed! She threw her hands up and quickly tried to cover her face, sure that whatever it was would inflict terrible damage. The thing fluttering against her hands had a strange waxy feel to it. It felt like hours passed, she and this thing in battle with each other, but in reality it lasted only seconds. Just as quickly as it had flown at her, it disappeared, swooping upwards into another dark hidey-hole that only the creature itself would know about. A bat. It must have been. Highgate Cemetery, as she'd told Zak on their first date, was home to one of the biggest bat colonies in London. Of course it was a bat! Ammonia. She could smell it, a stench that overrode even the pungency of damp and decay, such a peculiar odour, base somehow. She tried to laugh, still straining to see the offending mammal.

"Where are you?" Her voice echoed down the passageway. "Where've you gone?"

After a moment she got out of there and emerged into the rain, deliberately swallowing great lungfuls of fresher air.

She could still hear Firecracker barking in the distance, so she followed in that direction, straight into an area where tombstones and crosses of all shapes and sizes fought each other for space. Just ahead in a clearing, she came upon them, Firecracker clawing at the ground with frantic paws and a puzzled Bert standing over him.

"What's he doing?" she managed to ask between gasping breaths.

"Don't know, to be honest. He's acting as if he's found something." Bert knelt beside him. "What is it, boy? What's upsetting you?"

Still the dog whined and scraped.

Lucy bent down too. "Yes, what is it?"

As she'd done at the other gravesite, she felt compelled to reach out. When her fingers met grass and earth, more sadness overwhelmed her. There was an angry edge to it, though, developing into rage, an emotion seeming to rise up from the ground below and infuse her, as black as the soil itself. She stood, abruptly, and the dog had stopped, finally, to stare at her.

"I…have to go." Hastily she retreated, wading through greenery and foliage.

"Lucy!"

Bert was calling after her, but thankfully he didn't follow, perhaps realising she needed to be on her own. She drove herself further on; this part of the cemetery was very much off the tourist track, a place where tall grasses and relentless weeds still dominated. Here, stone slabs were pockmarked with lichen, their epitaphs barely readable, ivy hugging them close like the most possessive of lovers.

Looking up at last, she frowned. She hadn't ventured far,

not really, but what lay in front of her was a revelation. It was the statue of a woman in a simple summer dress, and she was kneeling with her hands laid upon her lap, her hair loose around her shoulders as she gazed outwards. A magnificent statute, so detailed. She'd known nothing about it and yet... Had she seen it before? She *must* have done, just not fully registered it. Again, that was a mystery, because the woman's craftsmanship alone was something to celebrate.

Kneeling too, Lucy read the epitaph engraved on the plinth that the statue sat upon. Amelia, that was who this grave was dedicated to, a woman born in 1863 and who had died in 1895 at the age of thirty-two. Beneath her name was an extract:

My life is like a broken stair
Winding round a ruined tower
And leading nowhere

If she'd felt desolation before, it was nothing compared to the feeling these words engendered. They not only overwhelmed her, they *defined* her.

No! Immediately, a part of her had rallied. *Those words are nothing to do with me!*

They were to do with Amelia; with the lost children of the Victorian era; with others buried here, perhaps, but not her. She was happy now. Love was within her grasp. Life wasn't *meant* to be futile. It was meant to be something good, something...magical. And that was why she'd decided that, yes, Joe must be helped, whatever it took. And no matter how proud a man Zak Harborne was, he must accept the help she was offering.

The extract had seared itself upon her brain. Even standing as she was now, with Zak's arms around her, she could recite it word for word.

Chapter Fifteen

Emma – 1972

Emma was so angry she could barely bring herself to look at Kev in the days that had passed since their second trip to Highgate Cemetery. His had been the hands that had torn her from bliss and plunged her, yet again, back into grim reality. He'd got spooked, obviously, but whether by someone real or just his own imagination, she had no idea.

Imagination. How hers had bloomed that night! Leading her not into dark corners and shadows but into what she continued to think of as paradise. She had felt so...complete there, especially towards the end, with Amelia. Before Emma's eyes she had come alive, had wrapped her not only in her arms, but also in love, something that nourished rather than depleted.

As she sat on her bed in her room, she remembered how she'd screamed at Kev as he'd pulled her along the path with such urgency, back to the area of wall they'd climbed over. "Why are we leaving? Get off! I want to go back to where I was."

"No, we've got to go. Loo and Ange were right, there's someone here, someone who's not quite...right. He was stalking me, I'm telling you, like...tracking my every move."

She'd frowned. What could he mean? He sounded higher than she did. Paranoid.

Still she had argued. "There's nothing to be frightened of in there. It's beautiful! It has angels, it has cherubs, the leaves on the tree dazzle you with colour, it has her."

"It's the acid, stupid. That's what's making you see all kinds of stuff."

Back on Swain's Lane, she had looked behind her longingly. "I saw such incredible things."

His voice was tired, bitter. "Lucky you. That's not always the case, believe me."

"Kev, I want to go back."

"I've told you, no."

"Kev!"

He'd stopped in his tracks then and turned to her. "I'm not going back in there, all right? It's the creepiest bloody place I've ever been in my life. I've had enough of it now; I've had it up to here, in fact. All that stuff you think you saw, it wasn't real, okay? Get that into your head. Stuff this hanging about in dead places with weirdos like you. It was fun at first, but yeah, the thrill's long gone. I can think of a million places I'd rather be than here."

And yet, it was the only place she wanted to be: in a cemetery, in the north of London.

She pondered his words again. All that stuff you think you saw, it wasn't real. And if it wasn't real, did that mean the emotions she'd experienced weren't real either? That she'd imagined them too, conjured them out of nothing? It couldn't be. Not that strength of feeling. It must have come from memory. Unconditional love. At some point in her life, she must have felt it.

Rather than torture herself any further, she jumped up from her bed, deciding to put that theory to the test. Looking in her purse, she checked that she had plenty of change – she did, 'shrapnel' as her father called it. Her tiny leather purse clutched in her hand, she left the confines of her room and strode down the hallway, not Led Zeppelin filling the air this time but a song by Leonard Cohen instead, a melancholy to it. Once outside on the street, she breathed in the fresh air. It was a bleak day, nothing inspiring about it at all, just an abundance of grey shapes and people, all melded into one mechanical mass. If this was what constituted real, it left her cold.

A few yards along the road from the flat, on the corner of the street, was a telephone box. She'd only used it twice, both times to call home, and both times it had gone unanswered. Would it be third time lucky? She raised an eyebrow at that. Lucky? That would depend on which way you looked at it.

The box was occupied by a woman speaking very loudly, laughing raucously at whatever the person on the other end of the line was saying. Emma shifted from foot to foot, impatient but also aware that the delay gave her time to change her mind and return to the flat, examine those photos of Highgate she'd taken for the umpteenth time. The shadow – it was so small it had to be a child. Had the camera been able to catch something that only drug-fuelled eyes could otherwise see? Her head began to hurt thinking about it. Who knew? Although nothing more than a shadow, there was something about it that nagged. That was the only way she could think to describe it. Again, how could that be? Was she – and she gulped at this – going mad?

The woman finished her call. As she turned around, Emma grabbed the door and held it open for her. The woman didn't acknowledge this courtesy but just carried on walking. *It's like I'm not a part of this world at all,* she thought for what also seemed like the umpteenth time.

As she took the woman's place, the smell of urine was ripe in the air, causing her to almost back out of there, especially as there was a puddle of something dark and wet in one corner, which she made sure to keep well away from. That she stayed was a sign of how desperate she was. Also ignoring a plethora of calling cards that had been stuck to the glass panes in front of her, those that promised the fulfilment of dark and delicious desires, she dialled her home number and listened to it ring…and ring…and ring…

It was no good; no one was in. She'd be able to prove nothing to herself.

"Hello…hello, who is this?"

She had practically replaced the receiver when she heard it, a tinny voice beginning to speak. Quickly she fed coins into the slot. "Hi, Mum, it's me."

"Oh, Emma. Hi." This was the first time Emma had managed to call home in three or four weeks; couldn't her mother inject a little more enthusiasm into her voice?

"I…erm…was wondering how you were," Emma said. "It's been a while."

"Yes, it has, darling. I'm…good, keeping well."

"And Dad?"

"He's at work."

"Yes, I realise that. But is he okay?"

"He's fine. Last time I looked, anyway."

Was she slurring her words slightly, trying hard not to but failing? Emma glanced at her watch; it was barely three o'clock in the afternoon.

"Mum…I miss you."

"Do you, darling?"

It wasn't quite the response she'd hoped for.

"Yeah, yeah, of course. Why wouldn't I?"

"I'd have thought you'd be far too busy to miss me. All those parties you must be going to, all the fun you're having."

"It's hard work, Mum."

"All work and no play…" Kev had said the same thing. "You've made friends, haven't you?"

"Of course I have." She fed more coins into the slot.

"Anyone special?"

"What do you mean?"

"A boyfriend?"

"No. Not yet."

Her mother laughed. Not only that, she slurped from something: a glass of wine, no doubt. "I don't know what on earth's taking you so long. When I was your age, they were queuing up at the door to take me out. Wonderful days, they were. God knows how I ended up with your father."

"Mum…I—"

"He doesn't deserve me. And it's not as if he doesn't know it, it's not like I don't tell him often enough. He goes to work early, comes back too late, never takes me out or treats me to a new dress or even a stupid bunch of flowers. Oh no, he does nothing like that, but he still expects his dinner on the table by a certain time, those bloody shirts of his ironed, and a clean house."

"Mum—" Again, Emma tried to interrupt her; this was not what she'd phoned for, to listen to another rant. Her mother, however, was on a roll, a *drunken* roll.

"If I'd known what I was letting myself in for, I would have run a mile. But he was handsome, wasn't he? Back in the day. He had a flash car. It's daft the things that can turn a young girl's head. Times are different now, though, aren't they? More and more women are able to make it on their own; they don't need a man." She sighed heavily. "If only I'd had the opportunities you've been given. I'm clever; I could have gone to university! And if I had, I'd have made sure I had plenty of fun, do you know what I mean?" More laughter, packed to the brim with bitterness. "You wouldn't catch me wasting time, ringing home, worrying about my parents."

"I love you, Mum." God, she'd had to force those words through gritted teeth, but now that she had there was relief in it. They'd been a long time coming.

There was indeed a pause at the other end, a silence that seemed to form an expanded bubble, like a balloon being inflated. And then came the furious sound of beeping. "Hold on, Mum, the phone needs more coins." It would happily eat all she had. Having rescued the call, she spoke again. "Are you still there?"

"Yes, I'm here."

"Oh. It's just—"

"I can't stay for long. I'm meeting Pauline."

"That's nice. What are you meeting for?"

"Oh, you know, a few drinks, a bit of a chat."

Pauline, a woman only slightly older than her mum, had an equally competitive appetite for alcohol.

"What's it like where you are, sunny?"

Emma shook her head. "Not particularly. Although it's not raining, at least."

"That's a blessing, then. Hate the rain. That's all it ever seems to do in this country, rain."

Why had they reverted back to small talk? Wasn't there anything else to mention but the bloody weather?

"Mum, look, I just wanted you to know, well, Dad too of course, that I—"

"I'm sorry, darling, I have to go. I'll be late for Pauline if I don't go now, and you know what she's like. I'll have to listen to her moan about how my time's more precious than hers. I'll...erm...tell your dad you called, shall I? And maybe we'll...see you soon. I'm sure we will." There was another burst of disingenuous laughter. "When you can spare us a weekend, that is! Look, have fun, won't you? Make sure you do. No one likes a killjoy. See you soon, darling. See you soon."

The phone went dead. Her mother had hung up.

I miss you, Emma had said, *I love you*. And her mother had heard her well enough; the latter statement had elicited a pause, filled with what – awkwardness, surprise? Even if that were so, she'd been given ample opportunity to say that she loved her back, her only child.

Emma replaced the receiver, then leant her head against it, growing used to the smell of urine; if anything, it suited the moment. *Why didn't you say it, Mum? Just say the fucking words!* Even if she didn't mean them, like Emma hadn't truly meant them. She could admit that now, here, in this stinking phone box, on the corner of an anonymous grey street in London. She didn't miss her mother or her father. And she didn't love them either. She loved no one, and no one loved her. She wasn't even sure if anyone *liked* her. She was alone, truly alone, in a city packed with people, in a world full of them. And yet, there was a place where she had found everything she had ever wanted, everything she had dreamed of.

A loud banging made her jump.

"Come on, love. Hurry up. What are you doing, daydreaming?"

Lifting her head, she turned to stare at the person who'd spoken to her, a man this time – shaved head, checked shirt, and jeans with braces. A skinhead, one with a sneer on his face.

She pushed at the door and let herself out of the cramped confines, the man grunting something at her; maybe it was thanks, most likely it wasn't.

She retraced her footsteps in something of a daze, reaching her flat on autopilot rather than by design, opening a front door whose peeling black paint always reminded her of some sort of skin disease. The smell in the hallway was similar to that in the phone box, permeated with weed, of course, which was a reliable constant. It came not just from her flat but several others too, all stuffed full of students. Doggedly climbing the steps, all the way to the top floor, the carpet beneath her feet was sticky and the handrail grubby.

Once inside the flat, she made her way to Kev's room and banged on the door before barging in, enjoying for once the role reversal.

Kev was in there, lazing on his bed, smoking. At the sight of her, he pushed himself upwards. "What is it? What do you want?"

It was a second or two before she answered. The brief silence was not one of awkwardness, as it had been between her and her mother, but filled with iron determination.

"I want more acid."

Chapter Sixteen

Grace – 1850s

She remembered so well the words that he'd said to her: "You are very pretty, *unusually* so. Some might say exquisite. Do you realise, Grace, how pretty you are?"

No, she hadn't realised. How could she? There'd been no mirror at home to gaze into; she hadn't even been able to catch her reflection in one of the room's windowpanes, as they were all so dirty. But more than that, no one had ever *told* her. Her Mam hadn't. All she'd done was warn her of the perils that faced young girls on the street. Dangers of a particular kind.

She closed her eyes as she had done that time at the bottom of Swain's Lane, in order to hide her tears, this time from someone who was more than a boy, who was grunting and sweating on top of her, foul blasts of hot air from his mouth coursing over her in waves. This man wasn't taking what he wanted, unlike that boy; oh no, this man had paid handsomely for it. Not that she would see any of it. All the money went to him, the gentleman, who had saved her. *For this?*

As the man on top of her – another that society would call 'gentle' and yet who was anything but, his hands before the act of penetration pinching, pulling, and punching –

continued in his endeavours, her mind returned to that first attack, as it did so often. How the boys had stepped out of nowhere to bar her way. And he had sprung from nowhere too, the gentleman, and beaten the boys from her, leaving the main perpetrator little more than a bloodied pulp. But he'd been too late to really save her. Deliberately?

She'd been defiled. And so, just as the gentleman had decided, why not continue along that path? She remembered also how he would come to sit by her in the days after the attack, when she had lain in a fever, the words he had spoken as he'd twisted that black jewelled ring round and round his finger.

"So beautiful..." Yes, he would murmur that, but other words too, a strange perfume on his breath, one she recognised: the smell of the street women. When she had seen him through the window, he'd been sniffing something from a bottle, some sort of medication, she had thought. Perhaps it was that, but it made his voice slur and his body sway from side to side. Funny how she hadn't noticed anything remiss all the times they'd met, or perhaps it was that she'd *refused* to acknowledge it, wanting only to believe in him. Oh, how she wished she could've turned her head when he'd leant closer. "I'm sorry for what happened to you, truly I am. I berate myself constantly for not reaching you sooner." There'd been no sincerity in his voice; even in her tortured state, she understood that. "But, dear girl, don't you see? The damage has been done. You are soiled goods. Your mother would hang her head in shame at the sight of you. No man would seek to wed you. And what a sin it would be for such beauty to go to waste."

She hadn't known the full meaning of his words, not

then. She certainly knew it now. The man on top of her gave a final grunt before collapsing fully, Grace barely able to breathe supporting his full weight. Still he lay there, oblivious to how short her breath was becoming, how laboured.

"Sir… Sir, please…"

How she hated having to call them 'sir', but the gentleman insisted. She was to be no ordinary working girl, as he labelled them, like the three that had accosted her in the alley, trying to turn a trick, any old trick with any old man, no matter the risk and the diseases that were rife, blotting out their cheap existence in whichever way they could. Grace was to service a much higher class.

"Because you see, they will pay for someone like you, an innocent."

She'd grown confused when he had said that. She wasn't innocent; he'd as good as said so. She was soiled, damaged, so what were they paying for, exactly, her so-called prettiness?

"It is your youth *and* your innocence," he'd explained, almost as if she'd asked that very question, "or at least the illusion of it. How men desire it. Not I, you understand, but…certain types. You shall stay here; there are plenty of rooms. I will clothe and feed you and look after you. You will see that I am not a bad man; I am a businessman. I shall make the most of you." Here he had laughed, a sound as gentle as his eyes. "Or, rather, my clients shall."

"But Mam…?" she had managed to whisper through a throat that felt like cut glass.

"As you have followed me, I have followed you," he'd informed her. "I know where you live, that terrible, terrible rookery. Ugh!" How appalled he had seemed. "In my opinion that place should be razed to the ground and all who dwell in it. Surely it would be a kindness to all concerned to end such wretchedness, but I am no politician, just a humble businessman, as I have told you, and so it is out of my hands. But at least you have been rescued from such squalidness. Your family, however, must persist, and so I will see to it that food is delivered to their door. I am happy enough to do it, although it is *all* I am prepared to do."

The words matched his façade of gentleness, but even so, she now knew well enough the threat that underscored them: *Don't push me, child. You had better not push me.*

And so, she had remained imprisoned at this house in Highgate, overlooking that fancy new cemetery, envying those who had found release.

Was it wrong to crave death? Would it visit her now and save her from this brute lying on top of her, not only having used her but intent on suffocating her too? She began to see so much black. If only she'd recognised it before being brought here, in the gentleman's face, in his eyes, in his manner; if only she had sensed how rotten he was beneath such a polished veneer.

Poor Mam! Would she refuse the food parcels he had promised to deliver to her? Would she summon strength from deep within in order to find out the fate of her missing daughter? Would Patrick cry for her as much as she had cried for him, missing so much his sweet baby smell when all around him was fetid? And Michael, would he miss her too? Was he looking after his little family, the head of the household now, keeping away from those boys in the yard that continually fought with each other? They would lead him into wrongdoing. Just as her mother had warned her, Grace had warned him, countless times: *Keep away!*

She longed to see them! She couldn't bear it if not. Even...even just as an observer. Perhaps that would be enough, just to know they were all right...to let them know that she was alive too. Many, many children went missing or were pressed into service, as she had been – all different kinds of service, the very worst kinds. She wouldn't be the only one, although she felt that way now. Acceptance was a key part of her life in the rookery, of death, of those who just 'disappeared', but not seeing her family again was something she couldn't accept; surely her mam must feel the same way? She mustn't succumb to the sanctuary of death, no matter how tempting.

"Sir!" Her voice was more strident this time. "Sir, please, I cannot breathe."

"What... Where...?"

As the man shifted from side to side, eventually rolling off her to lay on the bed, the smell of their mingled sweat was like a miasma, as thick as any London smog.

Able to breathe now, she gasped heavily, her chest pumping furiously.

"What the deuce...?" the man continued to say, a lord, apparently, his will something she must yield to. Certainly, he was a man with strange appetites; she was sure her skin bloomed with bruises from his rough handling, and she ached in places other than *down there*, where she always ached. Would her boldness in beseeching him to move somehow anger him again? Fearing this, she tried to calm her breathing, to lay still.

He had managed to heave himself up onto one arm now, the exertion causing his cheeks, as fat as the rest of him, to glow crimson. "I was asleep, girl!"

"Yes, sir. It was just... I couldn't breathe, sir. I thought–

–"

"You are not paid to think!"

She found herself swallowing hard. "No, sir. I'm sorry, sir."

"And you are paid well, girl. Higgins, I sometimes think, is guilty of fleecing us."

Fleecing? What did he mean?

Once again, the man moved his face closer to hers, his exposed teeth straight but stained.

"I paid for you, girl, to do whatever I want with you. And if I want to sleep on your soft pillows rather than the lumpy ones Higgins provides us with, then I damn well will, do you hear?"

She nodded. "Yes, sir. Of course, sir."

"Speak up, girl!"

"Yes, sir," she repeated, feeling tears sting her eyes again. She would not cry! She refused to! Not in front of Higgins – the gentleman's name – or this man, this lord, this *beast*, no matter what he did to her. It was the one thing she could control. He was more upright now, towering over her. She braced herself for what she knew must surely follow.

She was right. His hand had bunched into a fist and then smashed into her stomach, the force of it causing her to immediately double over.

"You insolent, insolent wretch!" he said as yet again he punched her, this time in the side of her head. Better that she had let him sleep, that she had suffocated. It was only the thought of her mam and her brothers that had made her dare to move him, because she had wanted to see them, so much. And yet now she saw that desire for what it was: futile, for surely she couldn't survive another attack. Her body, her poor beleaguered body, could only take so much.

She was curled up, her hands doing their utmost to protect her head, but he forced her to lie flat. She didn't want to gaze upon such a cruel face ever again, with its slits for eyes, its mouth too feminine, its crooked nose and flared nostrils, but that choice, like so many recently, was not hers to make. What was he doing? His hand was still a fist, yet this time he rammed it not at her but *into* her, causing her to scream out loud, to howl, to beg: "Please, sir, no more!"

Having retrieved his hand, she thought it was over. Not so. He repeated the action, tearing into her, with what intent? To rip her in two? For that's what it felt like, that he would destroy her. She tried to stop him, to hit out at him, but it was no use, there was so little strength in her own fists. All she could do was scream, those screams becoming hoarse, becoming nothing but whimpers. She would die here, in the gentleman's house. No…she wouldn't call him that anymore, for it was indeed a misnomer. His name was Higgins, and he had led her to this terrible fate; he had orchestrated it.

There was that blackness again, shapes within it, soft-edged, writhing, reaching out. Should she reach back, simply take their hands, forfeit her family? She should. Mam wouldn't want to see her anyway, not after all this. Perhaps…perhaps…she might visit them as a wraith. That thought, as the assault on her body continued, elicited just the briefest spark of hope that it might be so.

How long had she endured this imprisonment here? Weeks? Months? As when she had lain in her fevered state, she had no clue. Incarcerated in this room, not the room she had first been in but not dissimilar with its pretty patterned wallpaper and its dark wood furniture. Only the bed was bigger, made for two, her and a series of others – countless others, but none as bad as this monster, who had spit flying from his mouth and a look of frenzied enjoyment on his face.

Many men had 'kinks'. The maid had told her that, the one who had tended her from the beginning. Not an unkind woman but a cowed woman, perhaps she hadn't always been a maid either; perhaps she'd been something else in this household when younger, when prettier. Grace had asked her what 'kinks' had meant. "Certain tastes," the maid had informed her, "you know, in the bedroom. Ones that might seem peculiar to you and me. Don't question them," had been her advice. "Never question them." This man, this lord, was one of his kinks murder?

The blackness behind her eyes was becoming deeper, intense, the shapes more defined and…familiar too. Did she know them? Did they know her? Were those smiles on their faces, ones of recognition, of greeting? *Hold out your hand, you are done here.*

It was tempting! Their smiles promised so much. But then, hadn't she been fooled before by another smile that had promised so much? Look where that had got her. *Does it matter anymore? Go, now, go with them.* But Mam, what of her? She scanned their faces. These people – *dead* people she understood them to be, how she didn't know, but she didn't question it either – none were her mam. *Which must mean she's alive!* The consumption, or whatever ailment it was that afflicted her, hadn't triumphed, not yet. *I want to see Mam!* Just one more time. To cleave to her as she had done as a child, when she'd been truly innocent.

The smiles on the faces of the familiar strangers began to fade; they began to recede from her. Despite her resolve, she was bereft to see them go and almost called them back. *I've changed my mind.* Words she quickly concealed. As she drifted upwards, through layers and layers of darkness, not realising how far she'd sunk, she returned to something else: pain, and the sharp, raw edge of it. No, she wouldn't survive this, she couldn't. The man had succeeded in his intent; he'd torn her apart, the stickiness that she lay in and the flashes of red in the corners of her eyes proof that her life force, her blood, was being drained. Better not to hold on, then, to go. *Come back! Where are you all? Come back!*

Another noise assailed her. Not his grunting, his heaving, the whoops that kept escaping him, sounds of pure delight, but a door being thrust open, a voice. His voice? Higgins? Had he come to save her again, to tear this man off her? Such a peculiar saviour he was, delivering her from one hell only to plunge her into another. About to sink again, to give up, it was a voice apart from his that brought her back to consciousness, a woman's voice laden with such horror.

"Lord, have mercy on us! Help her! Don't just stand there gawping, someone help the poor girl!"

Grace tried to open her eyes, to see who it was. The figure of a woman was in the doorway, her hands clasped to her open mouth, her eyes bulging at the scene in front of her. There was also movement to her right and left, a man's indignant cries as he was hauled off the bed.

"What is this?" he kept saying. "What the deuce is this? I've paid for this; it is my right!"

"Get dressed, sir, and come with us," was the resolute reply. Another man, one in uniform – a policeman, that's what he was, one of those sworn to uphold justice. And yet still he'd called this man 'sir', just as she'd had to. There was more shouting, a voice she recognised that made her shudder.

"You are making a mistake, one you will regret! There are people who support me in this venture, important people. Do not cross them, for they will ensure you realise the severity of your mistake and that you too will pay for it. This is your last warning, Sister Christina – is that what you call yourself? I come from a fine family too, as do every single one of my clients. They have a right to spend their money in whichever way they see fit. These girls – *her* – they are taken from the streets and given an opportunity. You know well enough the hovels they come from!"

It was Higgins. What the woman said in reply, Grace didn't know. Her body was becoming more and more like a furnace, burning red, the fire that consumed it growing fiercer. Just how many versions of hell were there? Whatever opportunity she'd had to venture somewhere else – heaven, perhaps – was lost.

The woman had rushed over to her and was gazing down upon her face. Grace forced her eyes to remain open, swollen as they were, and saw that the woman was crying, tears falling from her cheeks and onto Grace's own, cleansing, she thought, like raindrops.

It doesn't matter, she tried to say out loud, wanting only to ease the woman's grief, but her lips remained still. The woman's eyes were so solemn, and yet there was a spark within them too.

Grace was being touched, kindly this time, not by the woman but by the others who tended to her, lifted her. The woman stepped back to make way, but her voice was ragged as she spoke again.

"Remove her from this…this…vile den of iniquity. May God have mercy on these men's souls, for in this moment, I can find no mercy for them in my own. You have tainted this ground, Mr Higgins, but you will not be allowed to flourish. We will fight back. Rest assured. We will fight."

Chapter Seventeen

Lucy – current day

Text conversations could sometimes be difficult, primarily when tone could be misconstrued. She'd pissed Zak off, but that hadn't been her intention. Looking at her mobile on her desk in her office, she picked it up again and scanned through the messages. Something she'd done several times already.

Joe's doing great, and it's in no small part thanks to you, but I'm unsure whether we should continue treatment or not. x

Why not, if he's doing so well? Therapy needs to continue, surely? xxx

You know why. x

Tell me. xxx

Because of money. x

What do you mean? Has what I've given you run out already? xxx

That's when there'd been a brief period of silence. Lucy hadn't wondered about it – not too much, anyway, as she'd been busy working on a letter at the time. When her phone had pinged, however, to indicate a reply, she'd immediately stopped what she was doing.

Forget I said anything.

That's all it said. No kiss at the end of the text as was

their custom, his one to her three.

Rather than reply further, she'd dialled his number. It went straight to voicemail. Frustrated, she had ended the call, trying again a minute or two later and then a third time. She hadn't wanted to leave a message – she wanted to speak to him – but, even so, she'd left one asking him to call her. When he still hadn't half an hour later, she could resist no more and sent him another text.

Where are you? Been trying to ring. Are you upset with me? xxx

I can't talk right now.

That text reply had been quick enough. So he was contactable, then, was checking his phone?

But I'm worried I've upset you. And I don't know why. xxx

Again, the reply was immediate.

Speak tonight.

He'd dismissed her, and inside she was cold because of it. That's why she kept re-reading the messages, trying to analyse why a normal conversation had suddenly come to a halt like that. *Has what I've given you run out already?* Had he taken that the wrong way, as some kind of accusation? It was the only thing she could think of. But if that was so, he couldn't be more wrong. She was simply asking if the funds she'd transferred across to his account had all been used – it had, after all, been a substantial amount, meant to cover costs for quite a while. If funds had run out, if that was the case, then *of course* she'd transfer more. He only had to say the word.

The hours had passed, and the tours were done. Another volunteer, not Bert this time but a retired woman named Gina, had left. Across the road at the East Cemetery, the entrance booth would still be open, but only for another half hour, and then Margaret would lock up and head home. So Lucy was alone, quite alone, and anxious. Unable to focus any longer on the tasks at hand, she did as she always tended to do at these times and got up and wandered over to the window.

Her gaze on the courtyard, she imagined the horse-drawn carriages with coffins laid upon them turning in a circle there. She could almost hear the animals as they whinnied, the clip-clop, clip-clop of their hooves. If mourners had been hired, paid to wail, and beat their chests in anguish, they'd have fallen silent once inside the cemetery, respecting sanctified ground. The family mourners occupying another carriage would then alight, weary resignation on their faces. The coffin would be borne to its allotted plot by pallbearers and by hand bier, with everyone duly following. It would be raining, she fancied, not heavy but a steady drizzle, for it was always difficult to imagine sunshine at a funeral. As the coffin was lowered into the ground, the wailing would resume, maybe more heartfelt this time as the loss of another living being *should* warrant tears; each person was unique, and no one could fill the void they left behind.

Once the mourners had left, then what? How long before visits to the grave became less regular? Time was a great healer – that was the saying; time could also make you forget. Hence why this once great cemetery had fallen into ruin.

As she continued to gaze out across the courtyard, her eyes travelled towards the steps that led up to the main path. Once again, her imagination was vivid. The mourners, clad head to toe in black, would return to their awaiting carriage after the service, one of the women dabbing at her eyes and nose. Lucy squinted. This light that was peculiar to Highgate was such a strange light, and today it had about it a grainy quality. Those people she envisaged? It was as if they were truly there, caught up in the raptures of grief. Shadows – that's all they were, of course, cast by the setting sun, a spectacle she was rather enjoying as it had taken her mind from her worries, had quite transfixed her. Shadows. Highgate was always so full of them.

She looked again, harder, and found herself leaning forward. Who was that trailing behind the mourners? No, not a straggler but standing at the top of the steps. She was more defined somehow, more real. *She?*

I know it's you out there...

A young girl, who couldn't be more than eleven or twelve, with pale hair that fell to her shoulders and features that even from here suggested great beauty. She was slight, though, painfully thin and dressed in a plain, somewhat ragged shift, and her feet were bare, inspiring pity.

The moment Lucy thought that, a protest entered her head: *Don't pity me!* Lucy found herself taking a step back because of it. Grabbing hold of the windowsill in order to steady herself, she blinked. Would the girl still be there when she opened her eyes? Not a girl, just a shadow, just an imagining. Yes, she *was* still there. Was she the same girl that had screamed at her the night she and Zak had consummated their relationship? Why had she screamed?

Who are you?

Her phone beeped. The noise, although not loud, was nonetheless startling in the silence that had fallen. It succeeded, at least, in snapping her out of the reverie she'd fallen into. The figure that had stood at the top of the steps, on the threshold, had gone. Feeling somewhat dismayed, and bewildered too, Lucy shook her head. This place! How it played tricks with you, bringing the past so easily to life. But that's why she liked it, why she'd been so drawn to it in the first place, the rich history of others making up for the plainness of her own.

Grabbing her phone, she hoped the text was from Zak, informing her he was home, perhaps, at her flat, as that's where they spent all their time for the reasons he'd explained. *Sound* reasons.

It wasn't from him but from her friend, the mutual friend, Karen.

Hey, Luce, how are you? Long time no see! How's it going with the delightful Zak? You're still madly in love, I hope. I've been thinking, it's been too long since we've seen each other. Do you think you could spare me an evening soon? I'm dying to hear how you lovebirds are getting on.

Her dismay deepened. As lovely as it was to hear from Karen, it was Zak she wanted a text from, explaining, perhaps, what a hard day it had been at work and that's why he couldn't talk to her earlier, but not to worry, because it was over now, and the shitstorm that went with it; all he wanted was to have a nice meal with her and just relax in front of the TV, as had become the norm for the pair of them, cuddling up together. Simple but happy.

"Damn!" she swore just as Margaret popped her head around the door.

"Everything all right, love?" her colleague asked.

"Yeah, fine." Lucy checked her watch. "Sorry, just…stuff

on my mind. You know, admin."

"Admin can wait. It's five o'clock already. You coming?"

"Of course, yeah. I'll grab my coat."

Margaret was right. It was time to go home and face the music.

* * *

You needed to be relaxed to sleep, and she wasn't. Every limb was rigid. He, however, had no such trouble; he'd drifted off as if he hadn't a care in the world, as if they'd indeed enjoyed a pleasant evening together, lightly snoring as soon as his head had touched the pillow.

How was it so? How could he just…sleep?

Her eyes stung with suppressed tears, a metallic taste in her mouth where she had bitten down too hard on her lip and drawn blood. The reason she didn't cry was because if she did, if she gave in to the tumult of emotions that stormed within her, she might choke, and that, in turn, might wake him. When all was said and done, it was far better he remained asleep.

When all was said and done…

Oh, the things that had been said that evening and the things that had been done.

She'd reached home, wary, she had to admit, of Zak's mood. Despite her wariness, she couldn't have predicted what did happen, how things would get out of hand so quickly. When she'd entered her flat, she had called his name, knowing he was there as his boots were in the hallway, right in the centre of it rather than to the side – something of a statement, she now realised, which had caused her to bend down, pick them up, and stow them more neatly. In the kitchen, there he'd been, leaning against the countertop, with a mug of coffee on the go. He'd had his back to her, so she had walked up to him and put her arms around his waist, intending to hold him. Just hold him.

"Bloody hell, Luce," he'd exclaimed, forcing her hands off him as he turned around to face her, "frighten the life out of me, why don't you?"

"I called out," she'd explained.

"No, you didn't."

"I did. You…clearly didn't hear me."

He had postured a bit then, huffing and puffing, making a fuss. "Just don't creep up on me, okay? I don't like it."

Hiding her surprise, she'd nodded instead. "Sorry, hun. I'm…erm, sorry."

He'd returned to his coffee and started slurping it. She could only see his profile, but the expression on it was so different to what she was used to, seeming entirely composed of anger. She also noticed his hands shook as he held his mug. Desperate to appease him, for things to get back on track, she started to speak again.

"You know, Zak, money isn't a problem. If you need more for Joe, then of course there's more."

She flinched this time as he slammed his mug down. "Really? You don't mind?"

"No, I've told you that before."

"Then why make me feel so bad about it?"

"What? I didn't! If it was that text, I think you read it wrong, I didn't mean—"

"So this is my fault, is it?"

"Your fault? I didn't mean that either. This is no one's *fault*."

He whirled back, so fast that he almost knocked the coffee cup over. It rattled precariously before settling back on its base. "Do you think I like having a drug addict for a son?"

"Zak—"

"Or having an ex-wife hell-bent on bankrupting me, who's basically stolen from me every single bloody thing I've worked so hard to build up. Do you seriously think that this is fun for me?"

"You're being silly."

"Silly? Oh, am I? Am I really? What exactly am I being silly about, Lucy?" His hand came up, his thumb and index finger held close together. "You made me feel this small, like shit. Everything you've given me has gone on Joe, to try and help pull him back from the brink. I didn't want your money, but you offered it, you *insisted* I took it. You said my problems were your problems because we're a *couple*, Lucy, and, God, I was so touched by that. I thought you meant it."

"I do mean it! You're getting het up over nothing."

"Over nothing? You *accused* me!"

So her hunch had been right; he'd stewed all day over this, over an imagining of his own.

She turned her back to him and shrugged off her coat and kicked off her shoes before reaching into her bag to retrieve her mobile phone. She held it up in front of him. "From now on, if we've got important matters to discuss, then we talk about it face to face or on the phone; we don't text each other. You've got the wrong end of the stick, Zak, completely. I was just amazed, that's all, at how expensive therapy can be, but if it's working, if they're helping your son, then that's great. I want it to continue, okay? I'm happy to help. I wouldn't say so if I wasn't."

"I don't want any more money from you, to be—" he paused for a moment and then spat the word at her "—*beholden*."

"Christ, Zak, just stop it, will you? This bloody stupidity!"

His blue eyes flashing, he grabbed the phone from her hand and hurled it onto the floor. That he'd done that was bad enough, damaged her property, but when he raised his hand again and slapped her so hard across the face that she crashed against the kitchen table, damaged *her*, she could barely believe it, despite how her skin screamed because of the impact. And it didn't stop there. He then grabbed her by the collar of her blouse and pulled her close, his face puce with the effort he exerted, the pupils of his eyes much larger than usual, practically obliterating the blue. Her face became covered in spittle as he yelled at her. "Don't fucking call me stupid, okay? Don't you fucking dare!"

"Zak, Zak, I'm sorry, I won't. I promise. Zak, stop, please."

"Who do you think you are?" he continued even though she was begging, pleading with him. "You're nothing without me, do you hear? You're just some sad old bitch who lives on her own, who'd probably *always* live on her own if I hadn't come along and taken pity on you."

Pity?

"Zak! Stop it! Now!"

The cry she'd emitted – one filled with as much horror

as the shadow child's – finally seemed to bring him to his senses. Something in his gaze cleared and became more focused. He blinked several times, slight tremors coursing through him before settling. "Lucy?" he said, as if he didn't recognise her or even recognise what he'd done.

"Zak?" Tentatively she'd said it. "Are you...are you all right now?"

"All right? Yeah...I..." He looked at one of the chairs that had scattered when he'd thrown her against the table. "I think I need to sit down."

She sat too, grateful for the opportunity as she wasn't sure her legs could support her much longer. He had his head in his hands, and he was muttering; several times she caught the word *sorry*. She didn't reply. She couldn't; her voice was stuck in her throat.

Suddenly he reached out and caught her hands. "I don't deserve you, do you know that? The way you put up with my—" he shook his head as though it hurt him to say it "—problems. Oh, Luce!" He was crying, as he'd done twice before. "You're so good to me. I'm sorry I got the wrong end of the stick. It's just getting to me, you know, this...situation with Joe. But he's on the mend, and it's all thanks to you and what you're doing for us. Thank you so much for funding his rehab, for *continuing* to fund it. I won't forget it, Luce, ever. Don't worry about your phone; I'll get you another. I'll do that tomorrow, okay? I promise."

And that was it. There was no reference to the fact that he'd hit her or insulted her, calling her a sad old bitch. He seemed to have brushed all that under the carpet as if he'd been possessed whilst carrying out the assault, as if it wasn't him at all. All he was concerned with was her broken phone, not whether he'd broken *her*. Oh, and that she transferred more funds, that she'd "make sure to do that."

And because he'd been so *normal*, she'd found herself doubting what had happened. He'd gone on to act so tenderly towards her that evening, so grateful when more funds had indeed been transferred: cooking her dinner, suggesting they catch up on a box set, taking her plate from her when she'd barely eaten a thing, not commenting on that either, returning to the living room to sit beside her as she stared blankly at the TV, placing his arm around her, ignoring or genuinely not realising how stiff she'd become. It was the evening she'd dreamed of, but with such a savage twist.

They had gone to bed. That was when fear had truly gripped her. Would he expect sex? She'd hoped not; she'd prayed not. Thankfully, her prayers regarding that were answered. He had simply kissed her on the cheek and turned over, and that was it. The day was done with.

For him, at least.

Chapter Eighteen

Emma – 1972

"Kev, you sure about this?"

"It's what she wants."

"Yeah, but you know more than anyone that that stuff's dangerous. One good trip doesn't guarantee another. And…well…she's not exactly used to it, is she, Miss Goody Two Shoes."

Kev and Danny were in the kitchen and Emma was in the hallway, listening again, eavesdropping. She could feel her whole body stiffen. What if Kev listened to Danny and refused her? She not only wanted to experience what she'd felt the third time she had visited Highgate Cemetery, she *needed* to. That Danny had developed scruples, that he suddenly seemed to give a damn – sort of – about her wellbeing, wasn't welcome.

Don't listen to him, Kev, just continue being your usual shitty self and give me the tab.

There was movement from inside the room, more talking, mumbling this time, words spoken that she couldn't quite make out. "Should I care?" was one such extract from Kev. "It's her life." She heard him mention something about Highgate Cemetery too; he was obviously telling Danny about their previous visit and that she intended to go again.

But Kev was right. It *was* her life, and with or without him she wanted to find meaning to it.

The door opened, and one of them was about to exit the kitchen. She started to walk, as if heading there herself. "Hi, Dan," she called when he emerged into the hallway. "Didn't know you were in."

He grunted in true Danny fashion. "Haven't been for long."

"Oh, okay. I'm just off to get a tea."

As they passed, Danny stopped. "Kev told me you visited the cemetery, just the two of you."

"Yeah, that's right," she said, feigning nonchalance. "We thought we'd give it another go."

"You took acid?"

"Just half a tab."

"If you go back, stick to that, okay? Go easy."

"Okay, maybe. *If* I go back."

He made to walk on and then stopped again. "Have a word with Loo too, and Ange, about what they saw." He shook his head. "Know what? As much as I enjoyed that visit, I wouldn't want to go back, so why would you? It's a cemetery, full of nothing but dead people. Oh, and a few tramps, of course. It's just...it's not a place that normal people would want to hang around in."

Normal people? A need to defend the place rose up in her. "I think it's beautiful."

Danny screwed up his face in disbelief. "Really?"

"You seemed to think so too when we were there."

A laugh escaped him, heavy with sarcasm. "Yeah, but I didn't see the real place, did I? I was...tripping."

"What did you see?" she asked, genuinely intrigued. "Tell me."

"Angels, cherubs, doorways opening, a light shining behind them. You know, all the usual stuff you'd see in a cemetery, when you're having a good trip, that is."

"And it was beautiful?"

He paused momentarily as if confused. "Well, yeah it was. But like I said, it wasn't real." Again, he paused and looked behind him, then turned back to her and lowered his voice significantly. "Look, be careful if you buy stuff off Kev. He's not fussy where he gets his gear. I keep telling him about that, but he doesn't listen. He's a law unto himself sometimes, plays by his own rules, you know? And if you do plan on going to Highgate, let the rest of us know, not just him, okay?"

"Okay," she answered, nodding. How strange to think he cared. Strange too that it didn't touch her at all; it was like rainwater falling onto the surface of her skin and just as quickly rolling off. *Dead inside.* She was truly beginning to think so. But she also knew what it was to feel otherwise.

She entered the kitchen. Kev was sitting at the table by the window, a notebook in front of him, which he stared at. He didn't look up as she approached.

"Hi, Kev," she said, forcing breeziness back into her voice.

"All right?" came the mumbled reply.

"Writing an essay?"

"Trying to."

"Want a cuppa?"

"No."

As she waited for the kettle to boil, she gazed at his

179

hunched form. Kev: the leader of the pack, who actually seemed as dead inside as she was. A kindred spirit? What an uncomfortable notion that was. There was anger in him, a violence, which skirted around the edges of so much dead stuff. She couldn't help but wonder what he'd experienced in his youth to make him like that. Or perhaps he was born that way as she sometimes thought she had been – was it possibly a case of nature not nurture, especially as she couldn't remember feeling any different? Except, of course, on one glorious occasion: Amelia. How kind she had been, a true mother.

Walking over, Emma reached into her pocket. "I've got the money," she said, holding it out to him.

When he still didn't look up, she laid it neatly on the table beside his book.

"Kev?"

"Yeah, okay. I'll have it for you later."

"Good."

Finally, he looked up, an expression on his face that made her recoil. Why did he hate her so much? Was it indeed because he was looking at a mirror image?

"I'm not coming with you this time, though," he said.

She nodded in understanding. That was fine by her. She wasn't going to ask him anyway.

* * *

With no street lighting, Swain's Lane was almost unbearably dark. Thankfully, Emma had a torch with her, but even that was having difficulty coping with such gloom. The high walls on either side of the lane lent it such a claustrophobic feel, as though she were not on a street but in a tunnel, one that was leading her ever onwards. No light at the end of it, just more darkness.

She'd taken a tab barely half an hour ago, knowing it would take a while to kick in. Not half, as Danny had advised, but a whole one, not wanting to compromise the experience. She wanted to make it even more intense, if possible. And she hadn't talked to Louise and Angela about what they'd seen; instead, she preferred to remember their happiness whilst behind these walls.

Their *initial* happiness, anyway. Afterwards, when Angela had grabbed her, when they'd joined the others and ran, it had taken a while for them to calm down. "There's something in there, something bad, something...*inhuman,*" Angela had finally admitted. But the next day – or was it a couple of days afterwards? – when Kev had mentioned it, she'd laughed it off, told him she couldn't actually remember what had happened, just that something had. "But before that," she'd continued, "it was lovely. Really kind of peaceful, you know?"

And that's what Emma found herself craving, that peace and love that had poured from Amelia and into her, to form something golden deep within. She could imagine it even now in this dark lane, vividly, in fact, causing her to stop and shine the light at her outstretched hand.

She gasped. Was her skin actually glowing golden? It was! The drug must be kicking in. She could see every vein and sinew that lay beneath the surface – her bones, even, all so brilliant and bright. This was perfect; this was what she wanted. Her laughter was something of a high-pitched squeal. It must have been that which masked another sound, one she'd heard before whilst traipsing in this direction…

Footsteps.

She turned quickly, determined to see who was responsible. A man, tall and dressed in black, was close behind her. She froze, feeling far from invincible suddenly. What did he want? Did he mean to harm her?

The figure, so difficult to distinguish – his face, at least, which was cast entirely in shadow – brushed past her before continuing on his way. She found herself breathing rapidly; in the absence of any other sound, it was so loud in her ears. Staring after him, he dissolved into the night, although her arm was still tingling from where he'd touched her.

Look at your hand again.

She did so, wanting, *needing* that distraction. There was no golden glow, not anymore. It was just a normal hand, a lifeless thing hanging limp before her, as if…he'd stolen the light from her somehow. Both disappointed and uneasy, she checked again for no further sign of him. Continuing her journey, she prayed it would stay that way, that their encounter was over.

The crumbled stretch of wall at last came into view. She felt like she'd walked forever, on and on, each tread seemingly getting her nowhere. Another effect of the drug, it had to be, and this time a far from pleasant sensation. Her unease grew. What was she doing coming back to Highgate at night, alone, and on acid? She, who couldn't even finish a cigarette. She wasn't someone crazy or rebellious; she was just a girl, a student, someone trying to get somewhere in life, to break the bonds of childhood, the *curse* of it. She shook her head. *That* was why she came here, to find a sense of true family, albeit amongst dead strangers.

Persisting with her plan, she'd climb over the wall, but perhaps she wouldn't venture too far. That way, if things turned bad, she could easily get the heck out of there. *But you want to find Amelia, don't you?* And Amelia was in the thick of things. *Just breathe, believe it will be all right.* And she *did* believe it. If only that man hadn't brushed past her, hadn't *infected* her.

"Stop it, Em!"

Her voice rang out in the night, echoing all around her. It was so silent otherwise, with no traffic and no birds calling to one another either. Her breathing *was* steady, although her heart felt odd, like a caged animal that wanted to break free. She daren't look at her chest, afraid of what she would see there: her sternum bulging and something red and fleshy behind it, oozing blood.

She couldn't do this, go through with it. *This* was madness. She'd turn around, go back down the lane and reach the Tube station. Home was a couple of stops along the line. Not a long journey. She'd keep her head low and her imagination in check, literally ride this thing out.

Her body had started to shake, her breathing once more inconsistent. She couldn't rid herself of the idea of infection. Her hand, the one that had pulsed golden just a short while ago, should she look at it again? What would she see this time, black rushing after the gold and devouring it? Christ, she shouldn't have done this! Far from dead inside, she was a riot of emotions, each one of them a demanding entity. *Turn! Go home!* But to venture down that lane that was so lonely, that stretched on and on, was it the better choice?

"Shit!" Fervently she wished that somebody was with her, someone who was straight. She even wished for Kev, despite their mutual loathing. That realisation startled her: that she actually *loathed* him. He'd given her this tab, just tossed it at her, told her to 'fill her boots' and then walked away, had left her, showing no concern at all. It was what she'd wanted at the time, but now it was the last thing. She was alone. All alone. Wasn't she?

Again, every limb froze. Were those more footsteps? That man, was he coming back?

A terrible thought! One she couldn't bear.

"Psst! Come here. Quick. Be quick."

Instead of looking behind her, Emma gazed ahead in the direction of the voice that had summoned her. There was a shadow, not tall, not him; it was much smaller than that.

She didn't even hesitate. "I'm coming," she whispered, shoving the torch in her jacket pocket and using both hands to haul herself over the wall and into the cemetery. "Wait for me."

Once fully inside Highgate, she retrieved her torch and started to run, the beam of light illuminating the ground in front of her in short, erratic bursts. *Be careful not to fall,* she kept telling herself, imagining that tall man leaping upon her if she did, his entire body covering hers.

"Wait!"

Where was the person who'd called her? Had he or she disappeared?

"Oh no, no," she whispered, not daring to look back, to see what else was nearby.

She continued running, staring not ahead but at the beam of light. What was that dancing within its glare? She squinted. Beads? Little black beads? A stream of them. Forcing herself to come to a stop, she leant forwards. That was when the beads changed: they grew wings, became bat-like creatures that now stared back at her, that flew upwards and straight into her face.

She screamed and dropped the torch, her hands swatting at them. Expecting claws and sharp teeth to puncture her skin, there was nothing, no pain at all. Slowly, tentatively, she lowered her hands. The light was shining in another direction now, and still strange creatures danced within it, as if trapped within its beam. Those that previously escaped had simply...vanished. But those were definitely footsteps she could hear, crunching over roots and leaves and coming closer. *Forget about the torch and run!*

She did exactly that. If she could find Amelia, all would be well. Amelia would protect her. Which way should she go? Where should she turn? *Just keep going forwards.* Amelia was somewhere here, waiting for her. As she ran, other things accompanied her, keeping to the edge of vision, and although they glowed, they were not pure white; instead, they had about them a yellowish cast, a *dirty* yellow.

Unable to resist looking, she turned her head. Angels, that's what they were, having come down from the plinths they occupied. One of the angels – on Emma's right – also twisted its head to look directly at her. As she did, Emma screamed. There was no beauty, no sweet joy or innocence; hers was the face of vengeance, of wrath, of hatred and spite. Desperate to see something different, Emma turned to the left. That other angel had come closer and was also looking at her, her eyes glowing red and pointed teeth bared.

Emma screamed, forcing herself to run faster. "Amelia! Amelia! Where are you?"

Aside from footsteps, another sound emerged – not the glorious blare of trumpets that had celebrated her presence last time but a low, rhythmic sound, the beating of drums, primal, a tune that only the depraved would want to dance to. It reminded her of something else, lyrics that had once upset her, the bitter truth of them: *Cryin' won't help you; prayin' won't do you no good.*

Breathless, she had to stop, sinking behind a tombstone and resting her head against the cold stone, wishing she could block out the endless drone, gain some respite from it. Panting, she lifted her head. Was something tapping at her foot? The ground she crouched on appeared to have split itself open, revealing a coffin whose lid was rattling. On either side of the lid were hands...no...not hands; they couldn't be called that. They were something skeletal with only gobbets of flesh hanging from them – *worm-ridden* gobbets. And they were reaching out, tapping at her feet, grabbing at them now, as desperate as she was, trying to drag her down so the corpse would have some company in its dark damp kingdom.

Screaming, she kicked out, saw the hands recoil before striking out again, faster than a snake.

The only haven was with Amelia; only she could provide protection from what Highgate had become. Emma had no choice but to continue onwards, jumping up and veering from the main path, which led to that strange Egyptian structure, whose vaults contained who knew what – more creatures like the one that had erupted from the ground, perhaps? Where did Amelia reside? This place was vast, endless, just as the lane that led to it had been endless, a world within a world.

Footsteps again. *No! Oh no!* Whatever she'd encountered here, what strange and gruesome sights, it was the tall man she feared the most – it was he that would be the undoing of her, she was certain of it, although why he should be so intent on capturing her she had no idea. He was a stranger to her, and she to him. Why couldn't he just leave her be? Was it him behind the trees, darting so quickly from one to the other, on her trail? She couldn't see him, but she could sense him, could *smell* him, just as Angela and Louise had, and it was the stench of something rotten that had been left to fester far too long.

"Come on, over here, follow! She's this way."

It was the voice from before, the one who had beckoned her. Just a shadow in the distance, small and quick. Could it see all that she could see, the horrors that surrounded them? Hear the beating of the drums, a dog's bark adding to it, another maddened beast come to life?

The child had been joined by yet more children, all skipping along, beckoning…gesturing for her to hurry…

As she followed, numerous branches from numerous trees scraped brutally against her face. Again, she imagined claws and had to clamp down on that thought, lest she breathed life into it.

Follow the cherubs. Keep your eyes ahead. Find Amelia.

Like a chant in her head, those words went round and round. *Find Amelia… Find Amelia…*

"Aargh!"

One of the boughs had bitten deep. She raised her hand to assess the damage, and it came away slick and bloody.

What if it became more than a cut, became a torrent? Briefly she closed her eyes, distraught. When she opened them, when she saw where she'd been led, tears joined the rivers of blood that surely poured down her face. It was – thankfully – Amelia. She was kneeling, her hands in her lap, her gaze ever wistful.

A mother to all.

Emma took a step forward and then another, not hurrying now, for there was no need, not anymore. All fear evaporated as if it had never existed. She was calm, even serene, sure that her face was no longer smeared red, that in Amelia's presence she was golden once more.

Nearing the plinth, she reached out her arms. Amelia would of course be eager for their embrace. The memory of their first meeting and the acceptance she'd seen in the woman's eyes warmed her through and through until she burned with anticipation.

"It's me; it's Emma. I came back. To see you."

Why was she so still?

"I wanted to see you again, so much. Amelia? Mother?"

Still the woman refused to move; she simply knelt there, gazing beyond Emma into what, another void? Slowly, terribly, it dawned. There was nothing in her eyes, certainly no vestige of love. Instead, there hung about her an air of such terrible melancholy. *My life is like a broken stair...* The words formed in Emma's mind to be joined by yet more. *Winding round a ruined tower...* Where had they sprung from, what could they mean? *And leading nowhere...*

Despite her desire to be close to this woman, Emma took a step back. There'd been a brief silence, reverent, almost – the respite she had yearned for – but now the beating of the drums had started again, and the cherubs, standing huddled to one side of her, were giggling, a far from delightful sound. They were laughing *at* her, at her hopes, her dreams, and her desires.

All I want is to be loved!

That wasn't quite true. She wanted to love too. But mothers with a heart of stone neither gave nor received.

The sound that escaped her was something primal too.

Cryin' won't help you...

With sodden cheeks she turned from Amelia, from the spite of the cherubs, and spun around, an action so quick that her foot snared in something – a root, perhaps, or something far worse?

"No! Get off me, please! God, dear God, someone help me!"

Prayin' won't do you no good...

The drums beat louder, the laughter became howling, the smell of death crept closer and closer, and there was no one to help. No God and certainly no Amelia, a statue erected to commemorate a woman who, if the words that had formed in Emma's head were to be believed, had been as much a husk in life as she was in death. Even so, could Emma bear the loss of her?

"GET OFF ME!"

Whatever had hold of her leg released it with such suddenness that it caused her to topple forward. There was no time to throw her hands out to save herself or indeed register the pain as her skull – amidst so many whoops and cheers – caught the edge of another plinth.

She lay there, as still as any statue.

Chapter Nineteen

Grace – 1850s

"Lie still, darling, don't fret. You're safe here. No more harm can befall you."

But who was it that had harmed her in the first place? Someone who had plucked her from the streets, who had favoured her. His eyes, though, what colour were they? Blue, yes…yes…that was right. And upon his face there was always a smile. She'd followed him, hadn't she? And because she had, she'd been delivered straight into the arms of hell. Now what should she do? Believe this second voice, a woman's, not his? But from the alleys she knew that evil was not present in the hearts of men alone. Would this woman prove just as despicable?

A hazy figure she was, sitting by her bedside. Having noticed her patient stirring, the figure reached out a hand. Grace flinched. She didn't want to be touched by anyone ever again.

"There, there, do not fear."

There was culture in her voice, and education. Why was a woman like her bothering with such a wretch? If only she'd asked herself that question of Higgins, not taken the gifts he'd bestowed on her and her family so readily. Of course he would want something in return, how naïve she had been to think otherwise. One thing was for certain: she was naïve no longer.

"Tell me your name."

Whore. Harlot. Jezebel. She hadn't been christened as such, but that's what she would be called now if she were to step back into society. From the highest to the lowest, all would scorn her. She had become her mother's greatest fear, the very person she'd been told to avoid. Her true name? It meant not a thing, not now, and it never had to Higgins, for if the woman was asking, then certainly he had not disclosed it. She had always referred to him as 'the gentleman', and in turn he had only ever called her 'girl', one of many, most likely, that he had ensnared, prized for their youth, their supposed beauty, not human but mere chattel.

There was evidence of movement in the room, low voices, the woman's and also someone else's, a man? What little breath she had caught in her throat. If she could force her eyelids to open further, she could see who it was, but the effort was simply too much.

Was this a trick? Another one? Did the second voice belong to Higgins? Did they...dear Lord, no...intend to *use* her again?

"Oh, look, she's trying to speak. Quick, Doctor Biddle, we must listen."

So hard she tried to push words out, clear in what she wanted to say: *You must leave me alone now. I am done with. I am spent. Just leave me be.* But all that left her mouth was a strange, low gurgling sound.

"Don't strain, little one. Another time we will hear you, when you are better, perhaps. Doctor Biddle, would you be

so good as to pass me a kerchief. I must wipe her mouth."
With the soft linen at Grace's lips, the woman continued
speaking. "Oh, Doctor, look at this, it has speckles upon it."

Was it like her mam's kerchief? Were the speckles blood?
Thoughts of her mam conjured her, in the confines of
Grace's mind, at least. Her mam stepped forwards out of
the darkness and into plain view.

Mam!

Grace's delight in seeing her was not shared.

Where have you been? What have you done?

*I'm sorry, Mam, but…terrible things happened. I couldn't
stop them.*

Evil? Is that what happened? You fell into its clutches?

How solemnly Grace replied. *Yes, I did.*

I told you, didn't I, to be careful!

I tried, but—

*You didn't try hard enough! And now look at what's become
of you. I can hardly bear to gaze upon you; you don't look like
my child anymore, it's as if evil has consumed you.*

Mam!

And what's to become of us, eh? Look at me, look! For the
first time Grace noticed beads of blood bubbling around her
mother's mouth, which she spat out, only for more beads to
replace them, one hand reaching up to smear them across
her face, making her look like something dredged from hell
too. *I'm not getting any better, not without enough food to eat.
I can barely move from my chair now. Certainly, I can't see to
sew anymore; my eyesight is failing rapidly. I shall die soon –
there, that's the truth of it, and then your brothers, they'll also
fall prey to evil—*

No, Mam! Not her dear brother Michael and sweet,

sweet Patrick.

They will! They will! Her mother's voice was as high as a banshee's. *You were supposed to be looking after them, stepping into my shoes, taking my place as the head of the household. Instead, you're lying in that fancy bed, fancy people at the foot of it, for what good it will do you. Because you're dying too, you realise that, don't you, Grace, that you're dying?*

Dying?

Yes. And don't think heaven waits, not for one such as you.

As quickly as her mother had appeared, she disappeared. Despite what she had said, Grace was sorry to see her go. She tried to lift an arm and reach out for her.

"Mam! Mam!"

"Oh, thank God, she's speaking!" The woman had come closer, so close that Grace could smell the perfume of her skin; it was soft and subtle, just how she imagined a rose to smell: the scent of the angels, not sickly at all. Grace relaxed. If she were evil, if she intended to trick her, she wouldn't smell as sweet, surely? And the man whom she'd been talking to – not Higgins, but a doctor – there was the same warmth and concern in his voice as there was in hers.

"If you could only tell us your name," the woman continued, "we could find your family and inform them. Where do you come from? What borough?"

Find her family? Would that be a blessing or a curse?

The woman held Grace's face in her hands, though she was careful not to move her.

"Your name, little one," she whispered. "Everybody has a name."

Perhaps, but not everyone had one so ill-suited.

"Tell me."

Because the woman was so insistent, Grace found herself trying to comply, to force her lips to move once again. What emerged from them caused the woman to cry out.

"Doctor Biddle, there is more blood!"

A frenzy of movement this time. The room was full of people, suddenly, crowding it. If they were truly there, however, they remained mute; only the doctor and the woman conversed.

"My dear Christina, I do not think there is anything more to be done for the poor child."

"Are you quite sure? Nothing at all?"

"That she has survived this long after such an ordeal is something of a miracle."

"A miracle? You call this a miracle?" The woman's voice was full of despair. "No! No! No! Too many are lost in this way. What is wrong with society that it accepts this?"

"I do not know," came the equally heartfelt reply.

Hands were upon Grace again, dabbing at her mouth, over and over.

"Hurry, Doctor Biddle, fetch a priest. She must have the last rites."

"A priest, Christina? I doubt one will—"

"Make them come!" The woman's raised voice, full of fury now, pulled Grace from the darkness she was sliding into. "Use your influence, your power, just as I have used the name of Rossetti in these circumstances, to save poor wretches such as her. No, it is not the children, the young women that are the wretches, but those that see fit to abuse them, men like Higgins, who will never pay for his crimes, because, damn him, he will use his power and his influence to avoid it. Now go, Doctor, please, make haste and bring back with you a priest!" Having issued her fervent instruction, the woman turned back to Grace. "There, darling, there. Soon all suffering will end. The priest is coming, and I will ensure your body is laid upon consecrated ground. Mark my words, you will rest in the finest of places." She was crying again, her voice as choked as Grace's own. "I am sorry, so sorry. *Suffer little children, and forbid them not, to come unto me: for of such is the kingdom of Heaven.*" Was it verse she was reciting, or were these her own words? "*Whosoever shall not receive the kingdom of God as a little child shall in no wise enter therein.*"

All words ceased, leaving just the sound of sobbing. The woman had scooped her up in her arms, had laid her cheek against hers. Grace wondered…fretted…about it. Wouldn't she soil the woman's skin and clothes, and she'd come away as bloody as her? But did it matter, any of it? The woman seemed to think not.

Suffer little children…

Incredibly, she *wasn't* suffering, not bodily. Where once she had burnt like fire, there was no pain at all; it was as if she were lighter, becoming quite detached from blood, bone, and sinew. There was no bodily pain, but for her mind, her heart, and her soul, it was different.

Whosoever shall not receive the kingdom of God as a little child shall in no wise enter therein…

She would not enter it. Her mam had said so, and if she could gain no entry as a child, nor would she ever. Somewhere quite different was waiting for someone as defiled, and there she would take her place amongst them: the damned. The terror that thought – that realisation – incited! If she could say her name, then perhaps this woman would remember her in her prayers, and if she did, would He finally listen, the God that presided over them? Would He eventually take pity on her and lift her upwards from the depths?

Whatever else was in the room crept closer. Who were they? The devil's henchmen, come to collect? They didn't look evil, though; they looked concerned, one man in particular who stood with his dog. Dogs weren't evil either, were they? This instinct to trust, it was the undoing of her. She should lift her hand, hit out at them, cast them back into the furthest corners of the room, but her strength was draining. She must save her last ounce for the purpose of saving her soul. Like her body, it was in this woman's hands now. A good woman. *Please, please let her be good.*

"Grace," she whispered.

"What? What was that? What did you say, darling? Say it again. Oh, please do."

"My name is Grace."

Chapter Twenty

Emma – 1972

"I knew it! I knew you'd take more of that shit than I told you. For fuck's sake, Emma! Look at the state of you."

Whose voice was that? Emma tried to open her eyes to see but couldn't. Whoever it was, why was he so determined to wake her? She didn't want him to! Oblivion was the last thing she'd experienced, no shadows within it, and no angels or ghouls. Just a perfect kind of...*nothingness*. That's what truly suited her and was where she belonged, at the heart of it. Perhaps the same was true for all those who were dead inside. But she wasn't dead on the outside, was she? Not if she could hear, and this man, he was angry with her. But who was he? Again, she tried to understand. There was a familiarity about the voice, but one she had trouble placing.

"Come on, try to stand, I'll get you back to the flat. After that, source your own fucking drugs if you want them. Jesus Christ, Danny knows I gave you them; he'll have a right go at me if you don't pull yourself together, although fuck knows why he's gone so righteous on me all of a sudden."

He was speaking about Danny? Then this must be...Kev. He'd come after her. But not because of concern, apparently, because…he was worried about getting into trouble with Danny? Righteous Danny? If she could have laughed, she would have done. So Kev wasn't quite the leader she'd imagined; he was accountable to others after all? There was no way she could muster even a brief smile, let alone stand. If he wanted her out of there, he'd have to carry her.

His hands were upon her now, trying to lift.

"Aargh!" The pain that shot through her when he tried was like a riptide. "Don't…"

"What's that? What are you trying to say?"

Stop!

"Fuck it. Come on, Emma. Meet me halfway here. Help me!"

His hands released her, and she slumped back, not against anything hard-edged this time but the softness of mud, grass, and ivy. She was thankful for it; it was like a plump cushion in comparison, its verdant smell pricking at her senses, trying to enliven them too.

"Look," Kev said, "I can't wait around here all night. You've got to get your act together. Why'd you want to do this anyway, come back here again?"

It was your idea. How she wanted to say it. *Initially. All this was your idea.*

"You're obsessed, all this death stuff, and it's not just because of some essay; that's just an excuse, I reckon. You're just… It's like I said…there's something wrong with you, badly wrong." The cry he gave was one of anger. "Jeez, how long's it gonna take for you to come round?" His hands were on her again, not trying to haul her up this time but prodding and poking at her, and not gently either. She could imagine his fingers sinking into her flesh and getting stuck there, the two of them fusing. *Get your hands off me!*

He was so close now, his face mere inches from her as she could smell his weed-laced breath.

"We could have got on together, you know, if you'd been different. You're not a bad-looking girl, not really, if you bothered to put on a bit of make-up, make the most of yourself. If you hadn't been so uptight. We could have been friends – proper friends, I mean."

Proper friends? What was he talking about?

"What happened to you to make you the way you are? Did your parents never love you or something?"

No, her parents had never loved her; was it so obvious? Or if they had, she'd never *felt* that love. But could they be blamed?

Kev's hands had stopped prodding and poking at her. What was he doing instead? *Stroking* her? She dragged the question she'd asked of herself to the forefront of her mind again. Could her parents be blamed for not loving their only child? Was it possible to love something that was incapable of love itself? Because that's how she felt: incapable of such a vast emotion – that age-old argument emerging, nature versus nurture, which was it? Had she been born with a gaping hole where a heart should be?

Kev? Kev, what are you doing?

Still he stroked her, had managed to peel back part of her jacket to expose the smock beneath it.

"Kev!" The cry she gave was guttural, a half-dead sound dredged up from the pit of her.

He ignored it, was lifting her smock now, his breathing becoming heavier.

"Yeah," he muttered to himself. "You're actually quite pretty. Maybe it's not too late, maybe we *can* mean something more to each other."

It had been so comfortable hiding deep within that emptiness, but now that had to change; she had to resurface. The sound of something – a zip, was that it? Being forced down – filled her with dread that was as cold as winter. Was he trying to force himself upon her? Was he trying to…rape her? Every bone in her body stiffened. *No, I mean it, Kev, get off! Not that! Anything but that!*

It was no use; her eyes wouldn't open and her mouth refused to scream. Damn this useless shell she was occupying. She must force it to work. She had to. *Leave me alone!*

His hand had reached inside her jeans, was forced lower and lower…

NO!

"What's that? Who's there?"

Suddenly – thankfully – he stopped. Something else had caught his attention.

"Don't bother hiding. I heard footsteps. I know you're there."

Was there someone there? And if so, would that person save her or… No, she wouldn't think of the alternative, of who it could be. The tall man, whose footfall she had heard too, for he was a worse foe to deal with. It wouldn't just be rape on his mind but something else entirely.

Still Kev was shouting out. "I'm telling you, mate, stop hiding! I can see you; you're behind that tree, aren't you? Watching me. Stop doing that!"

His shrill voice pierced her. He'd definitely taken more

than weed. LSD, perhaps, the drug that didn't agree with him, that fed his paranoia?

"Come out, you fucker. Come out now."

How quickly hysteria overcame him. All she wanted to do was escape him and the shadow that he insisted was stalking him. If she could just force some life back into her limbs, ignore the knife-sharp pain that jabbed, jabbed, jabbed at her skull, she could crawl away, get out of there. To go where? The flat wasn't an option, not anymore with Kev there. Where, then? Her parents? Again no. Let them continue to tear each other apart without her as their silent witness.

Put simply, there was no place to go. She belonged nowhere. *You belonged here.* True. She had. Once. If she could get away from him, she wouldn't be able to venture too far anyway, not just yet, but there were plenty of places to hide, just until she felt better. She could wait for daylight, a much easier time to navigate these sinuous paths, which, after much twisting and turning, could deliver her into the real world again, the one in which she was anonymous, and better to remain that way. *Come on, Emma, you can do it. Move.*

Kev was truly in a blind panic. "Where are you?" He was yelling at the top of his lungs. "There! There you are! No, no, it's not you. It's someone else. Oh God, oh shit! How many of you are there? Hiding behind every fucking tree. *What* are you? You're not…human. You can't be. The way you move…it's quick. Too quick. No one fucking moves like that. Leave me alone. Get away from me. I'll kill you if you come closer. I mean, it, I'll fucking kill you."

There was a rush of movement. Was it Kev spinning

round and round, trying to fight off those he imagined were intent on assailing him? She had managed to open her eyes at last; they were at half-mast, the world around her grainy and reminding her so much of the photographs she had taken. But yes, it was definitely Kev spinning, his fists held up in front of him, his curls flying as his head seemed to spin on his shoulders too. How his eyes bulged! The look on his face told her that even if the threat was imagined, it didn't matter; it was genuine enough to him, at least.

She finally staggered to her feet and peered ahead. She could see no one in the distance or close by; it was all just grainy darkness and stones – no life to anything, not anymore. Kev had forgotten about her, she could turn, try to get away, blend into the darkness, become it.

His terror, though, had been so awful to witness.

She stepped forward. "Kev?"

She was falling again, yet more pain exploding in her head.

"Emma? Oh, it's you. I thought… I thought it was one of them. Emma? Emma!"

He had thrown his arms out, had hit her. And back down she had gone, into the darkness, which didn't feel so velvety this time or as soft.

How her head hurt; how every limb ached!

He was crying. Yes, he was! Loud sobs punctuated by the words, "Fuck! Fuck! Fuck!"

And then, quite suddenly, there was silence. It stretched on and on… Again, there was no peace in it; rather, it was ominous, as though she were waiting. But for what?

There was movement at last. And muttering.

"… can't let you ruin…life…too late for you…not

me…it's just beginning."

It was Kev. She recognised his voice easily enough this time despite how low it was, as if her hearing had intensified somehow, becoming pin-sharp. If he'd left her there, he'd returned. What for, to truly save her this time, not assault her? Hope flared, but it was ragged at the edges. There was something unusual about the way he moved, she realised. It was no longer frenzied, as she remembered it – when was that? It seemed like such a long time ago. Her eyelids flickered. It was daylight. Definitely daylight. How long had she been lying there, her body growing stiff and cold?

There was a rhythm to his movement; that's what was different. A kind of pattern: *one, two, three, one, two, three*. And then a grunt, followed by more muttering. *One, two, three, one, two three*. She could open her eyes no more, nor her mouth to tell him she was awake. As before – *worse* than before – her body was a thing apart.

One, two, three, one, two, three.

The drums were beating in time with him.

What was he going to do to her now?

There was a splash on her face. Was it rain or something else…his tears?

He'd come closer, was lifting her…not lifting, *dragging* her.

Kev? What are you doing? You have to stop. I'm hurt but not dead. You…you didn't kill me.

"Sorry. Sorry. Sorry." That was all she could hear. "No one has to know, though. Who comes here anyway? People will think you've packed your bags and left, that's all. I'll see to it that's what they'll think. Who'll miss you? You've got no friends; you're a loner. It's your life or mine. If I don't do this, they'll lock me up. They won't realise I came here to help, just help. They won't listen to me, they'll throw the book at me, and I can't have that. I *won't* have that." More tears, more dragging. "You shouldn't have come here again. Normal people don't come here." Again, a brief silence. "There are *things* here."

She was falling, not so far this time. Her body landed with a thud, the pungent smell of soil invading her nostrils. Sound and smell, those senses were working well enough, but all others – those that could save her from this appalling fate – were paralysed completely.

Kev, no! I'm alive. Look at me. Look! I'm alive!

There was a pause. Had her thoughts somehow had an impact? Had he realised his mistake?

Kev?

"No, you're dead. You have to be dead. It's just... It's *easier* if you're dead."

Kev!

Something landed on her face, more soil, the first of many handfuls to be heaped upon her.

I'm not dead! I'm not!

More soil rained down.

You belong here.

Kev had said that to her, and she had thought it herself. Once.

But not like this.

Never like this.

Chapter Twenty-One

Lucy – current day

The days passed, the weeks and the months, all of them in a blur. How had this happened? How had she fallen into such a terrible trap? And so easily too; that was the thing. She'd been so stupid, so dumb. She'd believed everything Zak had told her, that he loved her. She could still remember the look in his eyes when he'd first said that, how the blue of them had brightened further, and she'd replied in kind. *I love you too.* But now, just as she despised herself, she despised him. The trick was not to let him know that, because if he did… She rubbed at her arm, felt how tender the skin was. Only this morning his fingers had dug into the flesh there.

"Come straight back after work, do you hear? I don't want you going anywhere."

There was no one she could turn to; her brother was too far removed, and her friends had their own lives to worry about. Surely they'd pour scorn on her for what she'd done to herself, what she'd willingly walked into. The whole world would. What was it Bert had said? *Sometimes the buck has to stop with the person who made those choices.*

Lies, all of it. Everything Zak Harborne had told her. It was Karen who'd opened her eyes to that, who'd finally made her realise. And yet Karen had been blinded by him too: the good-looking, hardworking Zak, a man who'd been shat upon by his greedy bitch of a wife, but who was such a good father to his kids, his two *young* kids.

Standing in her office, she gripped her coffee cup so tight she wondered if it might shatter in her hands. It was mid-afternoon, and she was alone. Bert was busy in the grounds of Highgate conducting a tour, Firecracker alongside him. A rainy day at the beginning of April, the weather didn't put people off; they simply came kitted out with umbrellas or rain macs.

Lucy scanned the courtyard and the steps that led to the higher ground – there was no low light, not yet, just greyness. And there were no shadows cast either. She felt bereft, more alone than ever. A victim. That's what she was, shame escalating in her because of it.

The conversation she'd had with Karen – how long ago was it now, two months? Slightly longer? Certainly, she hadn't seen her since. It had been such an eye-opener.

Zak hadn't known about her plans with Karen because she'd closed the office earlier that day, all tours done with, and hurried into Highgate Village, where Karen had come to meet her. She'd told Zak once that the area surrounding the village had a colourful history too. There were many haunted pubs there, most notably The Gatehouse, which was home to several resident ghosts, apparently, Mother Marnes included, a woman who'd been murdered for her fortune in the seventeenth century. Lucy shuddered to remember it.

Bypassing the pub, she'd met Karen at a coffee house, itself close to another famous site, that of a mangling shop.

Nothing to do with washing or laundry, oh no. This particular establishment had operated out of an old house whose proprietors had made their living by deliberately disfiguring children and adults so that they might command more money as professional beggars. Money, was it the root of all evil?

Karen had already been *in situ* and, on spying Lucy, rose to kiss her on both cheeks.

"Hi, Luce. You're looking well. A bit of romance clearly suits you."

She was right; it had, up until now. In the first throes she had fancied she looked younger, her skin pinker, her hair shinier, and her eyes with more life in them. If what Karen had said was true, though, could it be that fear suited her too?

Lucy ordered a coffee – an Americano, black, no sugar – and sat down opposite her effusive friend.

Was that what Karen really was? A friend? They'd met a few years back, when Lucy had worked another job, in another office, in the centre of London amidst the hustle and bustle. They'd got on well enough and had shared various lunches and evening drinks together, discussing their often similar gripes with various work colleagues, and because of that 'bond' they had kept in touch, met up on occasion, probably once every three or four months, kept the friendship going. But was it now just perfunctory and superficial? Was Karen someone she could confide in?

"So, come on, tell me everything. You're still with him, so it must be going well, right?"

"It's…erm…yeah, we've been seeing a lot of each other."

"That's amazing! You must be over the moon!"

"I…"

"Oh, come on, you're always so cagey about your private life. I remember that from when we worked together. No need to be coy now, spill the beans."

Karen was younger than Lucy, in her late thirties. She had long, dark hair, green eyes, and a zest for life, that latter quality having attracted Lucy to her in the first place. Lucy found herself wishing she could be more like her, lighter somehow, not so preoccupied with…morbidness. No matter that such a preoccupation had led her from her former office job, one she found so boring – other people's insurance of no interest to her whatsoever – to a job she loved and a place she loved, somewhere that was so special. But morbid.

Yes, it could be called that. It was *often* called that. It wasn't just Zak who'd raised his eyebrows when she'd first told him what she did. So many in the past had made similar judgements, made their excuses and veered away from her. And who could blame them? No one wanted reminding of just how mortal they were, that one day they might not live and breathe either. It was the only thing in life that was bound to happen – death – and yet so many denied it in the modern world, in the Western world. Ultimately, though, Zak had stayed; he hadn't been put off after all. And she'd thought it such a miracle…

Ignoring her coffee, which the waitress had finally delivered, Lucy leant forward. "Karen, how much did you know about Zak before the night of your birthday gathering?"

Karen sat back in her chair. "Know about him? Well…just what I told you, that he's a divorcée, or soon to be, anyway, and he's got a couple of kids. Why?"

"How many times had you met him before?"

"Erm…well, I hadn't, not really."

"Which friend of yours is he a friend of?"

"Jon's. Do you know Jon? He's a friend of Lara's."

"Lara who? Jon who?"

Karen shrugged, clearly puzzled by all this questioning when she'd been looking forward to some juicy gossip. "They're just…friends, Lucy, that's all. People on the same scene."

The same scene? He was a stranger to Karen too, then? Or as good as.

"How do you know about the wife and kids?"

Her face relaxed a little. "Jon told me about that. He said they'd been chatting about it. Jon's in the same boat. He's going through a messy divorce too and has kids. They were probably sympathising with each other or having a good moan. Jon can be a bit like that, can't he?"

I don't know Jon, remember? she wanted to scream at Karen, but with great difficulty she restrained herself. "I know about his kids, Joe and Maia."

"Is that what they're called? Have you met them yet? Got the dreaded introductions over and done with?"

Lucy shook her head. "No, I haven't met them." *Although one of them I've been funding.* Again, she had to clamp down on what she really wanted to say. After all, whose fault was it that she'd been doing that; she was the one who'd offered initially, who'd *insisted.* She'd let him know that she had savings, that she had plenty. In fact, that was the exact word she'd used: *plenty.*

Now she did come clean about her situation, an aspect

of it, anyway.

"Zak's son Joe is having trouble with drugs. I've been trying to help a little. Financially, I mean. He's in rehab. It's…costly. I've been giving him money."

Karen's coffee cup had been halfway to her lips when she burst out laughing. "His son is having trouble with drugs?"

Despite being taken aback by her reaction, Lucy nodded.

"Oh, Luce, I hardly think so."

"Why? What do you mean?"

"I know kids start all that shit pretty young nowadays, but not around five or six they don't!"

"Who's five or six?"

"His son, Lucy! And his daughter's even younger."

For a moment Lucy had been unable to speak. She'd just stared at Karen, at the amusement that danced in her eyes. At last she found her voice. "How do you know their ages?"

"Again, through Jon. He's met them. They're cute kids, apparently. But then they would be, wouldn't they, with Zak as their father. He's not exactly hard on the eyes."

"Jon's met them?"

"Yeah, at some kids party. One of his kids is the same age as one of Zak's, something like that." When Lucy failed to reply to this statement, some of the amusement in Karen's eyes faded. "What is all this you're saying about drugs and rehab, Lucy? I don't understand."

That makes two of us. Lucy's eyes had started to smart, and briefly she squeezed them shut, ensuring no tears could fall. Oh, what a fool she was! How desperate she'd been. Not once questioning Zak or even thinking to, instead believing so readily all the excuses he'd used to fob her off, to prevent her from finding out anything about him other than the scenario he'd fed her. Karen was talking again, her green eyes a slightly darker hue than before, more clouded.

"Jon also told me about Zak's wife."

"That she's swindling him?"

"That's it, that's right. You know, that must be tough. Shortly before he met you, Zak lost his job at some big firm in London. He worked in construction or something. Is that right? Anyway, there'd been a wave of redundancies, and he got caught up in it. He's been down on his luck, *really* down. Maybe...maybe that's why he needs money, you know, for the kids, so that he can keep up payments for them. This drug thing you're on about, it must be some kind of misunderstanding."

Before Lucy had a chance to reply, to defend herself, Karen hurried onwards.

"He's a lovely bloke, honestly, Luce. If I wasn't already spoken for, you'd have competition. He's a real catch, or at least he will be when he's back on his feet, which I'm sure he will be soon. Maybe...talk to him, you know, about it all. I'm not saying that you haven't, clearly you have, but...try again." She laughed, nervousness to it, or was that just Lucy's imagination? "The trouble with men is they're such proud beasts, aren't they? They hate admitting they're in trouble. Zak Harborne's all right, honestly. You're..." She faltered. "Perhaps cut him a bit of slack."

You're lucky to have him. That's what she was going to say; Lucy was certain of it. This person that Karen actually knew nothing about, certainly not how readily he hit out or how quick he was to threaten. But then Lucy knew nothing about him either. If he was jobless, where did he go in the daytime? What did he do? As soon as she left for work, did he let himself back into the flat? Was he, in fact, homeless, sofa surfing before he met her?

She thought again about the night he'd walked her home, when there'd been something different about his smile compared to how it had been all evening. It was a smile that hadn't reached his eyes and a goodnight kiss that never happened, not even a polite peck on the cheek. He'd also made a point of enquiring about the neighbour upstairs, and Lucy had told him she never saw him, that he was never around…certainly not to hear any commotion should it happen to go on below him. She'd convinced herself he'd seen her home out of chivalry, but it was becoming all too clear that he'd done it for another reason: to see if she was the kind of woman to pursue further, for reasons other than romance. *You're so…perfect.* That's what he'd said, a much more sinister meaning behind it.

Karen had been the one to end their meeting. The conversation hadn't quite gone the way she wanted, that much was easy to detect. She'd made some excuse about having to visit her mother, stood up, grabbed her coat and bag and said she'd pay the bill on the way out. There'd been no goodbye kiss from her either, although her greeting had been enthusiastic enough.

And so, Lucy had also gathered her belongings and made her way back to Crouch End. He'd be home, of course, another thing she berated herself for – how quick she'd been to give him a key, again insisting that he take it, the architect of her own downfall.

Shame, there it was, coming in waves and drowning her.

Following on from that insightful meeting with Karen, Lucy had asked again to meet Zak's children, Joe in particular, and to be taken to his flat in Hammersmith. She'd also asked about his job and how it was going, whether there were any problems with it.

"I've told you plenty of times why you can't meet Joe; it's difficult. For Christ's sake, woman, he doesn't even know about you." His benefactor.

"And your flat?" she'd persisted. "You haven't moved much of your stuff in, have you? Perhaps we could go there and grab some more of your belongings?"

"I've got all I need," had been his curt reply. All *her* things.

"What about your job? You've still got a job, haven't you?"

Her voice had dripped with sarcasm. That was when, fed up with her questions, he'd reached out, grabbed her by the throat and shoved her against the wall of her hallway.

"You're getting too sassy for your own good," he'd spat. "Too damned confident."

Perhaps, but the black eye he'd inflicted as a consequence ensured it didn't gain traction. Thank God for makeup, although when she'd turned up for work on Monday morning, two days later, Bert had looked at her peculiarly, causing her to snap at him, to remind him not to sit around the office, drinking tea, that the first of the visitors had arrived, and he should go and see to them.

His hurt expression in turn hurt her. She'd never snapped at him before or even talked out of turn. The visitors were indeed filing in, but they were also early, intending to spend some time in the gift shop, perhaps, or just soak up the ambience of the place.

God, she was changing; Zak was changing her.

Here, in the confines of her office, a sanctuary of sorts, she let the tears flow. Finally. She wasn't given to crying, not usually – she couldn't remember the last time she'd allowed herself such an indulgence – and certainly she wouldn't cry in front of him. That was the one thing she had some control over.

Turning her back on the courtyard, she noticed the clock. In less than three hours, it would be time to go home. How quickly that time would fly. What mood would he be in when she reached there? Strangely, he wasn't always violent, or even moody; sometimes he was happy, the very embodiment of the man she had fallen in love with. That, however, was his cruellest trick – showing her what she could have, what she'd *thought* she had.

Sniffing loudly, she wiped at her cheeks with the back of her hand.

She'd go back. She'd cook dinner. Toe the line.

The nightmare on repeat.

Chapter Twenty-Two

The beatings had always been in private before. And apart from the time he'd blackened her eye, forcing her to wear so much makeup – blue and green eye shadow on the other eyelid to balance out such a wild array of colours, and cheeks covered in blusher – he'd been careful to mark only what could be easily covered up. Now, however, he'd lost his temper in public, had screamed at her and practically choked her yet again. Here at last was the evidence she needed; others would see what a terrible man he was, would understand she was at his mercy, be appalled by it and help her. So why had no one stepped forward yet? Why were those who stood around averting their eyes?

Can't you see what he's like? Lucy wanted to shout. *You saw him. He hurts me. This is what he does, all the time. He's destroying me.*

But these were his friends, and they clearly saw only what they wanted to see.

Lucy and Zak had gone out several times in their first weeks together, but they'd never been out as a couple with other people. She hadn't minded, not at all, because she'd only wanted to be with him anyway, not dilute their time together. If a nagging thought had risen concerning the peculiarity of it, she'd brushed it aside, thinking he felt the same way. But this invite had come out of the blue: would

Zak like to join Mark and Carly for dinner and drinks to celebrate Mark's birthday? Oh, and feel free to bring a friend – that 'friend' being her.

"Do they know about me?" she'd asked when he announced they'd be going.

"Know what about you?"

"That I'm not just your friend, I'm your..." She had wanted to replace 'girlfriend' with so many other nouns: *your victim; your punching bag; your living, breathing bank.*

"They'll get to know you soon enough," had been his somewhat terse reply.

The dinner party had been held at a flat in Shepherd's Bush, a nice street, one of the better ones around there. A good few people had attended, including several other couples, some of whom had looked enquiringly at her as she and Zak had walked in together. It was a Friday night, and the mood in the flat was upbeat, someone – she wasn't sure who – complaining it had been a long week and their boss had been a 'menopausal bitch' for most of it. That had elicited great guffaws. "There's nothing fucking worse, is there?" someone else had said.

Another person had sidled up to them, a woman in her late thirties, Lucy guessed, in a short, sprayed-on black dress. She was wearing high heels, yet still she only matched Lucy in height; without them she'd be tiny. Compared to her, Lucy felt like a frump. She'd suggested to Zak that she wear a dress to the party, and he'd shaken his head, told her jeans and a top would be fine. *Every* woman here was dressed up, not just the one who stood in front of her.

"Well, well, well," she purred, "thought you'd been a bit quiet lately, Zak Harborne. Who's this?"

Inwardly Lucy bristled. Why hadn't the woman asked *her* who she was? Instead, her eyes were solely on Zak, waiting for the introductions. The answer wasn't forthcoming straightaway as the two continued to smile at each other, some sort of silent message conveyed within that, perhaps.

Deciding that enough was enough, Lucy forced a smiled too. "Hi," she said, "I'm Lucy, pleased to meet you. What's your name?"

Both the woman and Zak looked startled that she'd spoken. "I'm Claire," she announced. "Erm...yeah, nice to meet you. So...how long have you been together?"

This time Claire's eyes flitted between Zak and Lucy, Lucy keeping hers firmly on Claire, not daring to turn her head towards Zak but sensing his displeasure nonetheless.

Ensuring her voice held a breezy note, she answered Claire. "A while now, nearly six months." That it had been so long both amazed and distressed her.

"Wow..." The woman appeared surprised too. "That's incredible. I hope you're very happy." Her eyes on Lucy again, she added, "it's time Zak found some happiness, after that bitch—"

"Never mind about my ex," Zak said. "She's history. Yeah, we are very happy together and all that jazz. Now come on, let's get this party started. I need a beer."

"Just a beer?" Claire once again became playful.

"It'll do for starters." Zak too had a wide grin on his face.

And it *was* just for starters. Several beers, followed by wine with dinner – a half-decent attempt at a chilli that everyone helped themselves to bowls of, standing around as they ate. And then came dessert, or what they all laughingly called dessert: white lines, laid out lovingly by Mark upon the dining table once it was cleared of plates and cutlery. From the way Zak inhaled his lines, bending over them, shutting off one nostril and then inhaling, Lucy realised: he was the one with the supposed drug problem, not any son of his – not yet, at any rate.

Lucy had never taken drugs. A fact she was proud of. How much cocaine did Zak and his mates intend to get through this night? She had no idea, only that it seemed copious amounts. The small gathering – twelve of them in total – became more and more animated, so much so that Lucy feared such a small space couldn't hold them. She was grateful when one of the men pulled open the kitchen door and some of them disappeared outside, despite the chilly night air.

Claire was by her side again, Zak having gone, having left her at last, to talk to one of his mates. "You not having any dessert?"

Lucy raised her glass of wine higher. "I'm happy with this."

"It's good stuff Mark's got in."

"Really," Lucy insisted, "I prefer wine."

"Your loss," Claire replied, shrugging. She'd started to walk off – drawn by loud chatter and laughter from outside, perhaps – when she stopped and turned back round.

"I expect you know this, but Zak can be a handful. A bit…wild."

She knew it all right.

"He's our mate, though," Claire continued, "and we've got his back. Okay?"

Lucy could feel herself frowning. What did she mean by that? That she knew what he was like? *Truly* like? How handy he was with his fists? And that she condoned it? Everything Lucy had heard about his ex-wife had been derogatory. That he had an ex-wife was something she didn't doubt, that part of his life not fabricated, at least – not even the children, only their ages and supposed problems. But who was the real villain of the piece? What were the reasons behind their split? He did disappear sometimes at the weekend, probably to see his children, but it was becoming more and more spasmodic, and his mood when he returned was something she always feared. But these people, his friends, they had his back. What kind of people did that make them?

Zak had come back in from the garden to fetch her, his grin something really quite inane and his blond hair limp rather than foppish, greasy, even. He was staggering, unable to walk straight, although he made it to her well enough, grabbing her arm and causing her to wince again.

"Come on outside, Luce. That's where the real party is." He gestured around him. There was one man left inside, slumped on the sofa, half asleep, and a woman dancing alone by the Alexa tower, although whatever tune it played was drowned out by the racket from the garden. Lucy tilted her head. Were the neighbours used to this behaviour? Did they dare not complain either?

She had no choice but to follow him, and no time to grab her coat either. It was so cold outside, but she seemed to be the only one to notice it as everyone else was coatless too and looking perfectly happy about it. On a garden table was a plastic tray with yet more white lines laid out, some guests queuing to take their turn at demolishing them whilst others had clearly already had their share and were dancing haphazardly under the cloud-ridden sky.

Zak still had hold of her arm and was leading her towards the tray.

"What are you doing?" she asked.

"Oh, loosen up a bit, will you? Take a line and see what you're missing."

"I don't want to." She'd told Claire and now she was telling him.

"You're being fucking rude."

"I'm not. It's just…not something I want to do."

Somehow she managed to disentangle her arm from his and returned to the shadows, as far away from these people as possible.

If she thought he'd leave her alone, turn his attention back towards the tray, she was wrong. Something flashed in Zak's eyes; even in the darkness she caught it - similar to that first time he'd hit her. He joined her in the shadows, the pair of them inhabiting such a bleak, cold space together. His hand again on her arm, he leaned closer. "You ungrateful bitch."

"Zak—"

"We're invited to someone's home for the evening, and this is how you act. You're so fucking stuck-up. Do you think you're better than us or something?"

"Zak, people are look--"

"I knew from the minute I met you that there was something wrong with you, do you know that? You were lonely, that was plain to see. Everything about you fucking screamed out how lonely you were, a misfit, someone who doesn't belong, not in normal society, who sits on the edge of it, who can't join in, who hasn't got a fucking clue what fun is."

"This isn't fun." There, she'd said it, or rather whispered it, tears blinding her.

His face came even closer. "How would you fucking know? I took pity on you, plucked you from your lonely life, gave you a chance, and this—" he threw out his hands, and she flinched, but it was only to gesture again, "—is how you repay me, by ignoring my friends and refusing to join in."

She knew she should keep her mouth shut, but something in her rose to the fore: indignation, a hurt so raw that she couldn't help but retaliate. She was a misfit, someone on the edge of society? Perhaps, but she was not rude; she was not abnormal. She strove not to be.

As his eyes bored into hers, she fought down sobs, determined to say her piece, to make him understand. "You've lied to me, Zak! You've taken my money, not to help your son – who I know is only five or six – but to line your own pockets. What for? This? Drugs after all? Not to help in the battle against them but to feed your own habit?"

Was that surprise in his eyes? Shock? "Who told you about my son?"

"I don't want to say."

He showered her in spittle. "Who fucking told you?"

She shook her head. "I'm not saying. Don't keep asking."

"Oh, so you've been doing some digging have you, gone all detective on me? I took you on and all you want to do is make a mug out of me."

She braced herself further. "You took me on, but now I want to be released. You might as well because from now on I won't give you anything more. I know you haven't got a job either, that you pretend you're leaving the flat each day to go to work, but you don't, you just stay put, the lie continuing. I wouldn't be surprised if there's no flat to go to, if you're homeless. You preyed on me, Zak, but no more of it. I'm taking back what's mine. I want you to pack your stuff and leave. I won't have you in my home anymore."

His hand moved away from her arm and travelled up towards her neck, his other hand joining it and beginning to squeeze, squeeze, squeeze, rendering her completely unable to even cry out or alert the others. In the shadows it was dark anyway, but, without any air to breathe, it was getting blacker.

"You don't tell me what to do. I tell you, remember? I'm not going anywhere. What's yours is mine, every last bit of it. I took pity on you. I preyed on you. So what? It's all the same. You had a flat; that'd do for starters, but then I found out about the money. Whoa! I'd only gone and hit the jackpot; that'd do *very* nicely. It'd keep my bastard dealers quiet for a while, anyway. They can get quite…antsy. And there's more to come, isn't there? Lots more." Still his grip was tight, her breathing sure to cut out at some point soon. Would she die here in the shadows? His voice, his *hateful* voice, continued, "So, baby, it looks like you're stuck with me, at least until the money's all gone. Because you see, you might not be having fun, but I'm having a blast!"

His hands released her suddenly, and she gasped for air, spluttering and waving her hands, trying to alert the attention of those that were closest. When no help came, she looked up. There were several people staring at her, at *them*, fully aware of what had just happened. As he sauntered off, she was sure one of them would rush over to her, ask if she was okay. Perhaps Claire would, one of the other women, anyone.

Her very core froze when she saw people go to Zak and ask if *he* was okay. Zak was shaking his head, his shoulders slumped slightly. A forlorn figure, he was the victim here, of an uptight girlfriend, just as he'd been the victim of his 'bitch' of a wife.

Regarding her, no one did a damned thing.

Chapter Twenty-Three

It was that time again; she should be packing up, locking the office and heading home. The tick-tick-ticking of the clock became more insistent, but still she couldn't do it. Instead, she continued to sit at her desk, her limbs rigid and her hands balled into fists in front of her.

Bert and Firecracker had come and gone. He'd been hesitant too, not saying anything but lingering far longer over his coffee than he normally did. She'd kept her back to him, sorting out paperwork, but she could feel his eyes on her well enough. At one point she was tempted to turn around and face him, tell him everything about Zak, what had happened at the party, the beatings, the threats, what he intended to do – strip her of everything, basically, both materially and mentally. How had this happened? How? She'd asked herself that question over and over.

Bert had eventually risen. "I'll be off, then," he'd said.

She glanced to the side. "Okay, have a good evening, you two."

"Unless you'd prefer me to stay?"

She shrugged. "No, why would I?"

"You've got my number plugged into that device of yours, haven't you? My home number, I mean. I switch my mobile off after leaving here."

"Yes, yes, I've got it."

"Although I suppose I can leave my mobile on too. It's no bother."

Still not fully looking at him, she'd insisted she was fine. The dog whined at such words as if, like his master, he suspected otherwise. But what was the point of involving them? Bert had also said once upon a time that people who got themselves into a mess needed to help themselves to get out of it. *They have to take responsibility.* She hadn't fully agreed then, but she did now.

"Well…" Bert had continued, "I'm on the other end of the phone, should you happen to need me."

"Thank you," she'd replied, willing him to go, to just leave her to deal with this.

Once alone in the office, she'd had to work hard to steady her breathing, panic threatening to overwhelm her. And so she sat, staring blindly at her desk and all that was laid out upon it before lifting her eyes and gazing out of the window.

It was now well past six o'clock but not yet dark. Instead, there was that light so peculiar to Highgate, the low light. Still striving to keep her breath regular, she stared and stared at the higher ground, willing herself to see something, the shadow that was so often there. *I know it's you out there.* Those words would revolve round and round in her mind, such mysterious words, a chant almost, another voice joining in, a child's voice, and then…just lately…another. Was it imagination, wishful thinking, or something more?

Where are you now?

Like an arrow from a sling, she fired the thought outwards.

Where are you when I need you?

Someone – *anyone* – who was on her side. A misfit, a loner, a woman who didn't belong, not in normal society – that was how Zak had described her. And, if she were brutally honest, perhaps it was also how she'd describe herself. Had she ever felt she belonged anywhere? Even in the bosom of her own family? Her parents hadn't been unkind to her, not at all, but they'd given most of their attention to her brother. Not that he hadn't deserved it; he *had*. When she was twelve and Stephen just ten, he'd been diagnosed with cancer: acute lymphoblastic leukaemia. He was a survivor, but even so; the prospect of losing him had shifted her parents' focus.

She was the healthy one, the one who could look after herself, who shouldn't make a fuss, because her mother and father had enough to worry about. And she'd respected that, accepted that. Like them, she had prayed constantly for her brother to get well. She'd been everything she had to be in order to support her family, but somewhere along the way, she had also become detached – a protection mechanism? Not just from her family, from friends and boyfriends too, everyone…except Zak. Their connection had provoked such excitement within her. She had called it love. How wrong she'd been. It was something dark and terrifying, but also – she squeezed her eyes shut – familiar. After two weeks she'd truly felt she'd known him all her life – the bloodsucker.

An alert on her phone drew her attention. She was ten minutes behind her usual arrival time home, and already he had started.

You're late. Where are you?

Over the course of the next hour, messages came through thick and fast, bombarding her.

Where the hell have you gone?

Are you meeting someone?

They got nastier and nastier.

Fucking answer me, you bitch! Where are you?

If you don't answer me, you'll regret it. I'm not going to warn you again.

I'm getting angry now, really angry. You can't ignore me. I won't let you.

He also tried to ring her several times, cutting the call and then ringing again…and again…

She ignored every single attempt, sitting right where she was, her eyes still on the higher ground. *Are you there? Were you ever there?*

Someone was; she had seen it, and yet how blind she'd been up until now, *wilfully* blind, ignoring the alarm bells that had started ringing on their first date together, the smile that hadn't reached his eyes. Something else Bert had said came to mind also, when they'd been sheltering from the rain – or, rather, a sentence he hadn't quite finished, and that she hadn't pressed him about either. She'd simply…brushed it aside, buried it, but not deep enough. *It's just when I met him, that time he came to surprise you…* What had he been going to say? What had he sensed?

It's different now, though. My eyes are open, and I want to see.

When still there was no shadow in the distance, no sign of life at all – Highgate had never looked so still – she blinked hard.

Please, I want to see.

227

Obsessed with death. Had her brother's illness been the catalyst for that, or was it something inherent in her, a facet of her personality? Zak didn't know about Stephen and what he'd endured; why dwell on it when it was no longer an issue? Had keeping quiet, however, been a mistake? If he had known, would he have perhaps been more understanding of her? Maybe not, considering she didn't even understand herself. *Obsessed with death.* He hadn't actually said those words to her, no one had. And yet there was a familiarity to them too, as if someone somewhere *had*. This place – Highgate – she'd become obsessed with it, certainly, first as a visitor and then as a volunteer and, finally, as an employee. *You felt you'd come home,* the healthy child, the robust one, the girl who'd never, apart from a common cold, had a day's illness in her life. Not only had she grown up close to the cemetery, she had then bought a flat a short distance away, just one stop on the Tube. The thought of moving further from it was abhorrent; she was meant to be here.

Why?

There it was! Finally! A shadow, a shape, beginning to form at the top of the steps, in the exact same place it always stood. She was slight, no more than a child. And behind her, what was that? Another shadow? This one taller and set a fair distance back, as if it was simply too afraid to come any closer just yet, a figure that was truly forlorn, traumatised. Both of them were; she understood that now, just as she herself was traumatised. Is that what they were, then – kin?

There came a banging at the main door. She didn't flinch; she'd been expecting it.

Bang! Bang! Bang! She could easily imagine the fist that was pounding against the hard wood, the fury that would be on his face, masking surprise, perhaps, and even a little fear, that this woman he thought he'd so successfully cowed had defied him. "When you finish work, come straight home," he'd so often said to her. "Don't go anywhere, don't meet anyone, don't even *look* another person in the face. Just get home. I'll be waiting for you; you can count on that."

And she'd obeyed. But not tonight. Not now. Not anymore.

She stood up and, grabbing her jacket off the back of the chair, she shrugged it on, a torch already in its pocket. Soon he'd try the handle and realise the door wasn't locked. He'd push it open.

Glancing one last time out the window, she saw the shadows were still there, waiting.

"I'm coming," she assured them.

In the corridor outside her office, she veered not to the left, towards where Zak would be, but to the right, to the door that led into the courtyard. Again, she would leave that unlocked. Before she turned, she noticed the entrance door. As she'd predicted, the brass knob started to turn, slowly...slowly... Which meant that she had to hurry. Behind her, the office light had been left on and a small radio was playing; he'd make his way in there first, her absence temporarily confusing him. Perhaps then he too would look up, out towards the courtyard. If so, he'd also see a shadow: hers, fleeing up towards the higher ground. His fury mounting, he'd leave the office and follow her, determined to make her explain her behaviour, to make her pay.

He'd do all that because Zak Harborne was predictable. The angry often were.

As she closed the courtyard door and hurried across the gravelled expanse, incredibly she found herself smiling. At the party she'd been in his world, and in it, amongst his allies, he could do whatever he liked, people turning a blind eye to his actions. Here, however, he'd be at a disadvantage. This was her world, and somewhere she suspected she had allies too.

Chapter Twenty-Four

The minute she was over the threshold, the world changed. It always did at Highgate, this higher ground, this Garden of Eden. Darkness had thrown a cloak over everything; there were no stars in the sky and no moon to light the way. No matter. She knew these paths; she had trodden them a thousand times.

Veering off the beaten track, she headed towards an interior that was still so wild. *All* of Highgate was wild. She understood that now. Even the areas that people tried so hard to cultivate and manicure. This was a place no one could dominate. Always, nature would rise up and reclaim it. Others could lay claim too, those that had fed the soil with their flesh and bones. All she was, all any of them were who worked here, was a custodian – although now there was a possibility she could become something more.

The shadows she'd spied from her office window had disappeared. Would she be able to see them again in the darkness? She looked all around her. *Where are you?*

Zak had done just what she'd thought he would. He was outside, shouting for her.

"Lucy, is that you up there? What the hell do you think you're playing at?"

"Over here…"

The second voice – disembodied – was definitely a child's. Again, Lucy turned her head to the right, for that was where the sound had come from, just past the coach driver's final resting place, past the grandest of monuments that lined the main path, into an area dense with headstones and ivy. She'd go in that direction, knowing that already Zak was at her heels, his boots crunching against gravel as he endeavoured to close the gap between them.

Although she'd brought a torch with her, she wouldn't use it, not yet. To do so would be foolish; it would give her away. Let him search; let him keep calling her name. Let him see what was going to happen here, just as she was curious to see what would happen.

Her tread was swift, but it was careful, her hands held out and coming into contact with stone, feeling her way around it, its hardness or its sponginess when covered in ivy.

This way. This way.

Rather than a whisper, the words were in her head. She told herself to trust it; after all, what other choice did she have? Certainly, she couldn't trust Zak or what he might do to her should he catch her. And he'd do his utmost to reach her; he wouldn't turn back or flee from here. He was a man who liked to beat others but not be beaten himself, not in any sense of the word.

She knew to whom the graves she passed belonged to, was able to recite their names off the top of her head: Maria Eaves, David Aaron Holmes, Clara Munday, Arthur James Jackson. They were not famous names like so many of Highgate's residents. They were just ordinary people who had lived and died, whose families had paid for them to be here – whether they'd scrimped and scraped for that privilege, or it had barely dented their coffers. She'd memorised so many names on her walks in these grounds, feeling a responsibility to remember them. She had stopped by so many, had read their epitaphs, tried to imagine them and the lives they had led, real people who'd run the gamut of so many emotions, some good, some not so good. Regardless, she would whisper a prayer for them. *Rest in peace.* Had there been a greater purpose to what she'd thought was such a simple task? In doing so, had she somehow created an allegiance with those that had gone before?

"Lucy! I know you're here."

Still his voice was strident. Was he frightened to be here? If so, his tone showed no sign of it – not yet. Was she frightened? Of course! Zak posed a true threat; she was under no illusion about that, not anymore.

Quick! Quick! Follow!

As she continued deep into the thicket, she heard the child's voice again – the *ghost's* voice, although she'd been reluctant to use that term before. Was it truly possible she was dealing with a ghost? And if so, what else would she encounter this night? Highgate was a place with a history, not just the cemetery but also the entire village. The mangling shop she'd told Zak about was only one such building that had stood in this vicinity. There had been asylums too, such cruel places in the Victorian era; you could be locked up for the slightest misdemeanour. Women particularly were vulnerable, never finding freedom again. Some of their bodies would have been interred here, those marked with a *P* if they'd been marked at all. She knew well enough some weren't. She had cried over that, and over others that lay here who'd met terrible deaths. Sarah

Wallace Smith was one of them. After Lucy had read about her, she'd sought out her grave to lay some wildflowers at the foot of it. In 1854, aged just nineteen, Sarah had suffered terrible injuries when her dress had accidentally caught fire. She'd lain in agony for several days before finally giving in.

Tragic deaths, deaths by suicide, murder, and deaths that were unexplained – all were here. Would their earthly suffering continue to affect them, their souls rather than their bodies? Could it turn them into wrathful beings, hell-bent on vengeance? For the first time Lucy hesitated. Was it best to take her chances with Zak after all?

"Lucy!"

He was catching up with her, but her feet would no longer move. *You're chasing ghosts, Lucy, for God's sake!* This was insane!

"Lucy!"

Soon he would be upon her, those hands of his closing around her throat, squeezing again. *What have I done? What should I do now? I'm lost...just as Amelia was lost.* So often she thought of Highgate as alive. What if it actually was? *I don't know what to do.*

Footfall. Just behind her.

She could bear it no longer; she swung around. It was yet another shadow, but unlike the others, this one was tall. What was that around his shoulders, some kind of cape? She stared at the figure, unable to comprehend. *Who are you?*

Something – someone – rushed forwards and grabbed her. "Zak?"

It *was* him, not a spectre. He'd found her and, oh, the

expression on his face!

"What the fuck do you think you're playing at? You're going to pay for this, Lucy. When I've finished with you, you won't pull a stunt like this ever again."

His words were chilling enough, but what continued to loom behind him was more chilling still. The tall shadow hadn't moved; it was still there, quite separate from Zak, although he had rushed forwards from it as if, indeed, they were one and the same. If that were so, he was an entity apart once more, flesh and bone, something more substantial, yet what was to the rear was growing, becoming taller and wider, getting stronger and stronger.

"Zak!" she screamed. "We have to move."

"You're going nowhere, I've told you."

"Look! Behind you!"

Despite having captured his quarry, Zak was unable to resist. Turning hesitantly, his grip on her relaxed. In its stead, something else reached up and grabbed her hand, something so cold it shot ice tentacles through her veins. Tearing her gaze from what was in front of her, she looked downwards and saw nothing, only felt it, heard its command. *Come on!*

Unable to think, only act, she gathered every ounce of strength she possessed and, with her free hand, pushed Zak from her, heard his cry of surprise as she managed to send him toppling back in the direction of the tall shadow. Whatever held her hand dragged her along, Lucy terrified she might stumble and fall, that she'd be caught again.

"Who are you?" she managed to say, her voice catching in her throat, perhaps unintelligible. There was no answer. What had hold of her was intent on one thing and one thing only: escape.

Her eyes alternating between the emptiness at her side and the darkened landscape surrounding her, Lucy was nonetheless aware of more movement, things that once again she couldn't quite see but could sense well enough. Whatever was happening here tonight at Highgate, she realised she had somehow forced it, a confrontation *and* a collaboration.

It's time.

She gasped. Was it the child who'd said that?

There's no turning back.

It must be the child! What did she mean by it? "Tell me."

She hadn't realised how far they'd run. The archway of the Egyptian Avenue was up ahead. Soon they'd pass beneath it and there would be vaults on either side.

We can hide there.

"Hide where?" All of the vaults were sealed, weren't they? She shut her eyes, screwed up her nose. All of them *were* sealed, apart from one on the left-hand side, second from the top. There'd been maintenance work carried out on that particular vault because the shelves inside had collapsed, the coffins that sat upon them tumbling to the floor. Decay. This place was full of it. The work was ongoing, although she hadn't been up to check it in recent days. That door wasn't sealed, not yet, not until full restoration had taken place. "Is that where we're going?"

We have to hide.

But hide in there? A tomb full spiders and skeletal remains? After all, who knew what else would rise up this night. If she entered that vault, she'd be trapped, more than she was already. The very thought caused a tidal wave of panic.

"I'm not going in there. No!"

They were at the door to the vault. She couldn't read the name that sat above the door and she couldn't remember it either, blind terror having erased it from her mind. All she knew was that it was dark in there, so dark that only creatures that could tolerate no light at all could exist within it.

Open the door.

"No!"

Open it!

"I...I can't."

"LUCY!"

It was Zak again. Clearly, he'd recovered from his fall.

"I..." Words failed her. Was any of this real, or was she dreaming, the nightmare she was caught up in becoming fantastical?

"LUCY, WHEN I FIND YOU, I'M GOING TO KILL YOU!"

It wasn't an empty threat, not this time. All that Zak Harborne had done before was toy with her. He was coming for her – not a person but something else, a raging beast, and the tall shadow was coming for her too. She looked from the vault door to the still-empty space beside her.

Open the door.

As she heard the crunch of gravel again, she succumbed to the child's will, ducking beneath the builders' orange-and-white plastic tape, yanking the door open, and disappearing inside.

Chapter Twenty-Five

She wanted to cough, to splutter, to purge her guts, anything to eject the smell clawing its way into the pit of her stomach. The smell of death, an unholy smell. How could the workmen stand it? It was all pervading. Let the shelves collapse and the coffins too, let them sink into the ground, for surely that was where the dead belonged.

Only the dead?

Was it the child who said that? Where was she anyway? Had she brought Lucy in here only to abandon her, as so many who had been laid to rest at Highgate were subsequently abandoned? Straining hard to see, Lucy had to admit defeat; the darkness was too vast, too thick. She stilled, her back against the iron door, not daring to take another step and become further entombed.

Remembering what the voice had said, she replied. "Yes, of course only the dead."

The reply was instant and again in her head.

Not always, remember?

Frowning at how mysterious the child was being, Lucy closed her eyes. This smell, it would…suffocate her. Yes! That's exactly what it would do. She couldn't stay. The child, the ghost, whatever she was, couldn't expect her to! *This place is meant just for the dead!*

A noise distracted her before she could sink further into

panic. Her eyes snapped open, and she held onto her breath. It came from outside not in, which gave her only a brief sense of relief. It was her name being called – an angry sound but blessedly muffled. Zak was also on the path outside, but she heard his voice travel past the vault she was hiding in, towards the Circle of Lebanon.

She was safe – from him, at least – her breath returning in shallow gasps as her hand flew up to cover her nose, to protect her from ingesting anything that was in here. With Zak having passed, there was silence again, and it seemed to wrap itself around her as much as the darkness, as much as these walls had wrapped themselves around its inhabitants. *How can you stand being in here?* She had to remind herself that 'they' were dead, over and over, forcing logic to reign over imagination. Imagination? Or was it really insanity? She had no idea, not anymore. The lines seemed to have blurred.

So many thoughts, so many questions, tumbled round in her head that it took a moment to register more noise, this time definitely coming from *inside* the vault. She held her breath, although the beating of her heart became louder and louder, a drumbeat with a pounding rhythm, one that hinted at familiarity. The other noise was ever so slight, but it was there, a rhythm to it also: a tapping, then a scratching, and then a shuffling. And it was coming towards her. Was it bats, a nest of spiders grown so big, or nothing that had breath to it – the occupants of this vault, as desperate for escape as she was?

If she had to stay here any longer, her heart would cease functioning altogether. Whatever was making that sound was something determined, something stealthy.

Her hair! Had something touched her hair? She reached up and grabbed at it, caught something in her hands, something bulbous. Dragging it out of her hair, she opened her hand, intending to throw whatever it was from her, but it scrabbled, made its way back up her arm – a spider, it had to be, its proportions growing in her mind until it became monstrous. When it reached her head, it would open its jaws, its teeth sharp as razors as it—

A light! There! In front of her. Not a light, but something glowing. Stricken, she could form no words, furiously batting at her arm and her head, although her eyes remained fixated ahead.

Was this yet another horror, something else to torment her? Only slowly did her breathing ease, becoming calmer. The light was bright, yet it did nothing to illuminate what else was in there: the broken shelves, the coffins, the creatures…something she was grateful for. Lucy watched as the light shifted and changed, as it took form. It was more than a shadow of a child; it was the child itself, a girl. She hadn't abandoned Lucy after all. Seeing this, a sob escaped her.

"I thought… I thought…" She couldn't continue. Whatever she had thought might happen when she'd lured Zak deep into the walled surrounds of Highgate, it wasn't this. She'd been desperate, unable to face confinement of another kind, being with Zak in her flat at Crouch End. She'd felt so vulnerable, so alone. All she knew was that at Highgate she wouldn't be alone, not anymore.

The girl was so ethereal, an angel but without wings.

A broken angel.

That was it! That was how Lucy would describe her.

240

"I have to get out of here," she cried, begging the apparition.

Sanctuary.

Lucy glanced tentatively around her, into darkness that was like a wall. Could this dark, damp, stinking place really be called sanctuary?

For some.

Lucy shook her head vehemently. "I have to get out. I'm going to suffocate otherwise. I can barely breathe. There was something in my hair! A spider, I think, I...I don't know. No, I can't stand it. I'll die if I can't get out, I'll die!"

She had already turned and started pulling at the door.

"It won't budge!"

She was about to scream, to hammer at it, call out for Zak, even – anyone – to get her out of there, but the child's touch stopped her. She hadn't realised the girl had come so close.

Lucy's bunched fist, held aloft, slowly, so slowly, returned to her side. The girl's soft glow seemed to flood through her, relaxing her limbs, soothing her, a balm when she needed it most. Lucy lowered her body too, crouched on that damp and dirty, cracked concrete floor until she was the child's height, until she could look into her eyes...and see.

* * *

There was a room, a squalid little room with rough walls, no decoration upon them, no paint, just patches where render had crumbled, had decayed, to expose the shoddy brickwork beneath. There was hardly any furniture either, just a bed upon which two people lay, a baby bundled between them, and another bed on the floor, a no doubt stinking blanket thrown on top of it, beneath which young children huddled. One child in particular, a girl, stared back at the voyeur within the room – for that's what Lucy was, surely, a voyeur, seeing through the eyes of another. Taken on a journey, away from the confines of that dark vault and into a world that was…just as dark?

The baby's cries captured her attention, the girl's too as she pushed herself up onto one arm, careful not to wake her sleeping siblings. There was something wrong with the cry, Lucy realised; it wasn't loud or lusty, more a pitiful whimper. The parents knew it too. The man tried to comfort his wife, tried to reach out and put his arm around her shoulder, but he was also weak, the action costing him.

The image faded but was quickly replaced by another, a series of images: hungry faces staring at a meagre fire, no food in their bellies, the mother so worn, so tired. *Less* faces, Lucy realised, not as many as before. Then she was outside the room, breathing in the air – not fresh air, not at all, but sour – and she was down by the river, gathering sticks, unable to see across the water to what lay on the other side, as the smog was so thick. There was much that could hide in it, plenty to be wary of, to watch out for. The girl's mother was always saying so. *There's so much evil…*

More images flashed by. A funeral, such a grand affair, black horses wearing black feathers, pulling along black carriages, one filled with the living, the other with the dead. Crying, wailing, and the beating of breasts; it was just as she'd imagined, the grandest of spectacles causing all who stood nearby to stop what they were doing and stand and stare. And then evil did strike; the girl's mother was right. A tall man, wearing a tall hat and a cape around his shoulders.

Lucy went from rapt to trying to turn her head away. She didn't want to see this, how wolves came dressed in sheep's clothing. Not everyone who was ugly on the inside was ugly on the outside. She couldn't look away, however, as though her head was held in a vice-like grip. Even if she closed her eyes, the images were still there – bold and dark-edged.

Don't listen to him! Don't be taken in! Run away!

But the man had what the child wanted, what she spent her days in search of: food. Lucy shook her head in despair; *always* they had what others wanted. Meetings ensued: under a bridge, down by the river again. Secluded places, shadowy, the child coming away with money in her hand or food to eat. Lucy almost smiled. *You're a curious thing, aren't you?* And she was pretty too, her hair so light, her skin dirty but otherwise unblemished. She was just a child. How old was she? Prepubescent, Lucy guessed, her chest as flat as her stomach. There were two boys in this latest image as well, little boys, again with such sweet but dirty faces and smiling at Lucy.

The boys faded, replaced by a darkened lane, long and steep. Lucy gasped. She knew this lane; she walked it almost every day. Swain's Lane, no streetlights apparent, and the child was hurrying up it. *Turn back,* Lucy wanted to shout, but deep down she knew it wouldn't do any good – what she observed were events that had already happened. There was no changing them now; fate had dealt its hand.

She rounded a corner, and a house came into view. That's right! That was so! There *had* been a house on that site, long since pulled down. 'Dracula's House' it used to be called, on account of its Gothic architecture. It had been run-down, derelict, but it wasn't so in this image; it was splendid, albeit splendidly *forbidden*. It didn't belong to Dracula, of course not, but did some other monster lurk inside?

The next few images were hurled at her: the house; someone looking out of the window; a man, although he was hazy, a mere shadow; and then it was back into the lane, encountering a group of boys, raggle-taggle boys. What were they doing? Had they ambushed the girl? Were they dragging her somewhere dark? *No! I don't want to see, not this!* As though the images were swinging on some mad axle, the attack – for that's what it was, vile and brutal – disappeared, replaced once more by the lane and a man walking along it, the same tall man, his pace leisurely despite the screams that filled the air. Only when he neared the group did he hurry, a smile on his face all the while, as if he was pleased, as if this fitted his plan.

I don't want to know.

Tears had soaked Lucy's cheeks, but still the images refused to abate. She was in another room, lying in a bed, supposedly recovering from the attack, bodily if not mentally. This room was replaced by another, in which a healed body was set to be abused yet again, a succession of so many cruel strangers creeping in there, all with the darkest of appetites, the girl being fed alive to each of them, to one man in particular, the *last* man. And all the while, the tall man stood in the background, observing, sniffing at something in a bottle, knowing full well what the child – just one of many – was being subjected to, calculating the monies paid, and smiling…always smiling…

Gradually, thankfully, the images faded until once more there was only darkness. This time Lucy was glad of it; she didn't want to see, not anymore, or acknowledge just how base man could be, lower than a snake that slithered on the ground. Was she terrified still or was she numb? Again, she couldn't tell. There seemed to be a maelstrom of emotions deep within her – churning in a fetid pool – but just as she was behind an iron door, so were they.

At the child's touch, she opened her eyes. The sight of the girl caused yet more tears to cascade down Lucy's cheeks. Such a pretty face. What a target it had made her.

"Who are you?" she said. "What's your name?"

You know so many names here.

It was true, she did.

You should know mine.

Lucy frowned. How could she know it? How could she possibly?

The girl's eyes burrowed into hers.

"I… No, I… Please, tell—"

Any further pleading died in Lucy's throat. She wasn't alone in here, she knew that; there was the girl, those who occupied the coffins, and spiders and bats lurking, but now there was something else, someone that rose up behind the girl and was so tall.

Although the girl was facing Lucy, she could clearly sense it too.

Go!

"But Zak—"

Go now!

An image of the girl on that bed, lying there covered in

blood, the walls also splattered, forced itself to the forefront of her mind, so vivid she could smell the metallic tang of it.

GO!

Lucy rose to her feet, yanked at the door, and fled back into the night.

Chapter Twenty-Six

Hurtling up the path, Lucy reached the Circle of Lebanon. The sensible thing to do was stop, take stock for a moment, plan on where to hide before calling the police and telling them that she feared for her life – but the latter, at least, was impossible. She'd only brought the torch with her, nothing else. That she'd done so was further proof that she'd forced this situation between her and Zak, and that whatever happened from here on in, it would mark the end of it.

Above her crows were calling to each other – *caw, caw, caw* – a frenzied soundtrack that suited the mood. The tall man hadn't been part of the equation, however, instinct telling her to avoid him at all costs. All too well she remembered the way he had grown in stature when standing behind Zak, remembered also that Zak seemed to have been a part of that shadow before he'd lunged at her. What did it all mean?

You know what it means.

The girl was in her head but nowhere to be seen. She looked for her, but all she could see were more vaults, housing who knew what, not just the dead but a shadow so insidious it could creep in anywhere, a sealed door no barrier. Reaching the steps at the back of the circle, she flew up them. Ahead was the mausoleum dedicated to Ada Beer, the door to which was most definitely sealed, so it offered no hiding place. The catacombs were also in front of her. She slowed to a halt, for that was where she was heading. She had thought she'd seen someone in there before, in broad daylight, another shadow scratching around... No, she wouldn't entomb herself again. She'd stay in the open. There were plenty of hiding places, the night continuing to cloak her. Who would tire first, her or Zak? She meant it to be him. Back into the heart of Highgate – that's where she needed to go, where Amelia was.

Intending to put that plan into action, she turned.

"Gotcha!"

There were hands on her, not icy cold this time; the warmth of human blood ran through them.

"Zak!" Immediately she began to struggle, causing him to grip harder. "Leave me alone, you...bastard!"

Fully expecting to hear a string of insults leave his mouth too, his spit soaking her face, she was surprised instead when he begged her to be quiet. "There's someone else here, not just us."

She pulled her head back slightly. "What do you mean? Who?"

"I don't know who! Someone! He..." His head swung as wildly as hers had earlier, and then he was able to fix his gaze on her again, lowering his voice to a whisper. "He's been following me."

"A man?"

Avidly, he nodded.

"What does he look like?"

"Impossible to see; he keeps to the shadows. But I know he's out there. He's keeping pace with me, every step of the way. You crazy bitch! You idiot!" There they were: the insults. "Why'd you drag us out here for? Into a fucking walled cemetery."

She'd done it because there seemed to be no other option. It was as simple as that. The real world was his domain; it was where people like him could get away with anything, even murder.

He'd begun to drag her, one arm around her neck, the other maintaining its grip on her arm. As hard as she dug her heels in, she was no match for him physically. "Where are you taking me?" she spluttered.

"We have to hide," was his reply, fury in his voice but so much fear as well.

It was good to hear: *him* afraid at last. That's what she had wanted, dragging him within high walls to knock down his own, to see what lay beneath, the coward that had to lurk there.

They were heading back towards the catacombs. That was another door she'd left open earlier, albeit not deliberately; sitting rigid in the office, she simply hadn't got round to closing it.

It wasn't just what she'd seen in there, what she'd experienced that made her reluctant to go back. The body that had once lain in front of it also came to mind, the stricken young man. Although she'd never in her life seen a picture of him, his image was as vivid as the others, not inspiring sympathy but more terror.

She struggled harder. "Not in there, Zak. We need to stay out here, in the open."

Of course he wouldn't listen; she knew that. He just continued dragging her, reaching a door made of wood this time, not iron, and booting at it, her heart sinking as it so readily flew open.

Once inside, he was braver. He slammed the door shut and then pinned her against the wall, not just fear in his eyes but something else.

"Zak," she said, "are…are you on something?"

His sneer was so derisive. "What the fuck do you mean?"

"You know what I mean. Drugs."

His laughter echoed around the chamber and bounced off every wall there. "I fucking need to, being with you, the shit you put me through."

"You didn't have to come here, to my place of work. You didn't have to follow me out."

"Did you think I'd let you hide from me?"

"Or escape. Is that what you were worried about, that your cash cow would disappear?"

The laughter was gone, but the hatred on his face only intensified. It lit something similar in her. She'd been lonely before he came along. Oh, what luxury loneliness seemed like now!

Forcing herself to straighten up rather than slump, she leaned forward slightly. "Whatever happens tonight, you will never see another penny of my money, do you hear? I mean it this time. I want you out of my flat; you're not welcome there. I will no longer be your punch bag."

The memory of what that girl had endured – suffering far worse than her own – returned. Men like Zak – predators – had to be stopped. Would showing him she was not afraid achieve this, playing on his fears instead, more *primitive* fears? Would it help to turn the tables?

He lunged at her. Again, it was such a predictable action. As he did so, his hands reaching for her neck again, she turned her head to the side, brought her own hands up to try to stay him.

"What's that?" she said. "Did you hear it?"

Her hunch proved right. Once again, he couldn't resist turning his head in the direction she was looking, along that long, dark passage that led to those interred deep within.

"There's nothing there," he said, but his hands were not quite as tight as they could be.

What drugs had he taken, she wondered, pills or weed? Even the latter could have hallucinogenic properties nowadays. She remembered a group of her friends saying exactly that in the office, where she'd worked, Karen amongst them, that marijuana could be mixed with anything. One or two of them related their own experiences, eliciting several hushed sniggers.

"A scratching…" she continued. "I heard like…something was scratching."

How wide his eyes were. "What's down there anyway?"

"What do you think's down there?"

Her sarcasm was perhaps a step too far. Quick as a flash he turned his head and looked at her again, his eyes not blue any longer, just black, pure black. "You're not getting rid of me that easily, you understand? I'm very comfortable being your *boyfriend*, thanks."

Now his was the voice dripping with sarcasm, and it cut her to the quick.

"I'm not who you think I am."

"A weak, pathetic, needy little bitch?"

"I was doing all right before you came into my life."

"You were desperate."

"*You* were the one who was desperate. Tell me the truth,

Zak, about your life. You have no job, no flat. I think…I think with your ex, you tried to destroy her too—"

"Don't you dare! You know nothing about it, nothing!"

"But I do know, don't I? That your children are far younger than in those photos you showed me, that you're the one who has a drug problem, that you're bitter and twisted inside, that you're lost." She nodded fervently as the truth hit home. "That's it! That's what this is all about! You're lost! Completely. And you wanted some kind of saviour, but in your head, your messed-up head, you've twisted salvation into something cruel, something callous and evil."

The crack of his hand as it flew across her face told her she was right – finally. The blinkers were off, the love she had for him as dead as those that surrounded her. *But not buried, not yet.* Blinking rapidly, breathing hard, she had to force herself again to straighten up.

"There's plenty more where that came from," he snarled.

She didn't doubt it.

Again, she drew a breath, started cowering. He hadn't raised his hand a second time, so her action would confuse him. "There's someone in here with us, listen! Can you hear them?"

"There's nothing—"

"There is! The man who was following you, do you think…?"

Deliberately she let her voice trail off. If something adverse was in his system, then suggestion would be enough. Let his imagination do the rest, feed his paranoia.

There was silence between them, heavy and stagnant. He had craned his neck, was peering into the gloom. Would this work? Or would he simply lash out again?

He left her and walked forward, just a couple of paces.

"What are you doing?" She feigned concern. "You're not going down there?"

"What is that noise?" was all he said.

"Zak, be care—"

"Shhh. Quiet. What is it?"

She could hear nothing. There *was* nothing, not this time. The bats, or whatever had been responsible last time, lying low. Her plan – such as it was – was working.

"Is it mice, do you think? Rats?"

"I…don't know," she answered. "It could be, or…"

"Or what?"

"I've told you I don't know."

When he had taken a couple more steps, big Zak, brave Zak, she spoke again. "What if it's the man, a tall man, isn't he? He moves…almost as if he's gliding. Who is he, Zak? More to the point, *what* is he? When he's close, all I can feel is blind terror. Is it the same for you?"

"But it can't be. We were ahead of him when we ran in here."

"There's a window at the back, though, a smashed window. It's been on the repair list for ages. It's big enough for someone to crawl through. Zak, why's he following you? What do you think he wants with you in particular?"

Reaching into her pocket, she retrieved her torch at last and switched it on. She hadn't realised that this was the purpose she'd use it for – shining the light on his face as he swung round – but now that she had, it suddenly made sense as to why she'd grabbed it above all else. *This* was what she'd so desperately wanted to see as well as hear: Zak

Harborne trembling with fear.

Committing the sight to memory, she then turned as suddenly as he had and ran to the door.

"Lucy! Lucy, what are you doing? Don't leave me alone in here, not with him!"

Darting through, she closed it behind her.

"LUCY!"

Of course he could run straight after her, and with no key to lock the door, he'd do exactly that. No matter. It had never been her intent to incarcerate him, just to see...only to see... He was human, after all, not what she'd built him up to be in her mind, at first a god and then a demon. Realising this gave her at least a shred of hope. And now she would continue fleeing, over the spot where she was now certain the boy had lain, and through the cemetery, reaching the office before Zak did, bolting the door from the inside and then heading out the main door into Swain's Lane. He could stay in the courtyard for what remained of the night, take shelter beneath the colonnade on the lower ground as opposed to the higher ground. In the morning she would call the police to have him removed from there – removed from her life full stop.

It was a plan, quickly formulating, making sense, all of it now, so much sense...

"Aargh!"

She'd barely reached the steps down to the Circle of Lebanon when she was tackled to the ground. For a moment she was nonplussed. Who was it? Not Zak, surely?

It *was* him. He must have moved with preternatural speed, much quicker than she'd anticipated, fear not freezing him for long but infusing him with an almost superhuman ability. He was on her, and his fists were pummelling, his voice as high-pitched as a female's as he screamed at her.

"What were you trying to do to me in there? You left me! With him! You left me."

She couldn't answer; all she could do was drag herself away from him, towards the steps, back down into the circle. From there she would take the path that led past the vaults, passing underneath the archway and into the wild centre.

As hard as he fought, so did she. She kicked out, she screamed, her mouth filling with dirt because of it. Dirt...in her mouth... It triggered something...a memory? What memory? Whose?

As if she was infused with superhuman strength also, she forced her body round and with her arms pushed him, managing to roll him off her before scrabbling to her feet. At the steps he caught up with her again, the pair of them entwined like the lovers they once were as they tumbled down them. Despite that, he was no cushion for her; her head struck stone over and over – his too, she hoped, sustaining equal damage – until they both came to a halt at the bottom.

How much time passed she had no clue, only that she lay still and so did he. Finally able to move her fingers, to wriggle them, she swallowed hard so as not to vomit. Inch by painful inch, she crawled away from him, fearful that he'd pounce again. Still he didn't move. Was he...? Could he be...? She wasn't going to hang around and see. Still inching, grunting with the effort it took, groaning loudly, she climbed first to her knees and then to her feet, staggering like a drunkard, arms held outwards.

Her eyes stung, what with? Rubbing at them, she quickly realised what it was: blood, hot and sticky. Bile rose in her again, threatening to expel itself with all the force of a volcano. The office wasn't far, not the impossible distance it seemed. *Put one foot in front of the other. Go. Whilst you still can.*

One foot…and then the other… One foot…

She was so busy concentrating that she failed to notice what else went on around her. Initially, anyway. Lifting her eyes off the ground, her vision was still blurred as if a layer of gauze covered her face, a shroud of some sort. Finally managing to focus, she gasped.

Highgate was more alive than ever!

Chapter Twenty-Seven

She'd wanted to see, and she had: the girl, Zak feeling the same emotion he was so fond of inciting in her, the all-encompassing shadow. But there was so much more to Highgate, a world within a world, always suspected but never witnessed…not fully. Until now.

The circle Lucy stood in contained so many vaults. Always they had about them an air of foreboding, so dark inside, as well she knew. But they were dark no more. From some a yellow light seeped out from around the door edge, and there were signs of movement behind – *life*. Such a realisation caused not horror, not even surprise. Rather, she felt the beginning of acceptance, something that had been in her all along, or at least a *willingness* to accept.

Something passed her, a fleeting figure, not fully caught. A child, not the girl she'd seen previously but another. There were, after all, many children buried here – lives cut short, the broken columns rising from their tombs a testament to that fact. The Lamb of God too, a symbol of innocence. She didn't flinch as the child passed, nor again as another did, the two of them engaged in a game, the light sound of laughter heartfelt and wonderful to hear.

The path that led from the circle to the archway, oh, it was dark! And yet she could see well enough, her eyes having grown accustomed. She no longer had to rely on prior knowledge or instinct. Although the doors to the vaults remained closed, all except the one she'd hidden in, what they tried to contain had ventured forth, to roam these grounds as she was. More sounds…not laughter this time. A woman's voice.

"Where are you, you little swines? Come here! You deserve what you got and what I'm going to do to you still."

There was such venom in it, such mad intent!

Immediately Lucy darted off the path to hide behind a tall stone.

"Where are you?" the woman continued. "I'll find you! See if I don't."

Who was she, and what was she going to do with those she sought? What terrible punishment did she think they deserved? Crouching low, not daring to peek out from her hiding place, Lucy also closed her eyes, opening them after a few seconds to find a child crouching in front of her, the one that had darted by earlier? She was young, about eight or nine, and her dark hair was matted. With no sense of urgency at all, the child lifted a finger and brought it to her mouth. *Shhh!*

Who is that? Is it you she wants?

The child lowered her hand and nodded, gesturing behind her to other shapes that crouched.

She wants us all.

Why? What have you done?

Was it strange that yet again she was able to communicate without words? No stranger than anything else happening this night. *Are you scared?*

If she expected the child to nod her head avidly, she was wrong. Instead, the girl laughed, the others joining her. Low

258

laughter, titters, the giggling of earlier.

Abruptly, the child turned away from her and back towards the others, signalling for them to rise, to continue running. It was hide-and-seek they played amongst the tombstones, a game they were clearly used to. In life the woman might have indeed caught them, but in death she could no longer inflict harm. Of them all, only the woman refused to accept that.

Left alone once more, Lucy tried to stand, the world fading in and out before full sight returned. The blood had run down from her head, past her eyes and into her mouth, causing her to hunch over and spit several times. She must press onwards, away from Zak. She'd left him unconscious, but if he should awake; if he should also stagger to his feet...

Each and every step she took was hard won. She became disorientated, unsure she was going in the right direction. The world had started to spin, and so she had to stop, hold on again to a hard slab of stone in order to steady herself. What was that in the distance? It was something...floating. Yes, that was right, a figure, just floating and staring at what? The sky?

You're such a curious creature. Lucy couldn't deny it; she was. And she always had been. Drawing closer, using other tombstones to support her, she had to know what the floating figure was or the mystery would plague her. A ghoul, a spectre – would it turn to face her as she neared it, revealing a face that was nothing but a skull, its hollowed eyes worm-ridden? It did no such thing; it merely faded, leaving nothing behind but a dreadful melancholy. That was the thing that wormed its way into you, to sit there like a slab of granite. *I must reach Amelia.*

She continued forwards as though being pulled now, as if an invisible cord had been attached to her, guiding her, ensuring she strayed no more. A flare of light to the right caught her attention – a woman was screaming, batting at her dress that was bright with flames. Sarah Wallace Smith! It had to be, reliving the torture of her demise.

You can't help her.

Who was here? Who had said that? The girl? "Is it you? Are you back?"

Still the cord tugged, although she couldn't see it or detach it.

You can't help her.

Only those words were repeated, their truth sinking in.

Lucy tried to drown out Sarah's cries, her screams. There was a howling too, like a dog's – the one from Thomas Sayers' grave, the dog named Lion? They were such pitiful howls, as if he too was distressed he could do nothing to save a girl who'd already died.

She had to crouch again, the low boughs of trees scraping at her forehead. Here the graves were much closer together, the ivy and bracken covering each and every one, the trees as huddled as the children hiding from the old woman had been, but soon it would clear to reveal the stone figure of Amelia – sanctuary? Could it be? A place to rest, just for a few minutes.

As she approached, Amelia's epitaph resounded in her head, the hopelessness of it. Like so many others, would the real Amelia be present, not just the carved residue of her? And if so, would her torture be as plain to see as the girl that burned?

The cries, the howls had petered out, and in their place another sound emerged. Footsteps, either Zak's or the other one in pursuit. She had to pick up pace and reach Amelia. She was just beyond the clearing she had stumbled upon recently – courtesy of another dog, Firecracker – where she had fallen to the ground and wept. Both were just ahead. So close...

She fell again, her legs refusing to support her any longer. More dirt found its way into her mouth. She turned her head to the side, instinctively spitting it out. It mustn't be allowed to enter, to fill her up, cover her, *suffocate* her.

"No! No! No!"

Tears as well as blood blinding her, she pushed herself up onto her hands and fell again as they slid in the mud.

"NO! NOT AGAIN!"

Lucy! Lucy!

"Help me! For God's sake, help me!"

Lucy! It's me.

"I need help!"

Lucy!

At last she lifted her head and saw who was calling her. The child, but not only her, someone else too, someone just behind her. The other shadow, an older girl. *I know it's you out there...*

The child was still calling her name, beseeching her, but the other one... She looked as terrified as Lucy felt. Eventually, however, she drifted forwards, Lucy gradually quieting as she knelt beside her. Just as the child had done in the vault, the girl placed a hand on her arm. And as she did, Lucy noticed two things: that the girl was also crying and that her mouth was filled with dirt.

* * *

Not a girl, but a young woman, she dressed in far more modern clothing than the child: jeans, a smock of some sort, and a jacket. Although not as striking as her younger counterpart, she was pretty enough, but it was her eyes – not her mouth this time – that Lucy noticed. Green eyes, wide and framed with long, fair lashes. Sweet eyes, or they should have been. Instead, Lucy wanted to look away because…because…they were hollow somehow.

Why? What's your story?

She'd asked the question, but she needn't have. The girl's story would be revealed soon enough. That was why Lucy had been drawn here, the sole purpose of it. As with the child, a series of images assailed her, sliding into focus before sliding out. Also like last time, they were relentless, the woman's life becoming *her* life, all else ceasing to exist.

How Lucy identified with her loneliness; it had been in this woman from the start. An only child, her mother and father had their own tale to tell, although Lucy was not privy to it, only the effects of it, the consequences. Had they ever loved their daughter? Had they ever loved each other? She doubted it – love was not something evident in any of the images. There was shouting, screaming, and arguing, much of it drink-fuelled but not all; alcohol only brought out what was already there, an emptiness that had bred yet more, a cycle too hard to break.

A dog ran into the scene, just a small dog, its white fur marked with black. Now this creature *had* inspired love, in the girl, anyway. When she was a child, it had become her companion. A double-edged sword, however, as its demise had only driven deeper the pain of all she'd lacked in her life.

With university came the opportunity for a fresh start. She'd no longer be a pawn for her parents to battle over, an excuse; she could be whoever she wanted to be. Bright? Yes, she was certainly that. She had a love of history, of...dead things. Was that correct? An obsession. Ah, so it was this woman that someone had said that about! That she was obsessed with death. Was it the man who slid into view? He was young – as young as her, maybe, with dark, curly hair and wearing a cap-sleeved tee shirt and jeans. What timeframe did they belong to? She focused on his tee shirt; there was a band motif on it. Led Zeppelin, was that who it was? *Cryin' won't help you; prayin' won't do you no good...* Those words – those *lyrics* – flared in her mind. Did these two belong to the seventies? Certainly their clothes suggested it.

Lucy couldn't help but recoil at the sight of this young man, just as much as she'd recoiled at the older man in the other vision, *the gentleman*, the one who'd stood and stared at all the child had endured, the world he'd created for her, hell on earth. Both of them, now that they were in her mind, seemed to take up residence as if they'd always been there, the horror of them.

The scene shifted from the man and woman sitting in a room – which in its own way was as squalid as the child's, a bare light bulb swinging overhead – to somewhere outside, somewhere wild and overgrown. A jungle it looked like, completely given over to nature and yet a place she recognised, that she had known would appear, just as Swain's Lane had appeared in her other visions. It was this place, of course. Highgate.

Slowly Lucy shook her head, not with denial but yet more acceptance. The woman had seen things here, good things; she'd seen Amelia, who'd held her face so gently between her hands, angels too, trees that glowed, and leaves that shimmered, the paradise that Highgate promised it would be. She'd been welcomed; she'd belonged. She had then gone on to see the dark side of paradise, a garden more savage.

The man – God, who was he? Like with the gentleman, why did she feel she knew him already? – had joined the woman, in the thick of Highgate, in the thick of the nightmare. Was he trying to save her? No. Oh no. Not that. He had *fed* off the nightmare. Yielded to it. The woman was injured, and he was burying her, beneath the patch of ground that Lucy lay on now! A grave dug first with wood and then bare hands, committing her to it. Aware…

Yes, he was aware she wasn't quite dead, he had *become* aware, but still he continued. *It's easier if you're dead.* Why was it easier? What could possibly have possessed him? Possessed. More than a word, did it constitute an answer? This woman had been buried, her living body consigned to a shallow grave that would only sink deeper and deeper. As the first handfuls of dirt hit her skin, her mouth was open to receive, to choke, to die – eventually – on dirt. Lucy witnessed the darkness as it blinded the woman; smelt the pungent soil; felt her terror, her despair, and her rage. A victim. And like the child, she always had been, rendered powerless when evil came to call.

As the images began to fade, Lucy started scrabbling at the ground. Deeper and deeper she dug, her actions similar to the man's but with a very different purpose. She wanted to reach in and pull her body out. There were unmarked graves at Highgate, the names of those who lay beneath not fully disclosed. But at least they'd been known about! She'd had no idea about this woman, and she was damned sure no one else had either. Her tears mixed with the soil, as if trying to wash it clean. An impossible task, for it was beyond tainted. *But not the one who sleeps here; you're not tainted. You don't belong, I promise. Not anymore.*

Only exhaustion caused her to stop. Rocking back on her heels, she looked over to where the statue of Amelia knelt. A stone mother, that's what she was, and a sister and a daughter. And yet still she'd felt so much despair, was feeling it now as she cried. Lucy was sure of it, for something on the statue's cheeks glinted silver in the darkness. Who did Amelia cry for? Herself or for all who suffered? The pain of others, in the end, becoming one pain.

Turning her head, Lucy once more set her sights on the child and the young woman.

"What are your names?"

She asked the question, but she didn't expect an answer.

She didn't expect it, because she knew.

"Grace and Emma," she continued. "That's what your names are."

Chapter Twenty-Eight

The sound of someone fighting their way through the undergrowth returned, heavy breathing too. There was nothing unnatural about it. It was Zak, on her trail, as bloodied a mess as she was, probably, and as intent on closure.

Emma and Grace remained where they were – ghosts, apparitions, spirits, *kin*. Lucy was connected to them both, and their sorrow was hers. It *defined* her and explained so much: why she was different, not just because she had to be for her parents' and brother's sake, as she had convinced herself. That was only part of a much, much bigger picture. An introvert – naturally wary, shy, someone who found it difficult to bond with people, to trust them – that was her. The slightest wrongdoing and she'd recoil, a shutter closing inside her, coming down...down...down... She'd been lonely, an outsider. Until Zak. He'd brought her inside a circle she was tired of being shut out of. And that tiredness had worn her down. Too quickly she'd believed in him. Damn it, she had loved him!

Just as Emma and Grace stood their ground, so did she. The flame inside her that was responsible for animating her, she supposed, was flickering dangerously, becoming pallid. She had to stoke it, get it to roar again, and they would help her, she knew it; they would lend her their strength and their determination. After all, you could only run so far and for so long.

The branches of the tree closest to her parted, and Zak appeared. As she had guessed, he looked as wretched as she did, dark patches of blood and sweat staining the top he wore. His mouth was twisted in a grimace, the fury in his eyes something tangible.

"Had enough of playing games?" His gritty voice sounded as if he'd been the one swallowing dirt.

His eyes were solely on her, she realised. Did he not see who stood with her? Had he not encountered all that she had? Was it *only* the darkness he could see?

He stepped closer. As he did, every bone in her body wanted to move, screamed at her to do so, but she listened to two voices only, and they told her to stay exactly where she was.

"I'm really, really tired," she replied at last.

"*You're* tired?" His laughter was deafening. "Look what you've done to me!"

She shook her head. "You did this to yourself."

The laughter stopped. "What the hell are you talking about?"

"All that's happened, all that's *going* to happen, is because of the choices you've made."

"All that's going to happen?"

"That's right."

How he sneered at her. "I should never have got involved with you."

"The money was too much of a lure, though, wasn't it? You thought I was a woman of means. But do you want to know the truth, how much I've got left in the bank? Ten thousand and fifty-eight pounds, that's all. Oh, and ninety-six pence. A lot to some, perhaps, but perhaps not as much as I led you to believe. And I did lead you on in that regard, I admit it, because, like you, I was desperate…not just because I wanted to help your son. I wanted to keep you. But there it is, that's the truth. I bet you wish you'd put your efforts somewhere more worthwhile now."

"I'm going to kill you," Zak breathed, limping as he closed the gap between them.

"Actually, I think we might end up killing each other."

So many times he'd laid his hands upon her, first in a gentle manner that had reeled her in further and then, once caught, becoming rougher and rougher. Now they were on her again, her hands on him too, both of them pulling, hitting, and scratching at each other. Closure. She yearned for it. Would it happen here, on this patch of ground? Where Emma's body lay but not her spirit, because that had risen, as had Grace's, the three of them refusing to be victims anymore.

She was becoming stronger and he was growing weaker – putting them on an even keel for the first time. He grunted, he groaned, spitting curses under his breath, whereas she strove to remain silent, focused, and intent. She pushed him and he fell, a tombstone breaking his fall. He rose quickly enough and lunged back at her. She also staggered, but something other than stone prevented her from falling – hands, not just two pairs, more than that. Righting herself, she glanced behind her. As well as Emma and Grace, there were countless others, in and amongst the gravestones. Those that had suffered too? That craved justice?

She couldn't help herself; she had to know. "Zak, wait,

look! Zak, please…can you see them?"

Dragging his hand against his mouth, clearly struggling to breathe, Zak looked up to where she pointed. "See what?"

"Them! People. So many." Some of them shimmered, she noticed. Emma and Grace too, their light the brightest.

"There's nothing there, you stupid—"

She swapped such a wondrous sight for a far less appealing one, grabbing a handful of Zak's jumper and pulling his face to within an inch of hers. "There is! They've come to help me. They're on my side, not yours, and this game, as you called it, is very nearly over."

"You delusional, lying bitch. You're not fit to walk—"

The expression on her face clearly stopped him from saying anything further, the horror she felt extending to envelop him too. Just as there were those standing behind her, there were others standing behind *him*. Not the great mass she'd seen before; rather, it appeared to have splintered into dozens – no, hundreds – no, *thousands* of blackened shapes. Violent things: things that were depraved, indulgent, spiteful, greedy, and self-obsessed. On her side were those weakened by life: the downtrodden, the unheard, the desperate, the frightened, and the pitiful. What if his allies surged forwards and attacked hers? They were beings that knew no boundaries.

She released Zak and he pivoted, following the direction of her gaze. In the ensuing silence Lucy's mind continued to work frantically. Zak hadn't been able to see all that she had, but would he be able to see his own kind? And if so, would they bolster him as she'd been bolstered, injecting him with a strength that would once again exceed hers?

As he turned back to face her, every nerve ending she possessed pulsated wildly.

His expression wasn't one of triumph as she'd expected. However, the horror remained.

"Zak?"

"We have to go, Lucy. I told you, didn't I? Before. We have to go."

Roughly pushing past her, he began his flight, the limp that had been evident before slowing him down only a fraction. Watching him for a second or two, she then turned her attention back to the splintered mass. They began to swarm towards her, having congealed into a cloud of hatred. Zak had seen it. Zak had belonged to it, and yet he had run. Was it possible he could outrun it? Could she?

She had to try. Taking flight too, Emma and Grace were beckoning, gliding backwards, their eyes still on her, only on her, all others fading, leaving a slight glow behind that all too quickly faded. She had to get out of this area and onto the path; that way was quicker. Once she reached the office, she could shut all this out and leave here. Although the thought of never returning...

No, she mustn't let her mind wander. Not when another battle was intent on being waged.

Chapter Twenty-Nine

The office lights shone in the distance like a beacon. They represented safety, normality. Electric light, as opposed to that of a more spiritual nature, illuminating not coffins, caskets, and tombstones but the wonderful mundaneness of desks, chairs, and computers.

The dark mass was behind her, surely it was, silent and stealthy, a deadly assassin. It was always there – unseen, usually, hidden but ready to strike out, to consume. It wanted to continue growing, to become bigger still, and it would bide its time, intent on doing just that.

That she'd seen it was difficult to comprehend, something so hideous become so real.

But you've seen it before.

In Zak, is that what the voice was suggesting?

In Higgins and Kev too.

Higgins and Kev? Who were they?

Part of the same fabric.

There wasn't the time to contemplate such a mysterious answer, not now. Having reached the main path, the one that would take her to the steps leading down to the courtyard, she became aware of movement on either side of her. Terrified of who it might be, she turned her head only a fraction, first to the left and then to the right. It was Emma and Grace, gliding as they'd done before. Oh, how she wished she could emulate them! Instead, she could feel herself slowing down, the injuries her body had sustained too much of a hindrance.

She pointed. "There's my office. I need to reach it."

There was no reply, only silence.

"Oh God," she muttered, her voice trembling as much as she was. "I should never have come here. I should never have set foot in this place."

Grace spoke this time: *You belong here.*

Lucy was almost at the steps. On the way up she had taken them two at a time, but now she had to grasp the railing in order to tackle them, her strength continuing to wane, her mind growing black at the edges. Was it possible none of this was real? It was…if not a dream…a stage set… Yes! That was it! And she was playing a part, an actress reading from a script.

You've played many parts.

That was Emma's voice, refusing to indulge her.

In the courtyard at last, she wanted to howl with relief; the sound that escaped her, however, was barely above a whimper. The office was so close, just a few feet ahead. So often she would gaze out from its window, to a point just above where she stood now, into the low light.

"I know it's you out there." She whispered to herself this time, not Emma or Grace. "I *know*…"

Almost at the office door, she didn't enter. Instead, she allowed herself to pause, letting the words she still repeated sink in.

After a few moments, she veered to the left and back into the cemetery. But not into the heart of it, not this time. She went towards a place she knew all too well – the unmarked graves, where perhaps the greatest injustice had occurred: the refusal of a headstone to mark ten buried prostitutes from the nineteenth century, the youngest only twelve years old. It was a world away from the splendour of other memories forged within this cemetery, and yet still it was a part of that world. No marker had been erected, not then and not now – their supposed sins still frowned upon, girls and women who had fallen and, in the eyes of society, could never rise again. The evil in men had claimed their innocence, and many had stood aside to let that happen, apportioning blame where blame should not be placed.

This was where the final battle would take place, then, the dark mass continuing to swarm through the trees to gather there. Zak had arrived too. She could hear him as he approached. As she had muttered to herself, so was he, in between gasps and sobs.

Stand your ground.

She needed no instruction. This time she would.

The darkness wants you too.

Of course it did. It wanted so many.

We're with you.

They were. Grace and Emma. More than kin, they were a part of her soul, who she used to be and who she still was. Grace smiled to see Lucy no longer denying it. Emma's eyes, however, were still so sad, the damage she'd sustained as Grace weighing her down, just as it had weighed Lucy down, the consequence of sin taking its toll through the ages. It had all led to Highgate and to this night, a confrontation *and* a collaboration, just as she had thought.

And here was their age-old foe, not in his guise as the suited and booted Higgins or as the young hippy student

273

Kev. He was Zak this time, in his forties and good-looking, with blond, foppish hair and a whole armoury of lies. Had she encountered him even before Grace, in yet another lifetime? Would they meet again in some as of yet unimagined future? What defined the past and the future anyway? Both seemed to collide, here at Highgate, to meld into one. She swallowed. No, they wouldn't meet again, not if she could help it. Enough was enough.

"Zak!"

She called his name, and he lifted his head, his expression one of surprise, as if he'd forgotten all about her. Peering closer, she realised there was something different about him; not just drug-addled or consumed with rage, he was something else entirely. Mad. What had happened here at Highgate had pushed him over the edge and into the abyss.

The abyss?

Not quite.

Not yet.

She hurried over to him. "Zak, listen to me. Try to focus."

Still he was muttering, a series of barely legible words. "Help me...can't...coming...see it? Can you see it...can't...no, can't...so big...so much...help...no, can't..."

He was looking not at her but through her, the blood on his face having formed a mask-like crust, making him look every inch the ghoul he was.

How slowly the darkness behind him crept forward, its leisurely pace a mockery.

It wants you too.

Again, she was reminded of this as she continued to alternate her gaze between Zak and it, tempted, so tempted, to take advantage of him in this vulnerable state. The sins he was guilty of were too many to count: he had let a young girl be torn apart and had buried another knowing there was breath left in her body, that there was hope. As for herself, he had systematically beaten and undermined her, made her feel more isolated and lonelier than she had ever felt. In his current state, he was the vulnerable one, and being so close, she could strike out before the darkness did. And it would feel so good, so wonderful; surely it would heal some of the pain inside her, fill the void that was, after all, his legacy?

She could feel her hands become fists, become something clawed, and she raised them higher and higher. *I could crush you.* This whimpering fool, not a broken angel but a broken demon instead. This was what she had wanted to see and so much more; this was success.

But if that were so, then how come the taste was acrid?

It wants you too.

And this was how it would get her, through vengeance and through hate. Not just continuing the cycle but contributing to it, through allowing herself to become…what was the word? *Infected.* Yes, this thing could infect you. So easily.

"It's not just me it wants, is it? It's all of us."

As well as risk herself, she risked Emma and Grace too; they would all get sucked in.

Even so, the temptation was still so great, the grief he had caused!

It wants you…

She forced herself to reach out, to grab his arms. Instead of screaming, tearing him apart with words first, she spoke slowly, steadily. "Zak, it doesn't have to be this way. None of it did."

He was shivering as if frozen. "Too late... All of it."

"It's not! It isn't! When you turned around, when you noticed the darkness, I thought...I don't know...that you'd recognise it and run towards it, that you'd *want* to be a part of it. The fact that you resisted, that you ran from it, perhaps" —it hurt her to say it— "there's something good in you."

He shook his head furiously.

"Zak, you love your children, don't you? Your wife, once upon a time did you love her, did you have hopes and dreams for a happy life together, aspirations?"

His trembling slowed, his muttering ceased. Hopeful that she was getting through to him, she continued. "When things go wrong, when life...takes a bad turn, it's easy to grow bitter inside, to hate the world and how unfair it can be; I know that, Zak, *I know*. Karen said that your friend Jon had seen you with your kids and you appeared to be a good dad. Forget how you used them against me; you love them deep down, don't you? Come on, Zak, tell me that you love them."

His breathing was ragged, the stench from his mouth reminding her of the vaults. It was dark all around them, not just behind Zak, and there was such a thickness to it, such...energy.

The darkest hour is just before the dawn – that was the saying. Was this that hour? They'd been here all that time, running, hiding, and fighting? Such darkness bore down

276

upon them until all else disappeared and all that remained was the two of them, suspended within it.

"If you can't tell me you love them, and, Zak, I know you do, then say something else. Say—" she swallowed hard, kept her eyes only on him, beseeching him, "—you're sorry."

Still no word from him, and he continued to look at the ground rather than at her.

"Damn it, Zak! You had plenty to say for yourself before all this happened, didn't you? You didn't hold back then, kept calling me names, undermining me. You hurt me, Zak, not just with your fists. You—" again she had to swallow hard as anger resurged, "—hurt all of us. What makes you think you can do what you did to another human being? What gives you the right? You're nothing special, you're just one of us, so why, Zak, why do you, and people like you, do it? I might be a loner, I might be a little bit different, I might be all those things you said I was: crazy, mad, a bitch. But one thing I would never *ever* do is hurt another person, not knowingly, not deliberately. I would never have hurt you. God, Zak, I *loved* you."

More images slid into her mind, as vivid as any that Grace and Emma had shown her. This time the subject was herself. There was Lucy as a child, with her family, on the edge of the group photograph as she always was, even before Stephen's illness. Disconnected. School, college, jobs; it was all like looking through a window into another world – a glass panel separating her from others, a brick wall that past lives had built. She'd had boyfriends, but they'd come and gone. She'd had friendships, but she was never a best friend. *Because inside – deep, deep inside – I couldn't be. My soul was still caught up in horror.*

And then there was Zak and an image of them together on their first date in the pub, a close-up of the look on his face, so different to the one later on, after he'd walked her home. In this vision he looked like the cat who'd got the cream; that was exactly how she'd thought of it. A look she had trusted but which she'd also misread. She'd trusted him. Just as Grace had trusted Higgins and Emma had trusted Kev to save her when he'd returned to Highgate, not bury her alive!

"Damn you!" As anger drowned out even despair, what surrounded them began to infiltrate. How cold it was and yet feverishly hot too, as if it would burn the flesh from her body, boil it right through to the bone. Zak began whimpering again, began gibbering. Panic edged its way back into her. What was happening? This force, or whatever it was, was eating away at them, soon to swallow them whole, ingest them. They'd become part of it, trapped within a place much darker than any vault could ever be. And in it would dwell more panicking, gibbering creatures; creatures that would thrash at themselves and at each other, that would tear at their hair and howl, begging and pleading for mercy but to no avail. It would all fall on deaf ears.

Tell him you're sorry!

"What?"

Was that Grace? Or Emma? Perhaps it was both of them, in her head and screaming at her. What did they mean, asking *her* to apologise?

Quick! You must be quick! It wants us!

It wanted him too and, as rage-filled as she was, could she consign him to such a terrible and eternal fate? He had to have some redeeming quality. She couldn't have got it so wrong.

"Stop! Stop!" she cried as what felt like razor-sharp teeth sank deeper into her skin. That plea also fell on deaf ears. "Say you're sorry, Zak, just fucking say it, will you? SAY IT!"

Finally, he looked up, his eyes two fear-drenched orbs and drool hanging from his mouth.

"This is your fault," he hissed, "all of it. It was *always* your fucking fault."

Staring at him, she could see beyond the madness suddenly, beyond the hatred and the anger, and what she saw there was something far worse, something pathetic, more needy than she or Grace or Emma had ever been – something that thought it craved the darkness but, now that the darkness was upon it, was just as scared as they were. He was a little boy that had never grown, not properly, that had neither developed nor evolved. A primeval thing that remained stubbornly senseless.

"I *am* sorry," she said, for how could she not be? "For everything you are."

The darkness crashed, no longer feeding but *gorging* itself. In the chaos, all she could hear was Zak repeatedly screaming, "NO! NO! NO!"

She held her hands up to shield her face, trying to save herself from being feasted on too, closing her eyes and seeing in her mind's eye Higgins' face – a tall figure in a tall hat and a cape swishing about his shoulders, his blue eyes flashing red. There was Kev – if not Higgins reincarnated, he was, as had been said, part of the same fabric, a facet of it. He had earth on his hands and no remorse in his heart, giving in so readily to evil, devouring it before it then devoured him too, and so quickly, right here at Highgate, the boy on the path outside the catacombs. And, finally, there was Zak – beautiful, blond Zak – another demon, even though she'd tried so hard to disprove it, right until the end.

Their faces faded. The instant they were gone, she could barely recall them. Their screams, their cries and their false smiles all faded too.

In their place was birdsong.

Chapter Thirty

Her plan had worked, up to a point. She'd managed to expose Zak. She'd rid herself of him. His body still lay on the path before her, however, just like Kev's had lain in another part of the cemetery – shrivelled, his matted hair stark white, his hands like claws, and that mouth of his that she'd kissed so often stretched from ear to ear. His eyes were closed, at least, and she was grateful for that, that she didn't have to look into them, see both the torturer and the tortured.

He was gone. Long gone. The darkness, the void that for a while had blotted out everything else around them, had also gone. Dawn had broken, and it was glorious! As well as birdsong – so much more melodious than the cawing of crows – each tree glittered in a light unique to sunrise rather than sunset; each leaf, no matter how entangled, was a thing apart; and each headstone, those that were majestic and those that had tumbled to the ground, marked a new beginning rather than an end.

"This was how I saw it once." Emma, as solid as Lucy was, had come to stand by her, was gazing into the distance just as she was gazing. "It's how it should be."

Grace stayed where she was, slightly behind them both, a child in rags, her head turned towards the right. Lucy knew what she was looking at well enough – the unmarked grave.

"I'm sorry," she said to Emma, "for what you suffered." Rotating, she also addressed Grace. "I'm sorry for what you suffered too."

"We *all* suffered," was the child's reply.

True words. Suffering that had both fragmented and united them. It united all those who were lost. Just as inflicting suffering on others had united Higgins, Kev, and Zak. Were they really one and the same person, repeating actions and behaviours over decades, over several lives? If it were so, then she had always been their victim. Worse than that, they had almost succeeded in turning her into a vengeful, wrathful thing too, for eventually she had wanted to strike out and maim and kill, to make Zak hurt as much as she hurt. If she had given into such dark desires, if she'd refused to evolve too, or rise above it, how many lifetimes would it take to rectify that mistake, or was there simply no escape, not once you'd fallen all the way?

How her head ached to think about it. Her head... Remembering the injuries she'd sustained whilst she'd tumbled down that long flight of steps with Zak – stone steps, chipped and jagged – she reached up to tentatively touch her forehead. The subsequent bolt of pain caused her to double over. At the same time, she became aware of other aches and pains, no longer subdued. Before panic could once again overwhelm her, Grace came forward at last and slid her hand into Lucy's. Not a cold thing, not anymore, there was warmth to it.

Lucy gazed down upon her. "I'm hurt," she managed to whisper.

There was validation in Grace's solemn expression.

Adjusting her gaze, she realised that Emma had also

reached out and placed one arm around her shoulders, knew too what it meant. "I'm badly hurt. I'm dying."

The shake of Emma's head was barely perceptible. "New beginnings, remember?"

The other part of her plan, to walk out of Highgate no longer crippled by fear, was not going to happen. She would never again venture into that long, steep lane and walk down it. The world – and all its angels and monsters – was no longer her home. Never more would she eat dinner in front of the TV, roll her eyes at some daft reality show, sit shoulder to shoulder with others on a packed Tube or bus, or decide on which book to read to pass the hours that Sunday always seemed so full of. Her time as Lucy Klein – *solely* Lucy Klein – was over.

The day continued to brighten, promising blue skies and moderate heat. The birdsong amplified, yet there was no shrill note to be heard; rather, it soared and dipped in perfect harmony. What shone in the distance – a light of another kind – was so tempting, so welcoming. In it she could rest awhile, just rest. But not before achieving another segment of her plan, at least, one that had suddenly sprung into being, becoming urgent. Failure to carry out that part would mean she *wouldn't* be able to rest, not fully. The light and all that it represented – a true home, where each hour was filled not with loneliness but joy – would have to wait. Glancing at Emma, she saw a smile hover on her lips; Grace too was nodding.

"We have to go back to the office," she told them.

Although they helped her, each step she took involved a supreme effort, her heart impatient for its last beat. Crossing the courtyard once again, she could hear something else: the whinny of horses above the sound of the birds. She could sense their sure tread as, dressed in fancy feathers, they entered such a hallowed space and turned in a circle there. The cargo they pulled in a carriage behind them was of course the dead, delivered so gracefully to their final resting place – their bodies, at least, and, yes, their spirits also, for some lingered, *a lot* did, for reasons of their own.

Where are you, you little swines? How long would the old woman hunt for them? Would the children always insist on teasing her? And the one that drifted face upwards only to disappear once approached, how long would it take before they could truly see what lay beyond? The darkness too that stalked grounds such as these, *burial grounds*, would it ever leave? Perhaps not, because here it had a stronghold; Higgins, the origin of that particular evil, a being so depraved, had ensured it was so. It would continue to stalk and to prey, to attract as many blackened souls as it could, to grow in whatever way possible, to infect. At Highgate, just as many hid from the light as they did the darkness, but for some, that hiding might be over.

Pushing at the door that led to the office was another monumental feat, one she couldn't have managed if not for the help of Emma and Grace and…others? Although she couldn't see them, many had pitted their ethereal weight against its oak heaviness, and eventually it yielded.

"I must be quick." She said it as much to herself as them, dragging limbs that resisted further.

Her office: her domain and her refuge. It had been. Once. Reaching her desk, she stood, not daring to sink down upon the chair for fear she'd never be able to rise again. She shook her writing hand as vigorously as she could, tried to force some life back into it, to focus eyes that kept growing hazy. With her pen poised over a sheet of paper, she looked at Emma and Grace in renewed wonder. *I'm not who you think I am.* She'd said that to Zak. But she wasn't who she thought she was either; she was so much more.

"Tell me your full names," she asked and readily they obliged.

"Emma Jane Matthews."

"Grace Derby."

Beside Emma's name she scribbled notes and a diagram. *Look for Amelia,* she wrote. *Amelia looks over her.*

"I need more names, Grace, not just yours." When Grace remained mute, Lucy continued to beseech her. "Grace, please. You know their names." She'd shared a grave with them long enough, nine others, just like her, whose names history had only partially recorded, until now.

It wasn't Grace who obliged this time but another girl, who stepped out from behind Grace, one of those who had helped earlier, perhaps, to open the door for Lucy. She was slightly older than Grace but just as ragged, cheeks that should glow red streaked with dirt instead.

Lucy waited patiently for her to open her mouth and speak.

"Mary Holmes," the girl said at last.

"Thank you," Lucy replied, writing again. "Thank you so much."

Yet another girl appeared, and then another…and another. She counted them. Including Grace, there were ten girls and women in total. What they represented, however,

285

was more than the sum of their numbers; it was all who had not just fallen but been *dragged* into hell on earth, there to reside amongst devils.

"Your names," she whispered.

"Sarah Evans," came the next reply, "Anne Murphy," another. On and on they went. "Jane O'Donnell, Mary Elizabeth Connor, Catherine Clark, Lily James, Ada Potter and Flora Brown."

Ten who would be acknowledged – she knew someone who'd make sure of that. Ten plus Emma, the shroud of secrecy that lay over them all finally cast aside.

Satisfied, Lucy smiled. "Help me."

The words had barely left her mouth before her body crumpled to the floor, a battered, bloodied, and lifeless thing. Lucy watched it fall, her eyes widening. She could still see the room around her, she could hear the clock that ticked, and the gentle whir of the printer as it burst into periodic life. She could see it, but she was no longer a part of it. She was now a part of something else.

Help me...

The crowd before her surged forwards, Emma and Grace at their helm, and at the back were two others. One was wearing a summer dress, no sadness in her eyes. No hopelessness at all. As for the other, her smile held such kindness. Although as Lucy she had never seen them, not in this guise, she recognised them instantly. One had been a stone mother for so long, the other a living, breathing angel – Christina, who was standing there with tears in her eyes, happy that others would now be remembered alongside herself.

Chapter Thirty-One

"Crying, my little one, footsore and weary?
  Fall asleep, pretty one, warm on my shoulder…"

The day was a drizzly one, but Bert paid no heed to that fact, standing straight-backed at the graveside of the ten women and children who finally had a headstone. Firecracker, as always, was a fixture by his side and listening as intently. How solemn the priest's voice was when it should hold nothing but joy, for this was a landmark occasion – a battle hard-fought but won.

Still the priest's voice droned on.

"I must tramp on through the winter night dreary,
  While the snow falls on me colder and colder."

No matter that his voice didn't fit the occasion; it was but a mere technicality. Instead, as the second verse of 'Crying, My Little One' was read out, Bert recited the words in his head, the way that he'd say them, not grave, not sombre, but full of hope.

"You are my one, and I have not another;
  Sleep soft, my darling, my trouble and treasure;
  Sleep warm and soft in the arms of your mother,
  Dreaming of pretty things, dreaming of pleasure."

Bert had chosen the poem for its simplicity and also because it was by Christina Rossetti, a woman who had worked so hard for social reform during the time she'd lived. She had put herself on the front line, and, in doing so, Bert didn't doubt the horrors she'd seen.

These whom they presided over now were those that Rossetti had striven for, females pressed into an occupation that would surely kill them one way or the other: prostitution. It had no doubt been her influence that saw to it that these unfortunates were at least buried in consecrated ground, but influence could only stretch so far. For more than a century, there'd been no marker as they'd lain, one beneath the other, so deep into the ground. Now everyone would know their names, and it was all thanks to another woman, his friend and colleague: Lucy Klein.

Remembering her, Bert's eyes finally moistened. Firecracker sensed his upset and began to nuzzle him. What a terrible find that had been! Coming into the office that bright morning, ready to take the first tour, only to discover her, slumped on the floor, her hair with so much blood in it, her skin so bruised.

Immediately he had called the police, not leaving her body in the interim as he'd squatted beside her, and damn the arthritis in his legs, which he duly ignored. He had taken her hand and held it in his, Firecracker doing then as he did now to him: gently nudging her.

When the police finally arrived, Firecracker had started barking loudly. He had then shot to the door that led into the courtyard and started to scratch at it. One of the police officers had gone to investigate. After a few minutes that same officer had returned, red-cheeked and breathless.

"There's another body, Sarge," he said. "Out there. A man!"

That man was later identified as Zak Harborne, Lucy's

boyfriend. Bert had only met him once, but that had been enough. He remembered trying to tell her about the feelings he'd experienced on encountering Zak outside the office. Even though it was brief, he'd felt tainted by his presence, *infected*. Concerned how he would explain such a thing to an obviously smitten Lucy, he'd been saved from doing so by Firecracker, who'd bolted from the catacombs, where they'd been sheltering from the rain.

Bert had rushed after him and Lucy joined them later, but her attention had been on Firecracker clawing and pawing at the ground. That site was where another cadaver was found, that of Emma Jane Matthews, a girl that had gone missing in the early seventies – no wooden casket surrounding her and, of course, no marker. Lucy had known about her as well, had left careful instructions where to find her, had said she'd been murdered by the young man whose body was found at Highgate by a group of school kids in 1972, a lad by the name of Kev Walsall. The police had found that both had shared the same address during that time, and an investigation was currently under way.

One mystery solved, perhaps, but so many still left. Just *how* exactly had Lucy known about Emma, about Walsall, and the full names of the ten children and women? Wondering about it often kept Bert awake at night.

Regarding Zak, it came to light that he had a history of violence, his wife having put in numerous complaints about him before starting divorce proceedings. Latterly, when he saw his children, it was in the company of social workers, although apparently he had never harmed a hair on *their* heads, at least. When the media had got hold of the story of the 'Highgate murders', they had run with it, unearthing all the dirt on Zak and dubbing Lucy a 'vulnerable, lonely spinster,' such a terrible term as far as Bert was concerned, an insult to a once vibrant and caring woman. What she'd achieved in death, recognition for so many, they'd simply glossed over. Bert, however, would tell the tale to anyone who'd listen, having carried out her wishes in full.

Bert, she had written, *I've hidden my last will and testament here, in this office. It's in the safe – you know the combination. Will you please preside over it? I'm leaving the sum of my assets to the Friends of Highgate and also the stated drug charities. Please see to it that some funds are also used to erect a stone for the ten girls. As for Emma, I don't know where she will be taken once she is discovered, what cemetery she will be buried in, but please erect a stone for her too on my behalf. Perhaps I can be laid alongside her? I'd like that. On each stone it should read 'Remembered'. I trust you, Bert. Thank you.*

The priest was scattering holy water on the gravesite now. Soon, other volunteers and grounds staff that had joined Bert for the ceremony would return to work or to their respective homes. For now, a volunteer was covering Lucy's post. It'd be filled soon, no doubt, but it would take a special person, a devoted person just as Lucy was, her remains indeed residing at a cemetery alongside Emma's – at Brompton, another of the Magnificent Seven.

To have this headstone erected, here at Highgate, had taken some deep detective work on Bert's part. "We have to have some evidence that those names are truly factual and not fictitious," had been the general consensus. Not an unreasonable request, although it had taken him hours and hours, weeks and weeks to provide the desired proof.

Eventually he had found an article written by Christina Rossetti for a London newspaper, *The Morning Post*, in 1860. In it, she outlined the plight of 'fallen women', as society insisted on calling them, pointing out that many of them were not women but children, and calling for readers to change their attitudes towards them – not to condemn them but to assist in the work of the institution she volunteered at, St Mary Magdalene House. That if they knew what 'terrors' these girls endured, 'surely you would take pity on them'. Reading the article further, Bert had scarce been able to breathe when he'd seen her detail a case that 'haunted her', concerning one child in particular. 'She was known as Grace. What her surname was I do not know and nor will I ever, I suppose. The fate that befell her was an abomination. In no way could she have provoked it. I held her in my arms as she took her last, agonised breath, begging all the while for her to tell me her name. Grace. It is for her that I carry on, and for all those like her. If I cannot prevent it, not wholly, I can strive for justice and recognition on their behalf. It is the least I can do.'

Proof of Grace's identity had carried the others, and approval was finally granted. It had been hours and hours, weeks and weeks well spent.

"You all right, Bert?" Neil, one of the gardeners, crossed over to stand by Bert now that the service – which Lucy's funds had also paid for – was at an end.

"As well as could be expected, Neil, thank you."

Neil nodded towards the headstone. "Incredible day, shame about the weather."

"The drizzle?" Bert disagreed. "The sun will come out soon, I'm sure."

"It's odd here without Lucy, isn't it, she was such a part of Highgate. Although…" Neil paused. "Having said that, I never really knew her. She tended to keep herself to herself. If only she hadn't, eh? Perhaps Harborne wouldn't have been able to get such a hold on her. Lovely smile she had. I miss that about her."

"I'll miss it too. She was one of life's good 'uns."

"Yeah, yeah, she was. Best get on, eh? Lots to do. Working over at the meadow today, pulling up weeds as usual. God, they're rampant, aren't they? No sooner you've cleared one area than they're back again, squeezing the life out of everything. Ha!" For a slight man, Neil had one heck of a laugh. "That's one way of putting it, I suppose. Very apt, considering."

Again, Bert disagreed. Plenty bloomed here despite the relentlessness of the weeds or other things that might seek to choke them.

After making the obligatory fuss over Firecracker, Neil continued on his way, the others dispersing too. Bert shook the priest's hand and then gave him a cup of tea in the office before showing him to his car. Afterwards, he returned to the bench that was placed just a few feet from the girls' burial site, and sat as he had done so often, this time to admire the brand-new headstone rather than lament the lack of one. How long he sat there, lost in thought, he had no idea. At one point he believed he must have dozed off, because he woke to a noise that startled him, the sound of Firecracker jumping from foot to foot and barking.

Bert looked quizzically at him. "What's the matter with you this time?"

The dog leapt forward before stopping again, his tale

wagging frantically.

"What on earth is it?"

Knowing to trust the dog rather than dismiss his actions, Bert struggled to his feet too, scanning the horizon of the Cuttings Road. The sun was much lower in the sky than he'd anticipated it would be, the hazy light shimmering almost.

"Don't know what you're making such a fuss for, boy, there's no one—"

His voice died in his throat. There *was* someone there, a shadow of sorts, tall...

Or did she only seem tall because she stood next to someone smaller than her? *She?* Bert found himself holding his breath as another shadow joined them, amounting to three in total.

Who is that out there?

If only it were brighter, if the sun had come out for them as he'd hoped earlier, he might be able to see them better. In this low light it was difficult.

"Come on, Firecracker, we need to get a little closer."

Firecracker took advantage of being given the go-ahead. The distance between them and the shadows, however, remained stubbornly the same.

Slowly Bert realised that any endeavours to close the gap would be in vain.

Three shadows, or was it? Desperately he tried to ascertain. Not three shadows, not any longer – there were two now, the hand of the smaller shadow reaching up to take the hand of the taller one. As it did, the taller one disappeared. No...not disappeared; it was as if...the smaller one *absorbed* it somehow, just as it had no doubt absorbed the other. Where once there were three, there was now only one.

Fearful that the shadow child would disappear too, Bert cried out. "Don't go. Tell me who you are."

If she heard him, she gave no sign, unless...that laughter he could hear...such innocent laughter...that had struck up so suddenly and was all around him...unless that was indeed the child.

Rather than ask another question, Bert started laughing too, his belly shaking with mirth. What a joyous moment! What a wonderful moment! There was nothing but pure pleasure in it.

As Firecracker sat – he too clearly realising he had no hope of crossing such a great divide – the last of the shadows faded entirely. Rather than be consumed by sadness at her departure, Bert continued to laugh. He couldn't be sure who the child was, or the two adults that had flanked and then become her, but one thing he knew for certain: they had walked out of Highgate.

They were free.

The End

Afterword

This tale, although fictitious, is dedicated to the ten prostitutes that are interred at Highgate, one beneath the other, yet have no marker. Buried in the nineteenth and very early twentieth century, this story is really theirs, and although I've changed their names in the book, the dedication reveals their real identity, thanks to research carried out by two volunteer tour guides.

A second dedication is to Christina Rossetti, who worked tirelessly to help 'fallen women' as they were known back then. You'll find her, her name unchanged, throughout the book too.

Sadly, since I started writing this book, the mighty Cedar of Lebanon tree at Highgate has been chopped down due to disease. I kept it in the book, however, seeking to immortalise it also.

The pedants amongst you may notice I've taken liberties with the layout of Highgate, but only slightly, and all for the sake of a good story. I hope you can forgive me!

The known phantoms of Highgate: the woman with the butcher knife, the floating figure, and, of course, the Vampire of Highgate, have all been acknowledged or alluded to, as has the sheer and unique beauty of this truly haunting place.

A hard story to write at times, centred around forced prostitution and domestic abuse, I hope it shines a light on those that have suffered and suffer still, bringing their torment out of the dark.

Also by the author:

Eve: A Christmas Ghost Story (Psychic Surveys Prequel)

What do you do when a whole town is haunted?

In 1899, in the North Yorkshire market town of Thorpe Morton, a tragedy occurred; 59 people died at the market hall whilst celebrating Christmas Eve, many of them children. One hundred years on and the spirits of the deceased are restless still, 'haunting' the community, refusing to let them forget.

In 1999, psychic investigators Theo Lawson and Ness Patterson are called in to help, sensing immediately on arrival how weighed down the town is. Quickly they discover there's no safe haven. The past taints everything.

Hurtling towards the anniversary as well as a new millennium, their aim is to move the spirits on, to cleanse the atmosphere so everyone – the living and the dead – can start again. But the spirits prove resistant and soon Theo and Ness are caught up in battle, fighting against something that knows their deepest fears and can twist them in the most dangerous of ways.

They'll need all their courage to succeed and the help of a little girl too – a spirit who didn't die at the hall, who shouldn't even be there…

Psychic Surveys Book One:
The Haunting Of Highdown Hall

"Good morning, Psychic Surveys. How can I help?"

The latest in a long line of psychically-gifted females, Ruby
Davis can see through the veil that separates this world and
the next, helping grounded souls to move towards the light
- or 'home' as Ruby calls it. Not just a job for Ruby, it's a
crusade and one she wants to bring to the High Street.
Psychic Surveys is born.

Based in Lewes, East Sussex, Ruby and her team of
freelance psychics have been kept busy of late. Specialising
in domestic cases, their solid reputation is spreading - it's
not just the dead that can rest in peace but the living too.
All is threatened when Ruby receives a call from the irate
new owner of Highdown Hall. Film star Cynthia Hart is
still in residence, despite having died in 1958.

Winter deepens and so does the mystery surrounding
Cynthia. She insists the devil is blocking her path to the
light long after Psychic Surveys have 'disproved' it.
Investigating her apparently unblemished background,
Ruby is pulled further and further into Cynthia's world and
the darkness that now inhabits it. For the first time in her
career, Ruby's deepest beliefs are challenged.

Does evil truly exist?

And if so, is it the most relentless force of all?

Psychic Surveys Book Two: Rise to Me

"This isn't a ghost we're dealing with. If only it were that simple…"

Eighteen years ago, when psychic Ruby Davis was a child, her mother – also a psychic – suffered a nervous breakdown. Ruby was never told why. "It won't help you to know," the only answer ever given. Fast forward to the present and Ruby is earning a living from her gift, running a high street consultancy – Psychic Surveys – specialising in domestic spiritual clearance.

Boasting a strong track record, business is booming. Dealing with spirits has become routine but there is more to the paranormal than even Ruby can imagine. Someone – something – stalks her, terrifying but also strangely familiar. Hiding in the shadows, it is fast becoming bolder and the only way to fight it is for the past to be revealed – no matter what the danger.

When you can see the light, you can see the darkness too.
And sometimes the darkness can see you.

Psychic Surveys Book Three: 44 Gilmore Street

"We all have to face our demons at some point."

Psychic Surveys – specialists in domestic spiritual clearance – have never been busier. Although exhausted, Ruby is pleased. Her track record as well as her down-to-earth, no-nonsense approach inspires faith in the haunted, who willingly call on her high street consultancy when the supernatural takes hold.

But that's all about to change.

Two cases prove trying: 44 Gilmore Street, home to a particularly violent spirit, and the reincarnation case of Elisha Grey. When Gilmore Street attracts press attention, matters quickly deteriorate. Dubbed the 'New Enfield', the 'Ghost of Gilmore Street' inflames public imagination, but as Ruby and the team fail repeatedly to evict the entity, faith in them wavers.

Dealing with negative press, the strangeness surrounding Elisha, and a spirit that's becoming increasingly territorial, Ruby's at breaking point. So much is pushing her towards the abyss, not least her own past. It seems some demons just won't let go…

Psychic Surveys Book Four: Old Cross Cottage

It's not wise to linger at the crossroads...

In a quiet Dorset Village, Old Cross Cottage has stood for centuries, overlooking the place where four roads meet. Marred by tragedy, it's had a series of residents, none of whom have stayed for long. Pink and pretty, with a thatched roof, it should be an ideal retreat, but as new owners Rachel and Mark Bell discover, it's anything but.

Ruby Davis hasn't quite told her partner the truth. She's promised Cash a holiday in the country but she's also promised the Bells that she'll investigate the unrest that haunts this ancient dwelling. Hoping to combine work and pleasure, she soon realises this is a far more complex case than she had ever imagined.

As events take a sinister turn, lives are in jeopardy. If the terrible secrets of Old Cross Cottage are ever to be unearthed, an entire village must dig up its past.

Psychic Surveys Book Five: Descension

"This is what we're dealing with here, the institutionalised..."

Brookbridge housing estate has long been a source of work for Psychic Surveys. Formerly the site of a notorious mental hospital, Ruby and her team have had to deal with spirits manifesting in people's homes, still trapped in the cold grey walls of the asylum they once inhabited. There've been plenty of traumatic cases but never a mass case - until now.

The last remaining hospital block is due to be pulled down, a building teeming with spirits of the most resistant kind, the institutionalised. With the help of a newfound friend, as well as Cash and her colleagues, Ruby attempts to tackle this mammoth task. At the same time her private life is demanding attention, unravelling in ways she could never imagine.

About to delve deep into madness, will she ever find her way back?

Psychic Surveys Book Six: Legion

What if evil won't let go?

Along a sheltered lane, deep in the Sussex countryside, sits a house that is sometimes called home, the tenants it has held unable to forget it. When Ruby Davis gets a distressed call from Rosie Cowell, the latest inhabitant, little does she know that her life too will change forever, from the moment she steps over the threshold.

Unlike other houses of its kind, such as Bolskine and Borley, Blakemort has no reputation. Indeed, there is no written record of it anywhere; its history is quite untraceable. But Blakemort exists, and it exists for one purpose only. To torment.

How do you fight a house like Blakemort? Even with a team on your side, and the light encircling you? Is it possible to take on a darkness this deep?

In Legion, Blakemort is back.

Did it ever truly go away?

Blakemort: A Psychic Surveys Companion Novel (Book One)

"That house, that damned house. Will it ever stop haunting me?"

After her parents' divorce, five-year old Corinna Greer moves into Blakemort with her mother and brother. Set on the edge of the village of Whitesmith, the only thing attractive about it is the rent. A 'sensitive', Corinna is aware from the start that something is wrong with the house. Very wrong.

Christmas is coming but at Blakemort that's not something to get excited about. A house that sits and broods, that calculates and considers, it's then that it lashes out - the attacks endured over five years becoming worse. There are also the spirits, some willing residents, others not. Amongst them a boy, a beautiful, spiteful boy...

Who are they? What do they want? And is Corinna right when she suspects it's not just the dead the house traps but the living too?

Thirteen: A Psychic Surveys Companion Novel (Book Two)

Don't leave me alone in the dark…

In 1977, Minch Point Lighthouse on Skye's most westerly tip was suddenly abandoned by the keeper and his family – no reason ever found. In the decade that followed, it became a haunt for teenagers on the hunt for thrills. Playing Thirteen Ghost Stories, they'd light thirteen candles, blowing one out after every story told until only the darkness remained.

In 1987, following her success working on a case with Sussex Police, twenty-five year old psychic, Ness Patterson, is asked to investigate recent happenings at the lighthouse. Local teen, Ally Dunn, has suffered a breakdown following time spent there and is refusing to speak to anyone. Arriving at her destination on a stormy night, Ness gets a terrifying insight into what the girl experienced.

The case growing ever more sinister, Ness realises: some games should never be played.

Rosamund: A Psychic Surveys Companion Novel (Book Three)

Could you find your way through Hell?

Ruby Davis runs Psychic Surveys, a high street company specialising in domestic spiritual clearance. Having inherited her ability to see beyond the veil that separates this world and the next from her mother, Jessica, she is busy helping grounded spirits to cross the great divide. In turn, Jessica inherited her gift from her mother, Sarah, and Sarah from Rosamund.

Throughout the early twentieth century, Rosamund Davis was a woman held in high regard concerning her mediumship abilities and her pioneering work with London's famous psychical society. She published many papers on psychic matters, although there are some that remain unpublished, for the eyes of the Davis family only. It is these unavailable works concerning the non-spirit that fascinate many – entities born of negative thoughts that subsequently take on their own energy. Entities known as demons.

But what caused her to write about such dark matter?

From her own notes, in her own words, this is Rosamund's account.

This Haunted World Book One: The Venetian

Welcome to the asylum…

2015

Their troubled past behind them, married couple, Rob and Louise, visit Venice for the first time together, looking forward to a relaxing weekend. Not just a romantic destination, it's also the 'most haunted city in the world' and soon, Louise finds herself the focus of an entity she can't quite get to grips with – a 'veiled lady' who stalks her.

1938

After marrying young Venetian doctor, Enrico Sanuto, Charlotte moves from England to Venice, full of hope for the future. Home though is not in the city; it's on Poveglia, in the Venetian lagoon, where she is set to work in an asylum, tending to those that society shuns. As the true horror of her surroundings reveals itself, hope turns to dust.

From the labyrinthine alleys of Venice to the twisting, turning corridors of Poveglia, their fates intertwine. Vengeance only waits for so long…

This Haunted World Book Two: The Eleventh Floor

A snowstorm, a highway, a lonely hotel…

Devastated by the deaths of her parents and disillusioned with life, Caroline Daynes is in America trying to connect with their memory. Travelling to her mother's hometown of Williamsfield in Pennsylvania, she is caught in a snowstorm and forced to stop at The Egress hotel – somewhere she'd planned to visit as her parents honeymooned there.

From the moment she sets foot inside the lobby and meets the surly receptionist, she realises this is a hotel like no other. Charming and unique, it seems lost in time with a whole cast of compelling characters sheltering behind closed doors.

As the storm deepens, so does the mystery of The Egress. Who are these people she's stranded with and what secrets do they hide? In a situation that's becoming increasingly nightmarish, is it possible to find solace?

Jessa*mine*
The Jessamine series Book One

"The dead of night, Jess, I wish they'd leave me alone."

Jessamin Wade's husband is dead - a death she feels wholly responsible for. As a way of coping with her grief, she keeps him 'alive' in her imagination - talking to him every day, laughing with him, remembering the good times they had together. She thinks she will 'hear' him better if she goes somewhere quieter, away from the hustle and bustle of her hometown, Brighton. Her destination is Glenelk in the Highlands of Scotland, a region her grandfather hailed from and the subject of a much-loved painting from her childhood.

Arriving in the village late at night, it is a bleak and forbidding place. However, the house she is renting - Skye Croft - is warm and welcoming. Quickly she meets the locals. Her landlord, Fionnlagh Maccaillin, is an ex-army man with obvious and not so obvious injuries. Maggie, who runs the village shop, is also an enigma, startling her with her strange 'insights'. But it is Stan she instantly connects with. Maccaillin's grandfather and a frail, old man, he is grief-stricken from the recent loss of his beloved Beth.

All four are caught in the past. All four are unable to let go. Their lives entwining in mysterious ways, can they help each other to move on or will they always belong to the ghosts that haunt them?

Comraich
The Jessamine Series Book Two

An extreme land breeds extreme emotions…

Comraich – Gaelic for *Sanctuary* – that's what this ancient fortress of a house in the Highlands of Scotland has offered its generations, a haven from the world beyond.

The nesting instinct kicking in, a pregnant Jessamin decides that Comraich, which she shares with her partner Fionnlagh Maccaillin, needs refreshing. Getting to work in one of the spare bedrooms she makes a startling discovery, one that pulls her into a world of the intense and disturbing passions of others that have been here before.

Jessamin has to decide.

Will delving deeper into Comraich's history bring hope and peace to this troubled house or return her to a darkness she's only recently left behind?

As much as I love writing, building a relationship with readers is even more exciting! I occasionally send newsletters with details on new releases, special offers and other bits of news relating to the Psychic Surveys series as well as all my other books. If you'd like to subscribe,
sign up here!
www.shanistruthers.com

Printed in Poland
by Amazon Fulfillment
Poland Sp. z o.o., Wrocław